MW00478860

WHEN D-DAY DAWNS
Graham John Parry

WHEN D-DAY DAWNS © GRAHAM JOHN PARRY
COVER ARTWORK © GRAHAM J PARRY

ISBN-13: 978-1533164025
ISBN-10: 1533164029

All Rights Reserved

For my children, Andrew and Alison, with love.

CONTENTS

1 Danger

Morning came to northern France, dawn's soft light lifting the gloom from Nazi occupied Normandy. That first blush of sunrise flickered, a pink-grey shimmer in the early mist. Shadows stretched, and then shortened, melting swiftly as the earth warmed, brightening. A lone cockerel called, and the soft meadows swayed, rustling in the breeze.

On the western Peninsula, a paved road twisted south from the town of Cherbourg. The highway wandered out through a land of ripening fields, hidden amongst the maze of ancient hedgerows. At a left fork beyond an apple orchard where the tarmac turned from sight, the surface of the road changed to that of a rutted track, vanishing at the entrance to a gated drive. Nestled behind the dense foliage, an old, red-tiled farmer's cottage glowed in the radiant sun. A haze of blue smoke curled from the stone chimney, and the fragrant smell of bacon lingered on the air.

In the large flag stoned kitchen, Lucille Fuberge, the young blonde haired farmer's wife, flipped the sizzling rashers and cracked an egg into the pan. Her husband finished tucking in his shirt, shuffled over to the calendar and crossed off yesterday's date. Today was Thursday the 1st of June 1944, just gone midweek and he was looking forward to a game of boules in the evening. He crept up behind Lucille and kissed the side of her neck. She giggled and half turned to meet his lips. He slipped a gentle hand inside the robe, ran his fingertips up her spine, and pulled her close.

She broke away, laughing. 'Jacques, enough! I'll burn the bacon.'

He grinned, eyes smiling. 'Maybe I like it burnt.' But the table needed to be laid and he searched through the cutlery for the knives and forks.

Then the piercing roar of a fast approaching engine broke the stillness. With a squeal of brakes a Swastika flagged Mercedes slewed to a halt outside the latched wooden gate. Three uniformed members of the Waffen SS clambered from the seats, the dreaded silver insignia glinting on their collars. Their officer, Oberleutnant Gerhardt Ziegler, a dedicated fanatic of Hitler's Fatherland, wore the Deaths Head and Winged Eagle on his peaked cap. Dressed in an immaculate black uniform, and displaying the much acclaimed Iron Cross under his chin, he waited impatiently beside the car.

Sergeant Klaus Gruber, a short, stocky miserable excuse for a soldier, ambled round to the far side. The jack-booted officer demanded Gruber open the gate and pulled out his pistol.

The Sergeant cursed under his breath. Klaus Gruber held a deeply ingrained hatred of officers. There were too many idiots like Ziegler; not a drop of common sense between them, and too quick to condemn a poor bloodthirsty soldier like himself. He struck the iron latch with the heel of his hand, and kicked the bottom rung. As the heavy gate squeaked open, he stood aside to allow the pompous bastard to swagger through.

Ziegler turned to the driver and waved his Luger at a small decaying barn. 'Corporal, check that building.'

Cocking his machine-gun, Corporal Hugo Adler, ex Russian front, did as he was told. With a caution born of experience he walked slowly to the crumbling barn door. He stepped inside to the smell of horse dung, saw the tethered animal peering at him from the gloom and gave the pungent interior a cursory glance. Against the far wall was a wooden cart, one axle chocked up and the missing wheel lying discarded on the floor. Near to that sat the leather bellows of a blacksmith's forge and the dull glint of an anvil. A stack of hay half-filled an oblong cubicle, a two pronged pitchfork standing upright from the mound. He walked over, grabbed the fork and stabbed at the straw. There was no resistance so he dropped it to the floor and made his way back outside. He shook his head.

'Clear.'

Gerhardt Ziegler gave a brief nod, strode up to the cottage and hammered the door with the butt of his pistol. After a few seconds the door creaked inwards and the farmer's worried face appeared, his young wife waiting anxiously behind.

Ziegler spoke in French. 'You are Jacques Fuberge?' There was only the faintest trace of a German accent.

'Yes?'

Ziegler jammed a highly polished boot between door and frame. 'You will come with us.'

'Why . . . , why me, what for?'

The Sergeant brushed past his officer and put a shoulder to the door, forcing it open. The barrel of his gun rammed into the farmer's stomach, forcing him to double up in pain, winded. Gruber shoved him roughly into the yard and the man fell to his knees fighting for breath.

Ziegler grimaced, a mirthless glint of teeth. 'Watch him,' he said to Adler. 'We will search the house.'

In the kitchen, Lucille Fuberge backed away clutching tightly to her robe, and the fat bellied Gruber leered at a glimpse of flesh.

'Sergeant! Leave her. Upstairs, now!'

Gruber reluctantly broke off from staring at the petrified woman, cursed under his breath and turned away to thump noisily up the narrow steps.

Ziegler stepped over to the kitchen stove, peered into the pan, and very deliberately removed it from the heat. 'Such a pity,' he said softly, turning to the woman. 'The bacon has burned.'

Lucille stared at him, uncomprehending.

There was a loud crash from upstairs, immediately followed by a heavy thud, and the Sergeant shouted in triumph. 'I have it!'

He came awkwardly down the stairs, machine-gun slung over his shoulder, both hands holding a leather suitcase across his belly. A pair of headphones dangled from a wire. He brought the case to the table, opened the lid and swivelled it round for inspection.

Ziegler took a pace closer, leaned over and studied the contents. He flicked a switch back and forth, and then absent-mindedly turned a rotary knob. He was staring at a British manufactured shortwave radio. His cold eyes switched from the case to the young woman and he scowled. She stood staring at the radio, mouth open, the colour draining from her cheeks.

'What have you to say about this?' His tone had changed, abrupt, menacing.

She shook her head, blonde hair swaying, unable to answer.

He took two paces across the room and slapped her face, hard.

She screamed and fell back in shocked surprise; the imprint of his fingers a red weal on her cheek.

A burst of machine-gun fire rattled from outside and Gruber spun round, weapon ready, watching the door.

A shadow darkened the opening and Corporal Adler walked in grinning sheepishly. 'The man heard her scream, came at me and grabbed for the gun. I had no choice.'

The Officer lowered his pistol. 'Dead?'

Adler nodded and drew a finger across his throat.

Lucille Fuberge understood enough to realise what had happened. She sank to her knees, hands to her face and sobbed.

Oberleutnant Ziegler holstered his Luger, brushed a speck of dust from his sleeve and planted his fists on his waist. 'Well, gentlemen, that is that.' He thought for a moment, surveying the room. 'Adler, bring the radio. And you, Sergeant, deal with the woman.'

'Will you not be questioning her?'

For a long moment Ziegler gazed at the small pathetic figure bent double with grief. 'It would be wasting our time. The wives never know anything.' He turned for the door. 'See to it.'

The fat Sergeant was disappointed. He'd been looking forward to extracting a confession from the woman; he'd learnt a lot about torture in Russia.

Corporal Adler slung the machine-gun, gathered up the radio and dutifully followed his Officer out to the Mercedes.

For the first time, Klaus Gruber found himself alone with the sobbing young woman. He clumped across the flagstone floor and pushed with the barrel of his gun, prising away her hands. Her robe fell open to reveal her naked body and for a moment he hesitated, ogling the pale flesh.

She looked up, hatred in the red rimmed eyes, teeth bared.

The Sergeant stared back in contempt; after all, she was just another French peasant. There were plenty more in the surrounding villages. He raised his gun to her forehead and pulled the trigger. The bullet smashed through and took out the back of her skull. A crimson shimmer of blood sprayed the stone floor, the force of the impact driving her backwards from the bent knees. She lay sightless, a violent end to her young life.

Gruber took a last sneering look and stomped out of the cottage. He ignored the farmer's bullet ridden, blood soaked body and left it where it had fallen. The leather cased radio had been loaded into the back of the Mercedes and the Sergeant was last to find a seat.

Ziegler gave the command and they drove away without a backward glance. Where only an hour before two young people had awoken to a life filled with love, now only the grotesque horror of brutal death remained. As the sun warmed the farmyard a stray mongrel sniffed the blood, a scavenging curiosity overcoming his fear. He tugged at the man's shirt and tasted the blood, tugging harder, eyes wide, ears flat. In the kitchen flies began to swarm, buzzing round the exposed flesh, the once beautiful blonde hair interlaced with a writhing mass of insects.

The Mercedes swept round the apple orchard and skidded onto the paved road. Oberleutnant Gephardt Ziegler glanced at his watch. It was an important day in Cherbourg. The 1st of June was the Admiral's fortieth wedding anniversary and his wife was holding a ball to mark the occasion. Everyone who was anyone was invited, and that included Ziegler, and the rare honour of a hand written invitation was propped on the dresser in his bedroom. There would be many ladies at the grand ball, pampered and perfumed, all dressed in their finest low cut gowns. He smiled at the thought. Good food, the finest Champagne and the chance to reacquaint himself with a certain young lady who's husband had been called to Berlin. It would be an evening to savour.

The limousine purred powerfully round a long sweeping bend and crested a small rise. Stretching out before them was the northern tip of Hitler's Atlantic Wall and the heavily defended port of Cherbourg. In a dilapidated French château close to the harbour, Ziegler's evening Dress Uniform awaited his arrival. A long hot bath and shave and he would be ready for the evening's entertainment. He leant back in the leather seat, closed his eyes and tried to remember the name of that woman.

Approximately one hundred miles to the north, beyond the waters of the English Channel, Great Britain's crowded shores teemed with the men and machines of General Dwight D. Eisenhower's three million strong Allied Army. Stretching the entire length of the Channel coast, a ten mile security zone had been put in place to house almost a million of those in uniform, and they waited now for the Supreme Commander to launch the biggest amphibious invasion in the history of armed conflict. 'Operation Overlord' was the codename by which the Joint Chiefs of Staff would initiate the long awaited assault on Nazi occupied Europe; the hazardous, not to be underestimated challenge of gaining a foothold in the enemy's camp.

One of those men waiting for the order was an American. He was a tall, capable Ranger, a veteran of General George Patton's 7th United States Army, and well experienced in the art of killing Germans.

In the heat of early June he'd set off on a training exercise and mid-morning found him marching up the middle of a wide open stretch of moorland. He paused to take a break from the long hike and ran a finger over his map, checking the grid co-ordinates. Ahead of him, pushing on through the clinging bracken, nine men of his squad walked on.

He caught sight of the sniper glancing back over his shoulder. 'You got us lost, Sarge?'

The tall Ranger grunted, non-committal.

The sniper eased his helmet and wiped sweat from his forehead. 'Guess you ain't sayin', huh?'

'Nah, I'm just working on a need-to-know basis, an' I'm tellin' you here and now, I sure as hell don't think you need to know.' He folded the map with a grin, tucked it away inside the flap of his thigh pocket, and waved them forward. Of one thing he was sure; this was to be their last day of training. Last night's briefing had laid it on the line. No more exercises. And anyway, it didn't take a genius to see that the invasion was imminent.

Early that morning, just after sunup, they'd hitched a lift in the back of a Dodge truck, and in the course of the journey had passed endless lines of parked up mechanised weaponry. First thing they'd seen were tanks, row upon row of Sherman tanks. And beyond them, evenly spread out in acres of moorland, self-propelled guns, half-tracks, field guns, anti-aircraft guns and ammunition wagons. And then the bulldozers and bridging equipment, jeeps, ambulances, headquarter caravans and field kitchens. To their eyes, it was a vast array of hardware, and yet, by all accounts, only a small proportion of the equipment gathered for the assault on Hitler's Fortress.

A tangle of bracken tugged at his boot and he jerked it free and looked up at his line of Rangers, hunched forward under the weight of their packs, five yards between each man. Beyond them the undulating rock strewn, featureless moors. His pocket compass showed they were on the right track, and according to the map, within four miles of the next waypoint. A glance at his watch told him they were making good time, but there was no harm in quickening the pace

With a wicked smile he called up the line. 'Step it out, we ain't got all day.'

It was late in the afternoon when a small 'Hunt' class destroyer pushed into the enemy held southern waters of the English Channel. Under the billowing white clouds of early summer, H.M.S. *Brackendale*, pitching and rolling awkwardly, thumped through the short, foam flecked seas. Standing on the navigating bridge, the man in command stepped forward to the bridge-screen and glanced down at the pair of four-inch guns projecting from the forward turret. On the cuffs of his jacket he wore three, faded gold bands of rank, two of which, the broader rings, sandwiched a third narrow one, generally known as the 'half stripe'. The man's name was Thorburn, Lieutenant-Commander Richard Thorburn R.N., D.S.O., and the uniform he wore, much like the ship beneath his feet, had seen better days. His old, roll-neck jumper, tucked untidily inside the shabby double-breasted jacket, sagged under his chin. On this Thursday, his seemingly unimportant warship had taken passage from Falmouth to patrol the dangerous waters off the coast of Normandy. Cruising at fourteen knots, *Brackendale* was reaching the end of her crossing.

Richard Thorburn stood gazing contentedly out beyond the ship's bow. He reached for his battered binoculars and raised them to the southern horizon, and there in the distance he found the vague outline of the Cotentin Peninsula. With the help of a fitful, late sun glinting off the buildings, he verified it was the French port of Cherbourg and lowered the old Barr and Stroud glasses to hang from his neck. His keen eyes narrowed in thought and he turned to the compass platform. Bending to the brass voice-pipe, he spoke firmly into the bell-mouthed cup.

'Starboard fifteen.'

The Cox'n's voice acknowledged from the wheelhouse below. 'Starboard fifteen. Aye aye, sir.'

Thorburn watched the bows swing right, one eye on the compass.

'Midships. Steer two-seven-oh degrees.'

'Wheel's amidships. Steer two-seven-oh, aye aye, sir.'

Thorburn crossed to the port wing and gazed at the far shore, his weathered face creased in concentration. He had personal experience of this coastline, albeit from some years ago, and in much less favourable circumstances. It was partly down to that previous knowledge that *Brackendale* had been selected for the patrol, her third deployment in as many days. He was there to provide a visible reminder to the Germans, if needed, that the Allied Forces had enough strength to dominate these waters. It also served as a physical deterrent to the Kriegsmarine's nasty habit of laying underwater mines in the area.

'Coffee, sir?'

He smiled his approval. 'Thank you, Sinclair.'

The steward bobbed his head and scurried away.

Thorburn balanced the mug against the ship's erratic movement, moved over to the bridge-chair and sat with one scuffed boot wedged firmly on a bracket in the corner. Hazardous though it was to be so far south in enemy waters, he had one big advantage at his disposal. It was the ability to call up air cover at a moments notice. Even now, the Royal Air Force were patrolling to his north, all part of the Allied operation to deny the Luftwaffe visual access to England's Channel ports.

He took a mouthful of coffee, smiled in appreciation and glanced again to his left, over that port screen. His sharp eyes took in the most northerly point of the Peninsula, immediately followed by the rocky outcrops of a distant headland. Above the half exposed, off-shore islands, circling seagulls swooped in the surf laden onshore wind. He drank the last of his coffee, lit a cigarette and lifted his face to catch the breeze.

It was four years since he'd last visited these shores, four long perilous years of war. Back then he'd been a young man in his first command; naïve, reckless and, according to his superiors, too argumentative for his own good. Now here he was all this time later, back in the same waters with the same ship. He was of course, well aware of their 'Lordship's' deep displeasure in his generally argumentative attitude towards the authority of the 'Senior Service'. Hence their decision to have him chasing around well out of the way.

The few opportunities for promotion had passed him by, and like so many around him, Thorburn had grown accustomed to *Brackendale*'s familiar surroundings. Now he rebelled at the thought of strange new beginnings, and to the annoyance of their Lordships, had always managed to somehow hang on to the one warship he loved. Many of the crew felt the same way. *Brackendale* was a bit long in the tooth now, but she was a tough, reliable little ship, and he wasn't about to relinquish the reins. He smiled. Out here, well away from the clutches of the shore based establishments, his diminutive, overworked dogsbody of a forgotten destroyer was free to enjoy the call of the sea.

'Periscope! Red, one hundred!'

Thorburn came to his feet in a rush, looked quickly over the port side. 'Action stations!' he called, and bent to the voice-pipe. 'Hard-a-port!' It was imperative he turn for the target, reduce the ship's profile, and upset the enemy's calculations. The indistinct ring of the alarm bells sounded faintly from below, urging the men to action.

The ship sprang to life as men scrambled for their stations; crowding round the pair of four-inch guns on the fo'c'sle below the bridge, and the multi-barrelled Pompom, perched high on the galley housing. They ran to 'Y' gun turret which enclosed the second pair of four-inch guns on the quarterdeck. And most importantly, the depth charge crews raced to their stations at the stern rail.

The wiry First Lieutenant, Robert Armstrong, a competent, well experienced 'Number One', acknowledged the calls coming in to the bridge. Chief Petty Officer Barry Falconer reported from the wheel, Sub-Lieutenant George Labatt confirmed his attendance with the depth-charge party, and Lieutenant (E) Bryn Dawkins, came on amidst the noise of the engine room. There was an abrupt, 'Gun crews closed up,' from Lieutenant John 'Guns' McCloud, and Armstrong returned the handset to the cradle. 'Ship closed up to Action Stations, sir.'

Thorburn nodded, snatched up the bridge handset to the Range Finder Director.

Situated aft, just above and behind the bridge, the Gunnery Officer replied. 'Guns.'

'There's a periscope just off the port bow. Have a crack at it.'

'Aye aye, sir.'

Thorburn watched the forward guns traverse left, lower a little and steady. A loud crash of smoke and a pair of shells streaked across the waves. Two plumes of spray rose from the sea, immediately followed by a second salvo.

With her bow wave flying, leaning hard to starboard, *Brackendale* swept round to the bearing, the ship's White Ensign flapping in the wind. 'Midships,' he ordered down the voice-pipe. A check of the compass. 'Steer one-seven-five degrees.'

The Cox'n acknowledged from the wheelhouse. 'One-seven-five degrees. Aye aye, sir.'

A flurry of spray drenched the bridge screen and Thorburn straightened away from the pipe.

'Periscope down, sir,' called the lookout.

Thorburn raised his binoculars to scan the sea. At any moment they might see torpedo tracks. He found none but felt some comfort knowing there were another dozen pairs of eyes doing the same thing. He heard the cease-fire gong in the turret below.

'Number One,' he called to Armstrong. 'Make sure Asdic are on the ball.' It was vital to have the underwater search system working. Then back to the voice-pipe to set engine revolutions for an attack.

The ship trembled, noticeably, her bow wave lifting. The thrash of *Brackendale*'s propellers amplified, and the Asdic's underwater dome pulsed out its own electronic 'ping'.

Sub-Lieutenant George Labatt's response in an emergency had been to find his way aft to the depth charge rails and after reporting in to the bridge, he found Leading Seaman Abbot chivvying his men into order. They were poised to alter the depth settings. Only once the detonators were set would the barrels be allowed to roll down the chutes over the stern. Either side of the quarterdeck a depth charge waited to be fired forty yards clear of the sides. Labatt hung on for instructions and watched *Brackendale*'s foaming wake.

On the bridge, Thorburn also waited. At any moment he expected to hear a contact report from the Asdic compartment. The setting sun made a momentary appearance, a golden flush on the breaking waves. He frowned at the sea ahead, searching the water, finding it hard to believe a U-boat could have penetrated the mined Channel.

'Asdic . . Bridge. Target moving left. Range, eleven-hundred. Course, oh-nine-oh. Speed, seven knots.'

Thorburn looked at the compass. The U-boat was moving east across his bows. He made a rapid calculation to intercept, cut the angle, and altered course. 'Port five. Steer, one-two-oh degrees.

Falconer acknowledged and the ship heeled to starboard and settled on her new heading.

Thorburn felt the urge to hear the echo for himself. 'Switch on the bridge repeater,' he ordered. Instantly the strident electronic pulse rang through the bridge space, a clear high-pitched 'ping' followed by the pronounced deeper bounce back.

'Depth?' Thorburn asked.

'One-one-oh feet,' came the reply.

Thorburn squinted in thought; the U-boat was still going down. He snatched up the handset for the quarterdeck.

Labatt answered. 'Depth charge!'

'Set for three-hundred, Sub.'

'Aye aye, sir.'

Thorburn listened to the Asdic's ringing tones, the interval between pulse and echo shortening as they closed in on the target. The 'T' was being crossed. Then came the call he wanted. 'Instantaneous echo, sir!'

The 'fire' buttons were pressed and the first depth charge plunged over the stern. To port and starboard two more canisters arced out and splashed beneath the surface. And then a fourth, followed by a fifth, tumbled over the stern into the white wake and sank from sight. A pattern of charges in the shape of a crucifix, probing the depths. Thorburn allowed *Brackendale* to run on, away from any possible damage, all eyes staring out beyond the stern rail.

When the first drum reached a depth of three-hundred feet, the pressure activated firing pistol detonated the 300lb charge of high explosive. On the surface a towering plume of angry water erupted into foaming spray. Seconds later, two deep explosions either side of their wake tore the surface apart and billowed skywards. A slight delay and two final rumbling shocks burst from the depths and the spray drifted, out and down.

Below the waterline, in the stifling confines of the engine room, the Chief Engineer, Lieutenant Bryn Dawkins, fussed over his dials and gauges. He and the stokers heard the hammer blows, glanced at the thin hull, and preyed.

'Starboard twenty. Slow ahead,' Thorburn said into the voice-pipe. The ship leaned and commenced a turn to the west. The boiling water stilled, calmed. Ultra smooth liquid pools met their gaze. But the surface of the sea gave up no evidence of damage. There was no sign of oil, no sign of wreckage, nothing to say they'd hit the target.

Thorburn worried his bottom lip, disappointed. It should have been their first U-boat 'kill'; he was convinced of the attack's accuracy.

'Lost contact, sir.'

'Keep looking!' Thorburn snapped, immediately regretting his outburst. Of course they'd lost contact. With that amount of underwater disturbance, it might be quarter of an hour before the Asdic could penetrate the layers.

On the quarterdeck, Labatt was overseeing the re-load, checking the throwers, watching the drums being manhandled onto the rails. Time was of the essence, the captain was waiting for these weapons

2   Menace

It was evening when an elderly Frenchman strolled across his neighbour's field to collect his usual two day supply of milk. He was surprised to find the wooden gate unlatched, standing ajar; he'd never known it to be left open before. A nauseous smell lingered on the air, an unfamiliar silence hanging over the cottage. Concerned by the lack of activity he let himself into the farmyard and immediately spotted the bloated body of Jacques Fuberge.

The old man was no stranger to death. Until recently he'd been an active member of the Resistance, accustomed to dealing with the inevitable consequences of guerrilla warfare. He was also well aware of the young farmer's involvement with the movement. Eighteen months back, an Englishman from the Special Operations Executive had parachuted in and trained Jacques Fuberge as a wireless operator. He became the area communications contact for the local organisation, his primary link being a codename in Cherbourg.

The old man narrowed his eyes and looked up at the red tiled cottage.

'Lucille?' he called softly.

Stepping quietly towards the front door he crept inside and entered the cool kitchen. Pots and pans hung from wrought iron hooks on the beams and a frying pan sat haphazardly to the side of the cold stove. He took another cautious pace beyond the kitchen table, and froze. The young woman was dead, of that he could be certain. There was a black hole in her forehead and a large pool of congealed blood on the flagstones around her head.

He searched for something to cover her naked body and found the farmer's knee length coat hanging on the back of the door. With great tenderness he draped the garment over her bent knees and drew it up to cover the once golden hair. Grim faced, he trudged upstairs and found what he most feared. The radio was missing from the hidden recess under the floorboards. A lapsed member he may be, but it was time to inform the comrades.

One hour later, having negotiated the five gruelling kilometres to the nearest dwellings he rounded one last hedge to see the church before him. The Chapelle de la Croix stood next to the Priest's cottage and the old man walked wearily to the door and knocked.

Claude Theroux knew all his flock and instantly recognised the old man. Seeing how distressed he was, the Priest insisted on him taking a seat, fumbled around to find a glass and offered him a large brandy.

'Now what troubles you, monsignor?'

The old man painstakingly spelt out the horror of what he'd seen and then sat slumped, chin on his chest to recover.

There was more to Claude Theroux than the bespectacled, portly image of a man of the cloth. He too had become a willing member of the Resistance and now the Priest did not hesitate. London must be informed. Calling for his wife to look after the old man, he grabbed his bicycle from the outhouse and peddled off to the nearby windmill. The miller who ground the flour also made deliveries to a man in Cherbourg. London would know before the day was through.

In England, as the evening light faded over Dartmoor's southwest corner, the ten man squad of US Rangers slogged their way back to base. The training exercise had seen them dropped off from the trucks at 06.45 hours and head out onto the rolling uplands.

Each man carried sixty pounds of equipment; a carefully compiled inventory of items which every soldier would need in the fight to survive the first twenty-four hours of D-Day. Other than the mundane necessities of a water bottle, dry rations and cigarettes, there was a long list of additional paraphernalia. It included chewing gum and French francs, a miniature heating stove, a pocket guide of France, insecticide powder, water purification tablets, gas mask, raincoat and candy bars. The Rangers also carried personal weapons, either a Thompson machine-gun or the M1 Carbine. The squad's sniper had a Remington with telescopic sight, and one of them looked after the Browning Automatic Rifle. Attached to their assault vests were the fragmentation grenades, bandoliers for the BAR, extra ammunition, entrenching tools and first aid pack. A bayonet hung in a pouch behind the left shoulder and a pistol hung from a holster on their belts. A steel helmet completed the ensemble, a string net stretched tight to enable camouflaged concealment. The sniper had twisted two yellow flowers into the mesh.

By midday the Rangers had marched twenty-five miles. Before they took a break they were ordered to stage an attack on a dummy gun emplacement. The afternoon saw them slogging on with the march, a compass and map to follow the complicated route home. Now, tiring from the day's exertions, nine of the ten men began to slow, dragging their feet. The tenth man was their Sergeant, the squad leader, and his lean features gave no hint of the genuine sense of responsibility he felt towards his men. But he had a job to do, and right now that job was to push his men to the limits, no slacking. He saw the pace fall off, noticed the heads go down and stepped in.

'Pick it up, pick it up, we ain't on no picnic.'

Up ahead the sniper looked back. 'Well how about you take a turn in the lead? Mebbe we'll all follow your fine example.'

There were a few mumbled agreements and the Sergeant hid a smile. The Rangers were taught to use their initiative and they weren't slow in voicing their opinions.

'Alright,' he said, 'but you're gonna have to keep up. Think you can manage?'

'If the old man can make it then I guess us boys will just have to dig real deep.' A ripple of subdued laughter fell away and the Sergeant moved up the front of the line. He turned to face them and grinned.

'Okay, Rangers. We got ourselves three miles of this here bracken to negotiate. Anybody drops behind and he'll be on short rations for a week. You hear me?'

A gloomy silence met his proposal. A solitary, 'Yes, Sarge,' came from down the line.

'Good, we're all agreed.' He hefted the submachine-gun to his shoulder and turned away. 'Move out!' he called in his best drill-sergeant's voice, and strode off at a hundred paces to the minute. This would wipe the smile off their faces.

On the northern shores of Nazi occupied France, a few kilometres from the port of Cherbourg, Colonel Otto Reinhardt, of the 709th Infantry Division, clambered out of his Kübelwagen staff car to make another check on the progress of his Engineers. In the orange light of the setting sun he marched impatiently to a knoll, where firm sand met the rising ground, and looked out with a critical eye. Down at the water's edge a few hundred metres away the detachment of men from a mine laying party splashed through the rising surf. He watched the sergeant place a Teller mine on one of the obstacles and another of his subordinates set up a booby trap. Reinhardt could see by their footprints they had already covered a thousand metres or more. It seemed a long time since early May when the beach defences had been inspected and passed. All was fine until three days ago, and then Field Marshall Erwin Rommel made a surprise visit. He immediately issued orders to extend the minefield below the low tide mark. This was the end result.

From his vantage point on the high ground, Reinhardt turned away from the shore and looked inland at the flooded terrain behind the beach. Controlled by a lock system, the waterways had been allowed to spill over. The low lying countryside had quickly turned into an impenetrable quagmire. That left only four possible exits from the beach, and those causeways were covered by a network of gun emplacements. He grimaced. If the threatened Allied invasion ever came to this sector of the Atlantic Wall, the assault troops would never make it past the swamp. They would be annihilated.

Colonel Otto Reinhardt made a final sweeping survey of the defences and strode back to the car. Surely Field Marshall Rommel would be delighted by the outcome. By nightfall there would be another thousand mines at the water's edge. He dropped into the back seat and tapped the driver on the shoulder.

'Drive on; we go to Sainte-Mère-Église.'

The driver found a gear and they bounced off along the rutted track. Down on the beach, the waves tugged at the sand, but twelve more mines had been set and their detonators armed.

In London, a mile to the northeast of Hyde Park, in an old Victorian three storey town house, General Scott Bainbridge sat in the long, empty Map Room and contemplated his options. He frowned in thought, touching the faded scar on his cheekbone, trying to fathom out his next move on what was effectively, his giant chess board of northwest France. With only a short while before the invasion he knew he was fast approaching the end game. But at least the Resistance could play their part. The last of the weapons drops had been accomplished, now it was just a matter of getting them activated on D-Day. Their British controller would meet them during the assault.

He stood up and walked across to the main window overlooking Porter Street, a side avenue running at right angles to Baker Street. The Special Operations Executive (French section) organised their underground network of agents from Baker Street. Bainbridge's department, set up to deal specifically with 'Overlord' and the Cotentin Peninsula, had been classed as a 'satellite' unit, and Porter Street was a conveniently handy location. Down on the street below the traffic ebbed and flowed, much as it always had. Office girls came and went and the 'bowler hats' strode briskly about their business, briefcases in hand. Little did they know what went on behind the slightly weather beaten façade of the old Victorian house.

He turned back into the bare room, drawn to the big map on the wall, pondering. A vital part of Operation Overlord would be the capture of Cherbourg's deep water harbour, imperative for the continued reinforcement of American men and materials. It was his agent in Cherbourg, with a wealth of information on the current dispositions of the German forces, who held the key to a successful attack.

Bainbridge rubbed his chin. Time to check on the latest updates. He left the office and walked downstairs to the ground floor. Behind a closed door in the hallway, a set of rickety steps took him down to the cellar. A single orange bulb offered just enough light to reveal a short passage leading to a solid steel door. Half hidden in the shadows, a man in a flat cap and dungarees blocked his way, but on seeing who it was, stood to one side.

'Morning, sir,' he said, and opened the door.

Bainbridge nodded in passing and the 'civilian' relaxed his hand away from the hidden pistol.

Inside the brightly lit cellar a dozen wireless operators sat listening to their headphones, the rhythmic chatter of Morse keys reflecting off the solid brick walls. From each station, cables led upwards to the ceiling and across to the outside wall. Bainbridge knew they passed up to the rooftop where the powerful arrays of antennae were disguised by being attached to three disused flag poles. He walked past the row of signalmen and stopped in front of Sergeant Dave Cooper. He was a thirty year old linguist and 'short wave' specialist. As Bainbridge drew level he was writing furiously onto his signal pad and the General waited for a break in transmission. The fingers on the Morse key vibrated to sign off, and the Sergeant looked up.

The signalman picked up the pad and flicked through a dozen or so pages. 'This came in at 05.00 hours, sir. From the Cherbourg operator, just the standard daily contact, nothing to report.'

Bainbridge nodded thoughtfully. 'When's the next scheduled broadcast?'

'Any minute now, eight o'clock, sir.'

The General thought about it and decided to hang around. 'I'll wait,' he said simply, turning his attention to the main message desk. A stack of signal slips were in the process of being logged and filed for future reference. He ambled over and read through a batch of the latest entries, pausing occasionally to read one or two in greater depth.

A movement made him look up to see Sergeant Cooper tapping out a transmission and trying to attract his attention. Bainbridge walked back and stood waiting, watching him briskly jot down the incoming signal. He saw a frown develop on Cooper's face; the eyes narrow as he scribbled faster. There was obviously something unusual coming in. After what seemed a long time the Sergeant hit the key to acknowledge and sign off.

Cooper pulled over a code book and began to unravel the apparently meaningless jumble of hieroglyphics. Finished, he sat back and rapidly re-read the decrypted message.

'Well?' Bainbridge prompted.

'It's Cherbourg, sir. Message reads, "Snowdrop dead. Probable raid by SS. Radio missing." He's waiting for instructions.'

Bainbridge felt a chill run through him. How much had they found out? Who was at risk? The assumption had to be all those in the immediate chain of contacts. Now he faced a serious predicament. He couldn't take a chance on leaving his main agent inside Cherbourg; he needed to arrange a quick exit. 'Let the operator know we'll send instructions on the morning call. I'll have an answer by then.' With a final glance around his hub of operations, he let himself out past the guard and ventured into the outside world.

Turning left in the sunshine he quickly entered Baker Street and strode off to Regents Park. He crossed the busy intersection with Marylebone Road and skirted a heavily sandbagged doorway protruding onto the pavement. The walk was doing him good and he arrived at the entrance to the park feeling re-energized. At the boating lake he stopped and reached for a cigarette, shielding the flame against the gentle breeze coming off the water. Having cleared his mind he meandered along the bank and began to address the difficulty of extracting the agent, watching the swaying barrage balloons.

A pigeon flew into the branches of a weeping willow, disappeared from view, and re-emerged at ground level before hopping into a cluster of ornate stones. Bainbridge stopped, staring hard at the formation of rocks, the way the stonework hid the bird. And then it dawned on him, a distant memory; the answer to his problem had just appeared. The cigarette burned down, hot on his tongue, and he dropped it the ground, twisting his toe on the stub. He allowed himself a small smile of satisfaction, pleased to have found his way out of the conundrum.

A short while later he was back in his office. Reaching for the phone he pulled out his book of contacts and dialled the number for a Nissen hut in Plymouth.

'Sergeant Foster speaking,' came an answer on the other end.

'Bainbridge here, Sergeant. Need to have a quick chat with my man. Is he around?'

'No, sir. He's up at Sigs HQ. I can have him here in a few minutes.'

Bainbridge knew the layout; the Signals block was just round the corner. 'In that case, I'll hang on. Make it snappy, Sergeant!' He heard him leave the hut and sat back to wait.

Sergeant Foster opened the door to the Nissen hut and stood aside for the officer to enter.

Major Paul Wingham swung lightly through the opening and strode across to the operations desk. With the phone to his ear he spoke with a clipped clarity of purpose. 'Wingham here, sir.'

The General's voice was distant, the line crackling. 'Change of plans, Major. Forget about your secondary mission. I need you to meet Foxcub.'

Wingham rolled his eyes to the corrugated ceiling. 'Foxcub, yes, sir. Where?'

'Point of rendezvous is 'Talon'. You meet there and report back here. Absolutely critical. Understood?'

Wingham frowned for a moment, remembering. It seemed all so long ago. That it was critical he vaguely understood. Quite why he hadn't a clue, but orders were orders. 'Yes, sir,' he said, sounding more confident than he felt. 'Rendezvous is Talon and bring Foxcub back to you.'

'In a nutshell, exactly that. Foxcub has vital information, important stuff.'

'Right, sir.' He hung on, listening to the crackling line.

'Well, that's it. . . . Good luck, Major.'

'Thank you, sir.' The line went dead and Wingham thoughtfully replaced the receiver. Something must have gone badly wrong for Foxcub to break cover. As for himself, it didn't make much difference. He'd always been tasked with two missions. If he survived the first, the second had just become a lot more interesting.

He sighed and headed for the door. Time to get back to the signals office and that bloody book of Morse codes.

As night fell on the County of Hampshire, the bearded, portly figure of Commodore James Pendleton R.N., D.S.C., sat in a sparsely furnished ante-room on the second floor of an early Georgian mansion. Nine miles north of the Royal Navy's Portsmouth Dockyard, and set in over three hundred acres of parkland, Southwick House had been requisitioned to serve as the Supreme Headquarters Allied Expeditionary Force (SHAEF). Pendleton, like so many others in the surrounding countryside awaited the forthcoming operation to invade Nazi occupied France. Out in the corridor the sound of clattering typewriters filled the air, and occasionally someone hurried back and forth between the rooms.

Pendleton sat stiffly upright, hands on his knees, wearing his best uniform. The jacket felt a little tight over his thickening waistline. He had made a particular effort to look the part knowing the man inside was one of the Operation's senior planners. He tugged impatiently at his full heavy beard, wondering why he'd been called at such short notice. It was four months since he'd been attached to 'Overlord' and, specifically, 'Neptune', the Royal Navy's involvement for D-Day.

The door to the office opened and a Naval Attaché hurried out with a briefcase. He disappeared down the corridor leaving Pendleton with a frown, his heavy eyebrows almost meeting in the middle. He glanced at his watch. Thirty-five minutes they'd kept him waiting, and yet the message had emphasised the urgency of the meeting.

Then the door reopened and a young Flag Lieutenant put his head round. 'Commodore Pendleton? We're ready for you now, sir.'

Pendleton rose to his feet and tugged the jacket down over the slight bulge of his waist. Cap tucked firmly under his left arm he strode into the main office.

Vice-Admiral Sir Hugh Stanford R.N., K.C.B., O.B.E., looked up from behind his mahogany desk and waved to a seat. 'Afternoon James. Sorry to have kept you waiting.'

Pendleton settled on a chair and watched as the Admiral flicked through a file and added his signature to the last page. The gold lace on his cuffs shone softly as he pushed the paperwork to one side, leant back and rubbed his weathered, deeply lined face. The clear grey eyes gazed calmly across the table and he smiled a gentle, apologetic smile.

'I'm afraid we've lost one of our destroyers. She cracked a boiler.'

Pendleton took that for what it meant, at least a month out of commission. 'Yes, sir,' he said.

Stanford pulled at an earlobe. 'We need a replacement, James, and quickly.'

Pendleton straightened in his seat, surprised by the lack of spare capacity.

The Admiral held up a hand and shook his head. 'I know, I'm well aware of our shortcomings,' he said. 'We did have extra provision but not at this late stage.' He stood up and wandered over to the window. 'Whoever you choose must be experienced. The assignment is for close support in liaison with ground forces, in particular, the Americans.'

Pendleton stroked his beard and considered his position. Just about every available destroyer outside of Overlord's requirement had been allocated. The Atlantic convoys, the Mediterranean, even the Far East. And of course, those patrolling the English Channel to prevent U-boat incursions.

'I'll need a little time, sir.'

'You have until 08.00 hours tomorrow, but that's it.' The Admiral narrowed his eyes; a clear indication there was to be no argument.

Pendleton came to his feet, cap in hand. 'In that case, sir, I'd better get on.'

Hugh Stanford nodded. 'Remember, James, absolute priority.'

Pendleton was quick to reassure him, and allowed the Lieutenant to show him out.

Beneath the dark waters of the English Channel an ocean-going German Underseeboot (U-boat) slipped silently west, riding an underwater current. For almost four hours the boat had twisted and turned to escape an attack by a British destroyer. The men of the U-boat had

31

survived the depth charges, heard the pulse of Asdic from overhead, and eventually wriggled clear. But now, with batteries running low and breathable air at a premium, it was imperative they surface. Unsure of their position, but running out of options, the 'Old Man' took them up to periscope depth. A careful, unhurried search of the dark night and a nearly invisible horizon convinced the commander to surface.

Three minutes later the U-boat's menacing presence emerged from the waves. A hatch in the conning tower was thrown open, quickly followed by the commander. His powerful binoculars swept the perimeter and only when he was certain did he lower them and call down to the control room. 'Start the diesels.'

Sixty nautical miles northwest of the U-boat's position, a single freighter struggled slowly out into the waters off Lands End. The *Glasgow Bay*, delayed from joining her convoy by engine trouble, had moored up in the lee of St Ives and made repairs. Although her Captain vehemently argued against continuing the journey, the ship's owners had insisted. His shipment of Landing Craft engine spares was of vital importance to the Weymouth command. So without an escort, and against his better judgement, the long-serving, very experienced Captain, had reluctantly slipped her moorings and headed south into the moonlit night.

3   Glasgow Bay

At two o'clock on the morning of Friday the 2nd of
June, Lieutenant-Commander Richard Thorburn
unwillingly called off the hunt. At midnight he'd run down
the engines and stopped, sitting in the darkness in an
attempt to lull the U-boat in to some kind of action. When
that failed he endeavoured to find the enemy by combing
the waters towards the south, careful to stay well clear of
the French coast. With nothing to show for his efforts,
having heard not a single response to the Asdic's continual
'ping', he turned *Brackendale* northeast to take up the last
leg of her patrol. He peered round the darkened bridge.
Officer-of-the-Watch, Lieutenant Langford stood close by
the compass, a signalman on the Aldis lamp, and a lookout
in either bridge-wing. In a few hours the ship would be at
her berth in Falmouth and they would be preparing for
another day on Cornwall's southern coast.

Thorburn went to his cabin, pulled out the Captain's log
and brought it up to date. With a gin and tonic in his
favourite tumbler he squinted into the clear liquid and
grimaced. Can't win 'em all, he thought. Maybe next time,
if there ever was a next time. That was twice the
opportunity had come his way, both in the English
Channel, and both times he'd failed. He swallowed the last
of the gin and lay down fully clothed. With luck he might
snatch a couple of hours sleep.

A short while before sunrise, the submerged Type VIIC
U-boat picked up the distant acoustic signal of a merchant
ship's thumping single propeller. On either side of the U-
boat's conning tower, the image of an open mouthed razor
toothed shark, represented everything the boat stood for.

33

From the moment a talented torpedo man had put away his brushes, the outlook for Kapitänleutnant Kurt Schneider and his forty-two man crew, had been transformed. The portrait of the shark changed them from being just another U-boat into a living entity, the embodiment of their spirit; the willingness to attack from the depths, without warning, in deadly assault.

Lying sixty meters beneath the waves the Hydrophone Operator sat motionless in his small listening room. He raised a hand for silence, a warning he'd made contact, and listened closely to the noise in his headphones.

Schneider edged his way silently over to the cramped office and raised his chin in query.

'Propellers, Kapitän. Maybe two kilometres.' He turned a hand wheel, redirecting the port and starboard locators to triangulate the direction of contact. He nodded. 'Northwest,' he said. 'I think he comes this way. Slowly.'

Schneider moved silently back to the control room. 'Periscope depth,' he ordered brusquely. 'Slow ahead.'

The bow planes changed angle, the big electric motors engaged the twin propellers to push gently forwards, and the submarine rose to a hidden depth of twelve metres.

Schneider indicated the Observation periscope.

With a quiet whine of an electric motor the tube was raised until the eyepiece reached head height and Schneider flicked the handles down to the horizontal. He swept the periscope round through 360° to check the immediate vicinity for any sign of danger. When nothing materialised he stepped away. 'Down periscope.' Now it was time for the Attack Periscope and Schneider nodded to his officer. 'My killing eye.'

As it slid up to a comfortable level, Schneider put his eyeball to the socket and focused his attention to the northwest. A faint, blurred object swam past the lens and he quickly backtracked. Then he found it, sharpened the image. A freighter, smoking from the funnel, and at a guess, maybe four thousand tons.

The twenty-four year old Schneider smiled thinly. This was too good a chance to miss. A bow shot using just one of his 'eels' would be enough.

'We begin,' he ordered.

The First Officer looked up from the Attack Table and prepared to enter the numbers his Kapitän would supply. It commenced with the time, 06.15, followed by the ship's course and then a pause, after which he gave the speed, range to target and lastly, the angle on the bow.

Schneider snapped the handles up and stood back for the periscope to be lowered. Small as it was, the periscope created a bow wave; the least time it was above water the less time a watcher had to detect it. He waited for his First Officer to analyse the stream of information and make his calculations. The findings were checked and logged, the initial estimate made. He glanced at the time and after a two minute interval, made his second examination of the target. He called out his new findings in the same order, all different, but written down in the respective columns. The 'scope was lowered and Schneider glowered impatiently. A fresh calculation was compared to the first; the corresponding results confirmed the target's progress. A final sighting would verify the speed of convergence, only then could the torpedo room set the angle on the gyro. At the end of another two minutes the periscope lifted clear of the waves.

He walked the periscope round the horizon, looking for danger, not wanting to be caught by surprise. Returning to the target he confirmed all the previous numbers and finally checked the angle on the bow. 'Set the gyro for three degrees to starboard.'

A moment's pause. 'Gyro set, Kapitän.'

'Load,' he ordered sharply.

A light on the panel confirmed the torpedo was in the tube. 'Torpedo is ready, Kapitän.'

Schneider grunted. 'Flood number One tube, I will wait for nine-hundred metres,' Schneider said. A wave obscured his view and distorted the lens. 'Hold steady!' He clarified the order. 'The depth is under.'

The First Officer glared at the guilty planes-man who quickly adjusted the wheel until the needle showed the correct depth.

Schneider's vision cleared and he found his unsuspecting victim. It was rapidly approaching the firing point. He watched the range shrink to one thousand metres.

'Achtung!' he warned. With the range quickly reducing, at nine-hundred and forty metres he started the count.

'Three . . . , two . . . , one . . . . Loose!'

At precisely nine-hundred metres the boat shuddered softly. The torpedo accelerated to forty knots. At the Attack Table a stop-watch activated and the hydrophones picked up the shrill whine of the counter-rotating propellers.

Schneider waited, sweating in the warmth of the control room. And then he saw the warhead strike. A mountain of water erupted skywards, an explosive fireball as the detonation ripped open the freighter's innards, a concussive, underwater thunder.

The *Glasgow Bay* faltered, staggered under the weight of the blast. Eight feet below the waterline the hull imploded and the detonation tore away the riveted plates, smashing through the bulkheads. In the boiler room, two stokers died instantly, cut in half by the scalding steam, obliterated. In the engine room the Chief Engineer, past the age of retirement, managed to guide another stoker up the ladder and followed him as the water chased them out.

The dying ship began to break in two, screeching to the tortured sound of twisted steel. Up in the navigating bridge, now hanging precariously over the jagged ruin of the main deck, the Captain turned to the quartermaster on the wheel.

'We've had it, Jim. Out you get.'

Jim stood clinging to the spokes of the wheel, disbelieving.

'Life jacket! Out! Now!' the Captain shouted, and pushed him through the portside door. They were swept off their feet by a foaming sea and pulled below, sucked under with the ship's dying plunge. By a quirk of fate, sheer chance, the waves spat them out to the surface and the Captain, face down, struggled in the turbulent sea. A pair of strong hands, the hands of a man who'd steered the ship for fourteen years, hauled him over, and Jim managed to force a broken crate under his Captain's chest. He gasped his thanks and they floated clear of the turbulent vortex.

Kurt Schneider snapped the periscope handles upright and pulled his eye away. Whatever the cargo, it must have been weighty, the ship's back broke in two, fore and aft sections sinking apart. Within minutes the remnants had sunk below the surface, gone. Inside the U-boat they heard the unmistakable sounds of the dying ship, the rending shriek of torn steel, the dull echo of collapsing bulkheads. Crewmen nodded in satisfaction, grim smiles of satisfied triumph.

'Surface the boat!'

They rose the last few metres and launched bow first from the sea.

'Man the guns!' Schneider ordered, and shrugged into his dark leather bridge coat. Two men squeezed up inside the tower and a deluge of sea water cascaded over their shoulders. In a moment they were out and Schneider reached for the ladder.

Eight hundred metres off the starboard bow the dying embers of the *Glasgow Bay* flickered fitfully in the debris.

Schneider allowed himself a savage smile. 'Slow ahead,' he called down the tower. They edged forward towards the pathetic remains of a once proud ship. Wooden spars and hemp cordage, a broken ship's boat and the sodden remains of a cargo net. The U-boat's diving planes nosed into the mess and Schneider saw a red and white circular life belt float past. One of the crew fished it out with a boathook and turned it over. *Glasgow Bay* was written in black letters on the other side. Schneider nodded. It would prove the tonnage sunk.

'Herr Kapitän!' A crewman called from the deck gun. He pointed across the starboard bow.

Schneider followed his outstretched arm and saw a movement in the water. A man's arm was waving to attract their attention while helping a second man stay afloat. Schneider frowned, caught in a quandary. He could not rescue survivors; there was no room in the boat. But if he left them to drown and somehow they survived, his boat would be identified. The grey fish on the conning tower was too obvious. It would be headline news for the Englander's newspapers, good propaganda.

'Stop engines!' he shouted.

Two of the men beside him gave a sideways glance of surprise. He avoided their eyes and stepped out into the circular guardrail platform with the twin barrelled machine guns. 'Move away,' he snapped at an ant-aircraft gunner, and took hold of the trigger. He swivelled the guns around to the starboard side and scowled through the ring sight, trembling with an inner rage. Three hundred metres away were the flailing arms, and he pulled the trigger. The twin barrels erupted into life, hammering out a fusillade of shells. A trail of water-spouts advanced to the target. The bullets found the survivors and smashed through human flesh. One of the bullets ripped through Jim's shoulder and tore away his arm. Another hit his chest and pulverised his lungs, and the water turned crimson red.

The Captain was hit by a tracer to his throat and a bullet scythed through his forehead and blew out the back of his head.

Even when all signs of life had been extinguished, Schneider hung on to the trigger and blasted shells at the human scraps. In the end, the guns clanged to a stop on empty magazines. He let go of the trigger and swayed backwards, surveying the gruesome remains. All eyes were staring at him, the crewmen stunned by the brutal execution.

'It was necessary!' he grunted. 'Don't you understand?' he shouted defiantly. 'I had to do it. We cannot take prisoners, there is no room.' He ran out of patience. 'Dive the boat!'

With the deck crew scrambling inside, Schneider took a last look at the swaying field of debris. The witnesses were dead and would be swallowed by the sea. He dropped into the conning tower and secured the hatch. Minutes later the U-boat swam away in sixty metres of water and turned south for Nazi occupied France.

On the surface, at the outer edge of *Glasgow Bay*'s splintered remains, the whites of a man's eyes stared in horror from his oil blackened face. The Chief Engineer took a firm grip of the wooden hatch cover, determined to tell the tale. For as long as he lived he would never forget the grey shark on the side of that conning tower.

4   Mission of Mercy

Falmouth Harbour brightened with the early sun and in the Captain's cabin beneath *Brackendale*'s bridge, Thorburn finished his shave, dried his face, and paused to study the mirrored reflection. There were a few more lines on his forehead these days, but the eyes were clear and the laughter lines at the corners not yet too prominent. Pity about the unruly hair, but that's what he'd been born with.

He put on a fresh shirt, shrugged into his shore side uniform, not quite as threadbare as his seagoing outfit, and gave himself a final cursory glance in the mirror. It would do. A quick check for cigarettes and he made his way up to the bridge.

'Morning, sir,' Armstrong said brightly.

'Morning, Number One,' Thorburn replied, breathing in the tang of dawn's cold air. He felt the throb of the engines being turned, steam pressure raised. Moving across to the portside wing he took in the busy jumble of dockside paraphernalia. The early sun, just clearing the horizon, cast long shadows over the old buildings and he noticed a spiral of smoke from the repair shops. Inside, the welders would be busy fabricating new parts to replace the damaged ships. A motley bunch of tradesmen in flat caps and overalls rounded the corner of the slipway, weighed down with an assortment of tool bags and lunch boxes.

He turned to Armstrong. 'Depth charges?'

'Yes, sir. Finished about an hour ago. All replaced.'

'Good,' Thorburn said, and stepped forward to the bridge screen. He watched a seaman walk along the fo'c'sle to the mooring lines and give one a tug. The chains and capstans met his critical gaze and he nodded in satisfaction.

Footsteps pounded up the bridge ladder. He turned to be met by the anxious face of the duty Telegraphist.

'Urgent message, sir.'

Thorburn took the slip and squinted in response. 'Acknowledge,' he said tersely. Turning to Armstrong, he grimaced. 'We're wanted, Number One. Distress call off the Thames estuary.'

Armstrong sprang to the tannoy. 'Special sea duty men close up for leaving harbour. All hands to stations. At the double.'

As the ship came alive, Thorburn stepped up to the compass platform wondering why *Brackendale* had been called on. It should have been the duty ship. It was only through bitter experience that Thorburn had issued instructions for the boilers to be brought on line before the sun was up. He knew that once daylight arrived the ship needed to be ready for any emergency. He checked his wristwatch and wondered if he had time to change into his seagoing rig. Smoke billowed briefly from the funnel as Dawkins raised steam. Mooring lines were slipped and hauled away, the gangway whipped aboard.

Thorburn stood by the compass housing and bent to a voice-pipe. There was a thrash of white water as she moved her stern out from the dock, the bow spring holding her head. As she angled out from the quayside, Thorburn changed from slow astern to engage a minimal amount of slow ahead. The spring slackened and a shore man let go the wire, and *Brackendale* reversed out into the harbour. On his orders the ship began to move ahead, and as she turned to starboard he felt the bows lift with power and the ship accelerated down river towards the estuary. With the bow wave curling and the surging wake disturbing the banks, the small destroyer raced out beyond the repair basins. At twenty-five knots it wasn't long before they left the coast receding in the distance.

The call had given the freighter's position as approximately seven miles southwest of the Lizard and Thorburn made a quick check on the coastal chart. Straightening up from the table he called a warning to the lookouts. 'Keep your eyes peeled. Any time now, off the port bow.'

Around the decks, those that could be spared strained to catch a glimpse of anything important. As *Brackendale* reached the last reported position, Thorburn bent to the pipe. 'Half ahead together, make revolutions for eight knots.' The forward impetus slowed and the bow wave fell away. A dozen pair of binoculars scanned the sea.

It was Leading Seaman Allun Jones in the port bridge-wing who raised the alarm.

'Objects in the water! Red, oh-one-oh. Two thousand yards.

Thorburn whipped up his old Barr and Stroud glasses and focused them fine across the port bow. Small breaking crests danced across his vision, flickering reflections making him squint.

And then he found the first signs of debris. 'Well done, Jones. I have it,' he said. He immediately decided to approach with the wreckage on their right, down the starboard hull, and bent sideways to the wheelhouse pipe. 'Port ten. Steady on on-nine-five.'

'Port ten. Steady on on-nine-five. Aye aye, sir,' came the Cox'n's acknowledgement.

Brackendale eased away, and as the helm steadied, settled onto her new course. Within minutes wreckage appeared, visible to the naked eye, a broad swathe of fragments filtering by the starboard bow.

'Slow ahead.'

'Slow ahead, aye aye, sir.'

They gently closed in on the sad remains of a sunken ship, and not for the first time in this war, the ship's company hung over the rails and searched for any sign of life.

Thorburn knew it was vital they make a thorough search, but at the same time, with yesterday in mind, he shuddered at the thought of a lurking U-boat, maybe watching them even now.

'Lookouts! Think U-boats,' he called, and guessed that would be enough. Nonetheless, he paced anxiously round the confines of the bridge space, peering intently over the starboard wing. A sad assortment floated past, an undulating mess of oily flotsam. Sodden remnants of clothing, a limp leather glove on a half submerged crate, and the skeletal remains of what must have been the ship's cat. A white Chef's hat, discoloured and torn, and the startling red header of the Daily Mirror, all reminders of a once living ship.

'A survivor! Someone's alive!' The shout came from the quarterdeck.

Thorburn jumped to the back of the bridge and looked aft along the starboard side. Gathering at the rail, the depth charge crew were pointing, gesticulating out beyond the stern. He watched as Sub-Lieutenant George Labatt shoved his way through the men and Thorburn saw him whip off his jacket and sea boots. A seaman tied a line under Labatt's shoulders and without hesitating the young man dived over the low side. The seaman paid out the line and Thorburn raised his glasses for a closer look. He found the survivor clinging to what looked like a hatch cover, a hand waving feebly in the air.

'Stop engines!' he called. God help them if a torpedo found them now.

Labatt, he knew, was a strong swimmer, but even he struggled in the choppy waves. More than once he disappeared, only to pop up splashing on through the water.

Thorburn saw him reach the man and pull him free. He turned him on his back, cradled him to his chest and signalled with his right arm. The men on the rail began to haul them in. Labatt's head and shoulders lifted slightly as the tow took hold, and the pair of them skimmed the water as willing hands pulled on the line. On reaching the side, they separated the oil caked survivor and dragged him over an open scrambling net. Tenderly, with gentle hands, they gathered him into the net and lifted him to the quarterdeck, carefully lowering him to the deck. The generously proportioned figure of Surgeon-Lieutenant 'Doc' Waverley pushed through the crowd of men and he crouched to wipe the blackened face. Someone draped a blanket across his legs and chest. The man stirred, opened his eyes, and tried to speak. Thorburn watched him choke and cough, shivering with cold. Then the Doctor obviously gave orders for him to be taken below, and Thorburn watched the crew disperse.

'Slow ahead, both,' he ordered, relieved to be on the move. They circled and searched for another fifteen minutes, all in vain. No one else was found, so Thorburn set a course for home and made his way below to find the patient. In the sterile surroundings of the brightly lit sick berth, the survivor lay on one of the operating tables. Two of the medics were doing their best to swab away the worst of the oil.

Thorburn raised an eyebrow to Doc Waverley.

'Not so good,' he said, out of the patient's hearing.

Thorburn crossed to the table and looked down, studying the man's face. He appeared to be in his fifties. The matted hair was grey and beneath the remnants of thick oil he could see a deeply lined forehead.

The man's eyes fluttered open and steadied, his breathing harsh, audible.

'A shark,' he managed, and coughed fiercely.

Thorburn frowned, wondering if he'd heard right.

The man tried again. 'A U-boat . . . , shark on the conning tower.' He gagged and wretched, a gunge of oil leaking from the side of his mouth. He reached up and grabbed Thorburn's arm, pulling him closer. The staring eyes bulged with the effort, desperate to speak. 'Machine guns,' he managed. Another pause, whistling breath. 'They surfaced and fired on the Captain, the Cox'n too.' His eyes filled with angry tears. 'Just bloody murdered them, in the water. Shot them to bits.' He let go of Thorburn's arm and sank back. 'A grey shark on the conning tower.' The effort had drained him and Thorburn let him lie. In the silence that followed, he looked up.

'You all heard that? He asked.

Waverly nodded and one of the medics confirmed it. 'Yes, sir.'

Thorburn straightened away and Waverly placed his stethoscope on the man's chest. He listened, then glanced up. 'Shock, hypothermia, oil on his lungs. He's lucky to have made it this far. Rest and warmth for now and we'll see how he goes.

Thorburn was only half listening. This was a witness to cold blooded murder and somehow he'd survived long enough to report what he'd seen. 'Right oh, Doc. Do your best.' He looked again at the oil soaked overalls and the drawn, lined face. You poor bastard, he thought. Whether you survive or not, I'll make damn sure your efforts weren't in vain. He turned away wanting to be alone with his thoughts, afraid of his emotions, and headed for the bridge. It occurred to him that the U-boat might have been the one he'd come across near Cherbourg. No way of knowing for certain, but he just had that feeling.

In London, underneath the house in Porter Street, General Scott Bainbridge handed an encrypted message slip to Sergeant Dave Cooper. 'Send that.'

Cooper took the paper and checked it through. It was a cursory glance, looking for obvious errors; he didn't expect to understand anything in the jumble of letters. 'Yes, sir.' With his right hand hovering above the Morse key, Cooper watched the clock tick round to 08.00 hours and transmitted the call sign. The air waves responded with the operator's signature, a distinct hesitation between two of the letters, a guarantee of authenticity. He nodded to Bainbridge.

'Then send it,' the General insisted, showing his impatience. The key clattered out a rhythmic pulse, the clenched fingers a blur of movement; and across the Channel, hidden in one of Cherbourg's narrow streets, a pair of ears listened and the signal was transcribed.

Cooper waited for the acknowledgement, and signed off. 'All finished, sir.'

'Well done, Sergeant. There'll be a reply to that, should be on the evening call. Make sure your relief keeps me informed.'

'Yes, sir. I'll let him know.'

Bainbridge touched the faded scar, hoping for the best, and for the first time since last night's call, felt a small sense of relief. At the very least, he should be able to recover two vital years of espionage, and with a grim smile he thought it just might save the life of an important asset.

At 08.55 hours, First Officer Jennifer Farbrace, W.R.N.S., opened the door to Commodore Pendleton's office and shrugged out of her overcoat. A westerly breeze had chilled the morning air, bringing with it the threat of rain. She crossed to the large window, drew back the curtains and rolled up the blackout linen. Before her the crowded waters of Portsmouth harbour rippled in the breeze.

Returning to her desk, she placed the gas mask within easy reach and checked her in-tray for anything new. Removing the cover from the typewriter, she made sure the notebook was ready to use, and then walked into the small room of filing cabinets. At a small sink in the corner she filled the kettle and made herself a hot drink. In the main office she paused by the window and nursed the steaming coffee. A vast array of shipping filled the harbour. There were cruisers and destroyers, minesweepers and corvettes, and dozens of landing craft berthed at the docks, in some places six deep. On the quayside to her right a column of Bren Gun Carriers lurched forward in unison lining up to board a Landing Craft Tank. An old V&W destroyer reversed away from her berth, and as Jennifer watched, a Swan class sloop edged forward to claim the spot. And, just for a moment she found herself wondering about Richard Thorburn. *Brackendale* had not been allocated a place in any of Operation Neptune's flotillas. Since leaving Chatham with Pendleton, and working within the strict confines of Overlord, she'd lost track of his whereabouts. Not that their relationship had ever become serious, but she felt comfortable in his presence.

A staff car pulled up on the road below and she watched the Commodore climb out. She pushed all thoughts of Richard to the back of her mind and returned to the desk.

James Pendleton made his weary way up to the office and swung in through the door.

'Good morning, sir.'

He nodded to Jennifer and walked through to his desk. 'Morning, young lady.' He reached inside the top drawer in the centre of the desk and pulled out last night's file. Although the decision was made before he left the office, he'd decided to sleep on it before committing himself to action. Admiral Stanford would know soon enough. Trouble was he hadn't slept much, worrying about all the implications involved. One of those complications was standing there with his coffee, First Officer Jennifer Farbrace. He reached out and took the mug. 'Thank you.' He nodded to the spare seat. 'Sit down, Jennifer.' He saw the surprise in her face and steeled himself to tell her of his decision. 'As you know, young lady, I was called over to see Sir Hugh Stanford.' He took a mouthful of the hot liquid. 'He informed me that one of the destroyers selected for close support has suffered a boiler failure. He tasked me with finding a replacement.' Jennifer sat and crossed her elegant legs, note pad at the ready, pen poised, and Pendleton marvelled at her cheerful efficiency. He held up a hand. 'No, don't take notes yet. This concerns you.' A flicker of concern crossed her face. 'I'm sorry, young lady, but I've had to make a decision to call in Richard Thorburn.'

Her face lit up. 'Oh I am relieved, sir. At least I'll know where he is. And there must be safety in numbers.'

Pendleton took another drink to hide his confusion. Women, he thought, you just never quite knew where you were.

'In that case we'll proceed. Take a message. "To *Brackendale*. Immediate. Proceed Portsmouth with all despatch. Report on arrival." Add my name, code it up, and get that off soonest.'

Jennifer smiled, snapped her notebook together and flounced over to her typewriter. Two new sheets of A4, a carbon between, and her fingers flew across the keys.

Pendleton sat with a cigarette and the last of the bitter coffee, and watched in amazement. In his experience she was as happy as he'd ever known her. It didn't seem to occur to her that Thorburn might end up in more danger with the amphibious assault than with his current duties. A minute later, with a copy in his in-tray, she swept out of the room to get the message sent. He shook his head, slightly amused. Then he reached for the phone and contacted the switchboard. 'Get me Admiral Stanford,' he ordered, and walked over to the window. Outside the sky had changed, weak sunlight through scudding clouds, not as bright as yesterday, he thought, bit windy.

H.M.S. *Brackendale* ploughed through a rising sea, pushing on for the south coast and that first glimpse of Pendennis Castle. The sea breeze had picked up from the west making for a lively passage but as Thorburn climbed to the bridge, the sun peered out from between the clouds.

Armstrong stood back from the compass platform and made his report. 'Course oh-four-five. Speed twenty knots. There's a small convoy ahead moving north past Falmouth, sir.'

Thorburn nodded. 'Thank you, Number One.' He moved to the bridge-screen and narrowed his eyes into the wind.

'Captain, sir?'

Thorburn looked round to find Leading Telegraphist Elliot at his elbow.

'Urgent signal, sir.'

Thorburn glanced at Armstrong with a wry smile. 'Never rains but it pours.' He took the slip of paper and pushed his cap back from his forehead. He read through and handed it to Armstrong. 'Read that.'

Armstrong read aloud. 'Immediate. "*Brackendale* to report Portsmouth with all despatch." and signed off by

Commodore Pendleton.' He folded the message and returned it to Elliot.

Thorburn looked down at his feet, remembering. James Pendleton, shore based staff with an outstanding service history behind him. *Brackendale* had been under his command in the early days, working out of Chatham Dockyard. And the Dover patrols, what became known as 'Hellfire Corner'. So, it was Portsmouth now, he thought, and Commodore no less. He gave Armstrong a sideways glance. 'Acknowledge,' he said to Elliot.

'Aye aye, sir,' the man said, and turned away.

Thorburn took a step across to the wheelhouse voice-pipe. 'Starboard ten. Steer oh-eight-oh degrees.'

'Starboard ten. Steer oh-eight-oh degrees. Aye aye, sir.'

Thorburn straightened and stared at his First Lieutenant. He motioned with his head for Armstrong to join him at the screen. 'If I'm not mistaken,' he said, looking out beyond the bows, 'we might be in for a bit of action.'

Armstrong smiled knowingly and nodded. 'I wouldn't be surprised, sir. Sunshine instead of rain.'

Thorburn grinned with satisfaction, ordered an increase in revolutions, and they braced against the rolling sea.

5   Portsmouth

Thorburn stood high on the ship's compass platform, one eye on *Brackendale*'s heading and one eye on Gosport's southern headland. He bent to the voice-pipe. 'Half ahead, make revolutions for twelve knots.'

'Half ahead, twelve knots, aye aye, sir.'

Brackendale ran in on the final approaches of the Solent, preparing to enter Portsmouth's naval waters. He glanced up as a squadron of Spitfires thundered low overhead, racing out to sea, and a flight of American Mustangs roared after them, peeling away over the Isle of Wight. Sunlight sparkled off a cockpit

'Hands to stations for entering harbour! Special Sea Dutymen close up!' The call rang through the ship's decks and the destroyer sprang to life.

Lieutenant Robert Armstrong made his way forward to the fo'c'sle. Tradition dictated that a destroyer's First Lieutenant oversaw the delicate task of mooring up to the quayside. Not that he had much to oversee. The Petty Officer and Leading Seaman in charge of the fo'c'sle party were well versed in their respective duties, and Armstrong's presence merely satisfied navy protocol. The important difference today was the fact that this was Portsmouth, and God only knew how many senior officers were watching their arrival.

As the first lines were deftly coiled and thrown to the waiting shore staff, Armstrong watched with approval. The heavy mooring wires quickly followed and he satisfied himself as to their security. The Leading Seaman made a final adjustment to a trailing coil, and straightened up in line with the others.

'Bow lines secured, sir,' said the Petty Officer.

'Very well,' Armstrong acknowledged in the traditional manner, and turned to face the bridge. He could see Thorburn checking on the stern lines, waited for him to look forward, and gave him an exaggerated nod. The Captain returned the nod and disappeared from view.

Armstrong heard the faint ring of the wheelhouse telegraph and felt the engines come to a stop. Tying up was complete. He turned back to the Special Sea Dutymen and dismissed them.

'Carry on.'

He let them go and stood for a moment studying the quayside. It wasn't always that easy of course. Not when it was mid-winter, rain coming in sideways, tide against, cross wind and slippery decks. Sometimes there were bad days, and then it took more than a little effort to berth alongside another ship in a fierce swell. But Armstrong was a competent seaman with a strong sense of duty. His primary task was to present the Captain with an efficient, capable, working weapon, ready to be used at a moments notice. And Lieutenant Robert Armstrong, experienced and tactful, had the happy knack of knowing just how to keep *Brackendale* performing at her best.

With the ship secured, Thorburn left the bridge and headed for his cabin. He entered and closed the door, leaning against it. The survivor's name was Edward Fitzpatrick, and Thorburn had entered it into the ship's log, along with the man's statement. Lieutenant-Surgeon 'Doc' Waverly had signed to say he was witness and all that remained was for Thorburn to report the matter to Commodore James Pendleton.

For the second time that morning he checked his appearance in the mirror, settled his cap firmly, and strode out through the passage to the main deck. Chief Petty

Officer Barry Falconer stood checking the restraints on the ship's motorboat and straightened into a salute.

Thorburn touched the peak of his cap in return. 'Remind Number One I'm going ashore, Cox'n. Off to see Pendleton.'

'Aye aye, sir,' Falconer answered and snapped up his best salute.

Thorburn nodded, touched the peak of his cap and stepped out onto the gangway. With an assured confidence he picked his way between the cargo nets and an assortment of crated supplies. A naval ambulance pulled up and the medics brought out a stretcher. He hoped Fitzpatrick recovered. If ever a man deserved a better future, then the Scotsman was first in line. An ammunition lorry drove past and Thorburn waited for it to clear his path, and then found himself saluting a party of seamen marching towards a minesweeper. He cleared the last of the obstacles and glanced back at the ship.

She was no longer the pristine newcomer to the fleet. The odd trace of rust marked her hull. Where once there'd been a distinctive 'dazzle' pattern paint job to camouflage her lines, repairs had taken their toll and she'd been reduced to Admiralty grey. But beneath that drab exterior, beneath the superficial dents and scrapes, Thorburn knew that *Brackendale*'s history singled her out as a remarkable ship of war. He gave an involuntary nod of appreciation. 'Battle hardened' is how one senior officer had described her, and Thorburn knew the truth of that. He half smiled at the thought and turned away to find Pendleton's office.

Fitzpatrick's story needed telling and he quickened his pace.

Hidden in the depths of the English Channel, Kurt Schneider's U-boat moved steadily towards the French coast. At irregular intervals, he came to periscope depth and checked his location against the navigator's predicted position. Rising to a shallow depth of twelve metres was a calculated risk, but in the grey-green, choppy waters of the Channel their chances of being seen from the air were negligible. The electric motors propelled them forward at a good five knots and they were on course to reach the French port of Cherbourg by nightfall.

Schneider leaned on his chart table and scowled in thought. He would have to put one of the men ashore, transfer him out of the boat. His had been a voice of criticism after the episode with the *Glasgow Bay*, and Schneider would not tolerate any dissent. The man would be confined in isolation. Then they would recharge the batteries, replenish the torpedoes and top up with provisions. A few hours of uninterrupted rest and he could return to the Channel and the south coast of England.

On the balcony of an old French chateau, FlotillaKapitän Werner von Holtzmann stood inside the large windows and stared wistfully out to sea. White fair weather clouds filled the mid-morning sky, stretching to the distant horizon. He took a puff of the Havana cigar, rolled the smoke round his palette and blew a perfect circle. For an instant the circle held together, then whisked away to nothing. He blew on the end of the cigar, thinking. Four years back he'd lost the use of his right arm. It had been hit by shrapnel, severed the nerves and paralysed his muscles. The surgeons had saved his arm but were unable to say whether he would ever regain full use of the fingers. So now, all this time later he used his uniform jacket as an improvised sling and tucked his hand between the buttons. As for his career in the Kriegsmarine, it had not been great. He'd lost his ship in the same battle and, in his opinion, to an inferior opponent. At thirty-five years of age, he'd been transferred to a desk job at Wilhelmshaven.

But now, four years later, he was about to attend a meeting in Cherbourg, and he was perplexed. Whatever could they want with a handicapped failure?

A field grey Mercedes pulled up in the chateau's pebbled driveway. Holtzmann tramped down the stairs and stepped outside. The driver opened the rear door and clicked his heels. Von Holtzmann touched the peak of his cap and sank into the leather comfort. Might as well enjoy the finer things of life for a while.

Forty minutes later the car came to a stop near a wide flight of steps in Cherbourg's town centre. Holtzmann climbed out of the car and took the steps two at a time. He strode through the big glass doors of the Grande Hotel and marched down the thick pile carpet to reception. An Oberleutnant wearing the distinctive SS collar badges stepped forward from behind the desk and threw up a formal Nazi salute. 'Heil Hitler!' he snapped. 'Papers, please.'

Holtzmann reluctantly succumbed to the impertinence and produced his identity card. The man took his time, giving the card a thorough scrutiny before begrudgingly handing it back and turning to open a side door. He saluted into the room. 'FlotillaKapitän von Holtzmann,' he announced and stepped back out of the way.

Holtzmann removed his cap with his good hand, took three paces inside the room, and clicked his heels to attention.

Two men sat behind the elegant, intricately carved desk; an old, overweight Admiral and a thin, greying Naval Commander, and initially they chose to ignore Holtzmann's presence, continuing instead to converse with one another in hushed tones. Eventually, the officers behind the desk finished their conversation and the Admiral looked up and entwined his fingers under his double chin.

Holtzmann felt the man's disdainful, hawk like eyes give him a dismissive inspection.

'Why is it Holtzmann that I have to find you something to do?' he asked quietly, menacingly. He shook his head in a show of exaggerated frustration. 'You lost your ship, did you not, and yet you had the temerity to survive.' He raised his voice in anger. 'Why did you not die when you had the chance? It would have saved me having to even look at you.'

Holtzmann gritted his teeth, tightened his mouth, and held his anger.

The Admiral snorted in disbelief. 'Nothing to say for yourself? He leaned back in his seat, contemplating a folder on the table. 'If I had my way, you would have been dismissed. Gone!' The heavy jowls wobbled. 'Unfortunately, the Kriegsmarine has lost many good commanders, men who have died for the Fuhrer, fighting for the Fatherland!' He shook his head. 'But it seems after all this time, you may be useful. So my thoughts are for nothing, I am overruled.' He reached forward over his ample paunch and opened the folder. 'Because we are threatened by the Allied invasion, you will go to Alderney,' he grimaced, and turned to the Naval Commander. 'No one in his right mind would want a posting there, eh?'

The Commander nodded, grinning. 'Only fit for the dregs.'

The Admiral picked up a typewritten sheet. 'It says here that you are to assume command of the island's Schnellboat Flotilla.

Von Holtzmann felt his pulse quicken. A new command. A myriad questions ran through his mind. How many boats? What was their role? Would he have sole command? Not that he would give them the satisfaction of hearing his concerns. He remained silent, totally impassive.

The Admiral fixed Holtzmann with a glare. 'Your job will be to maintain a constant watch to the north, night patrols.' He looked at the Commander. 'Have I missed anything?'

'No, sir, but I must add,' and the thin face scowled as he glared at Holtzmann, 'you are there to raise the alarm. Spread your forces, find the enemy, and raise the alarm. Are we clear?'

Holtzmann nodded. 'Yes, sir.' He wanted to be away, get to Alderney, but he was struck by a sudden thought. 'If I may ask, who recommended me for this command?'

The Naval Commander glanced at the Admiral, who looked away. 'Kriegsmarine headquarters at Bremerhaven, Admiral Mathias Krause.'

For the first time, Holtzmann smiled. Admiral Krause had been instrumental in giving von Holtzmann his last command. He was a powerful ally, an important marker for the future.

The Admiral saw the smile and stared angrily. 'Do you find us amusing, Holtzmann? Something we said? A joke perhaps?'

'No, sir.'

The heavy jowls wobbled and he waved a podgy hand. 'Then you are dismissed.'

Holtzmann clicked his heels and marched out of the office. He glared at the SS Oberleutnant, daring him to speak, and jammed his cap on his head. The staff car was still waiting at the bottom of the steps. He climbed in and ordered the driver to take him to the harbour. Settled in the back seat, he touched the Iron Cross at his neck, remembering the days of glory. There might yet be a chance to win more decorations.

At ten o'clock Richard Thorburn entered the old red

brick building, and after asking for directions, took the stairs up to Pendleton's office. He tapped the outer door and pushed his way in. First Officer Jennifer Farbrace looked up in surprise.

'Hello sir, can I help you?' Hidden behind the formality, her eyes twinkled, smiling.

Thorburn recognised the formality and winked. 'I'm here to see the Commodore.'

'He's expecting you, sir. I'll let him know you're here.'

She made a move towards Pendleton's office, but the door opened before she reached it.

The Commodore's ruddy, bearded features beamed into the room. 'Ha! I thought it was you, Richard. Come in, come in.'

Thorburn entered the senior officer's inner sanctum.

Pendleton gestured to a chair. 'Sit down, m'boy. I hear you were out looking for survivors, how'd it go?' He looked at Thorburn from across his desk, and the smile faded from his lips.

'One survivor, sir,' Thorburn said soberly. 'A fair bit of wreckage, what you might expect.'

'It wasn't a wasted journey then. At least you saved a life.'

'Yes . . . ,' Thorburn said, perturbed by what he was about to say. He shuffled his feet, uncomfortable. 'I'm sorry, sir, but I'm obliged to pass on a report from that survivor.'

Pendleton stroked the full beard, raised an eyebrow. 'Go on.'

'The man we pulled from the water is called Fitzpatrick. He was the Chief Engineer.'

'Right . . . ?

'He's a witness to murder.'

Pendleton rubbed the top of his nose and then pushed a silver cigarette box across the desk. 'Proceed.' He held out

58

the flame of a lighter.

Thorburn lit one and dragged in the smoke. As he breathed out he continued. 'The U-boat surfaced and machined gunned two men in the water. According to Fitzpatrick, they were the Captain and the Cox'n.'

Pendleton tugged on his beard. 'And they were killed?'

'Yes, sir, shot to pieces.' Thorburn sat forward in the chair. 'More to the point, Fitzpatrick knows what U-boat was involved. It had a motif on the conning tower, a large grey shark.' He sat back.

Pendleton sat stiffly upright, taking in the news. 'I take it you've written this in your report.'

'I have, sir. Doc Waverly is witness to the statement.'

'And how's Fitzpatrick now?'

'Fifty-fifty. Doc's inclined to think he'll pull through.'

Pendleton stood up and walked to the window, standing with his hands clasped behind his back. 'I'll let the Channel Patrol know, and I'll get Jennifer to type up your report, get a copy off to the Admiralty.'

Thorburn watched him turn into the room, felt Pendleton's eyes searching his own.

'I know how you feel, Richard, but right now, there's nothing you can do about it.'

'No, sir,' he said. 'Sorry, but I thought you ought to know soonest.'

Pendleton nodded. 'And you were right. Best thing, get it in motion.' He held up a hand. 'But if you remember I requested you report to me. Now you're here, we have a problem to resolve. Sit down,' he said, indicating the seat. 'Please.' He moved back to his desk and hovered above his chair.

Thorburn sat with a sense of misgiving. Now what?

The Captain stared down at his desk, hesitant. Eventually he looked up. 'I've had a meeting with a chap called Stanford, an Admiral; not that you'll have heard of him. One of the backroom boys.'

'Yes, sir?' Thorburn answered guardedly.

Pendleton swivelled in his chair, leaned back, stretched his legs and crossed his ankles. 'He ordered me to find a replacement for the invasion. You're it.'

Thorburn compressed his lips into a hard line and frowned. Surely this was a bit late in the day. No one in their right mind could fail to understand the invasion of Europe was imminent. At the same time, he couldn't help but feel a twinge of elation.

'To do what, sir?'

'You'll be joining Force U, known simply by the codeword 'Utah'. It represents the 4th Infantry Division of the American Army. It'll be the right flank of the invasion. *Brackendale* will actually form part of Operation Neptune, which means us, the Navy.' He extracted another cigarette from his packet. 'Initially, your job is to support the troops on the beaches. That means covering fire as they go in, and then any targets of opportunity.'

Pendleton reached for Thorburn's file and detached a large envelope. 'These are your orders.' He tapped the packet. 'They include order of battle, timings for departure, rendezvous, cleared channels, and 'H' hour, the time the infantry hit the beaches. There's a lot to learn and not much time to do it.'

Thorburn picked up the envelope and peered inside. There certainly were a lot of pages. 'Exactly how much time, sir?'

Pendleton fingered his beard and Thorburn could see he was struggling for the answer.

'One day . . . , maybe two at the outside.'

Thorburn grimaced. 'Christ Almighty!' He swept an arm out towards the sea. 'The rest of the fleet have had months!'

Pendleton shook his head. 'No, m'boy, not true. Most

of the commanders only opened their sealed orders the other day.'

It was tempting for Thorburn to begin reading, but he resisted. 'Anything else, sir?'

Pendleton nodded. 'As from now your ship is closed down. Except for you, no one leaves. There'll be no visitors, no mail, on or off. Telephone calls forbidden, no telegram cables. If there's a private family emergency then a wire is permitted, but only with your authority. Have I made myself clear?'

'Definitely, sir.'

'Good. Read through that lot and if you have any questions, come and see me.'

Thorburn stood to go. 'Thank you, sir.'

He saw Pendleton tug at his beard and Thorburn hesitated, raised an eyebrow.'

Before you go . . . , there's something I think you ought to know. There are an estimated 160,000 troops involved in this operation. This will be the greatest sea borne landing ever attempted. Operation Neptune has more than 6,000 vessels under its command.' He paused, catching Thorburn's eye. 'Just think of it. Battleships, cruisers, frigates, destroyers, the minesweepers, and all the other small boats to get the troops across and onto the beaches.'

Thorburn waited, but Pendleton looked down and continued to stare at the desk, so he left him to his thoughts and turned to find Jennifer in the outer office. That wonderful sense of relaxed familiarity pervaded his senses, a tenderness he'd never experienced with anyone else. It had been some time since they'd seen one another and yet there was never a moment of awkwardness between them. They just slipped back into that beautiful, warm relationship. Not that he took it for granted. From the first time she'd made her feelings known, he'd always wondered what it was she saw in him. She was not someone to trifle with, and it never occurred to him to even look at another woman.

She reached up and touched his face. 'Will I see you before you go?'

Thorburn swallowed and forced a smile. 'You probably know that better than I do.'

She stood on tiptoe and kissed him lightly. 'There's a chance, a final briefing for destroyers. Tomorrow, I think.'

Thorburn glanced at Pendleton's door and bent to her lips. She clasped her hands around his neck, holding him tightly. Slowly, he eased himself away and smiled. 'I bet you do that with all the sailors.'

Jennifer tilted her head to one side. 'And I bet there's a woman in every port you visit.'

He grinned, chuckled. 'Fat chance, I'm never in port long enough.'

They kissed once more.

There was a polite cough. 'When we've all quite finished,' Pendleton said from his office, 'I have a signal to send.'

Thorburn winked and she turned for her handbag. A quick glance in a small mirror and she reached for her notepad. With a wave of her fingers she was gone, leaving Thorburn to make his way out and back to *Brackendale*'s cabin to read through his vital new orders.

In the Channel Islands, on the northeast tip of Alderney, near the west coast of France, a pair of Schnellboats took it in turns to patrol the surrounding seas. In addition to the sailors and shore staff involved in their operations, a small detachment of navy personnel were stationed in the partial remains of an old fort. Their job was to provide radio communications with the Kriegsmarine's headquarters at Cherbourg.

Hans Keller, the senior German naval Telegraphist in charge, sat playing a game of chess with one of his watch keepers. The dials on the wireless transmitter glowed orange in the gloom, the pair of headphones propped on a biscuit tin to amplify their sound. As he moved a pawn to cover the threat of a knight, the hiss of background static cleared and he heard the dots and dashes repeated. He crossed to the rickety seat and grabbed the telegraph key. He rattled off his acknowledgement and reached for a notepad. The Morse code message began and Keller scribbled each combination of letters onto the pad. Finally the buzz of telegraphy stopped and he toggled the Bakelite knob in response to the transmission and signed off.

Shaking his head at the unintelligible grouping of letters he moved over to the decoding machine. He sat himself squarely in front of the glorified typewriter, checked the calibration of the Enigma's four drum rotors, and began the laborious task of punching in the letters from his notepad.

Twenty minutes later he stood up with the decrypted message, read it again and dropped it in front of his chess partner. The man scanned it quickly and glanced up with a soft whistle.

'They won't be happy with that, too many changes.'

Keller nodded, grinning. 'The Oberleutnant's problem, not ours. Take over,' he ordered, and strode off to find the officer in charge of Schnellboats.

Far away in England, deep in the heart of rural Buckinghamshire, a member of the Intelligence section, a 'code breaker' began to decipher the signal.

6 Jeopardy

Mademoiselle Marianne Legrande walked self-consciously along the cobbled street on the southern outskirts of Cherbourg. In the crook of her left elbow, covered with a red checked cloth, she carried a wicker basket for her shopping. The sound of an engine made her step to one side and a German army despatch rider bounced his motorbike over the uneven surface, helmet and goggles hiding his face. She looked away, not wanting to attract attention, just another peasant-woman going about her daily chores. The motorbike smoked past and she felt the draft on her bare calves. Mindful of being followed, she glanced cautiously up and down the street before crossing to the narrow path opposite. Her destination lay round the corner of a side street, the patisserie of Monsignor Francois Toussaint.

As Marianne pushed open the half glazed door the bell tinkled on the wall inside. She was greeted by the warm smell of freshly baked bread and the jovial figure of Toussaint. He wiped his red face with a corner of his apron and smiled broadly.

'Bonjour, mademoiselle. What can I get for you today?'

Marianne inclined her head and spoke softly. 'Bonjour, Monsieur Toussaint.' She looked around as if confused. 'I think that two of your farmhouse loaves would be wonderful. Which ones would you suggest?' She removed the check cloth and placed the basket on the counter.

Toussaint beamed cheerfully, bent to a bread cabinet and selected two well risen loaves. He positioned them neatly within the wicker basket and straightened up. The genial host of moments before changed. The smile disappeared. He glanced at the window then held her eyes. He leaned in a little closer and patted the top of the loaves.

'A very wholesome choice mademoiselle.' He dropped his gaze and ran his finger over the rough handle. 'There is much goodness inside a well baked loaf.' He raised his eyes to hers, a faint smile playing about his lips.

Marianne nodded and tucked the check cloth neatly round the bread.

'Thank you, monsieur, I always enjoy your baking.'

Toussaint lifted the basket and handed it to her. 'Even more so with these, I assure you,' he said, and gave her a final, significant look.

The movement was minimal, but she understood the implication, instinctively held the basket closer, not wanting to share with anyone. She felt in her skirt pocket for some coins.

The door crashed open behind her, the bell ringing loudly. A pair of tall Wehrmacht soldiers stomped in, brushing past to the counter. They were young, in their early twenties, a corporal and a gunner. The corporal turned to glower at her and she shrank inside. Given the opportunity she could handle herself, but not now, and definitely not here.

'And what have we here?' he said in broken French. He grinned, nudging his comrade.

The gunner leered over the corporal's shoulder and said something in German. The corporal took a pace towards her and she backed away to the door. He stepped beyond her, blocking her path.

She felt his hand on her arm and shook it free. 'You are not allowed to touch me!' she shouted. 'Your officers have given the order.' She knew the German Command had decreed a policy of non-aggression towards the civilians. Only if they had reason to believe they were dealing with the Resistance could they ignore the order. The corporal understood enough to stand clear, but the gunner was not so timid. He laughed aloud at the corporal's reluctance and made a grab for the basket.

Marianne pulled away, and bumped into the corporal behind. The gunner slid an arm round her waist and drew her closer. He tried for a kiss and she turned her face to the side, his foul breath on her cheek.

The corporal said something, a sharp order, and the gunner hesitated, then let go and stepped back. He glared at her, angry. The corporal intervened and pulled him to the counter where Toussaint stood waiting to serve them.

Marianne fumbled with the handle of the door behind her back, managed to undo it and slipped out before they could stop her. She ran out of the side street and back to the cobbled road, retracing her steps and crossing over where the motorbike had driven by. To avoid any unwanted attention she forced herself to walk and glanced over her shoulder in case the men had followed. The road was clear and she drew a deep breath to regain her composure. Up ahead a married woman with her two laughing children emerged from one of the terraced houses. An old man came into view pushing a bicycle, and beyond him at the Café Royale the owner swept the pavement in between the tables and chairs. She breathed a sigh of relief. Normality, she thought, the everyday life of the townspeople.

A few more paces and Marianne turned left into the cul-de-sac where she lived. The house lay back on the right. A final check to see if she'd been followed and she slipped down the tiny alleyway that separated the buildings. The side door was almost at the rear of the house and inserting the key she let herself in. Through into the kitchen she removed the lid of the bread bin and carefully placed the two loaves inside. From a drawer of the old wooden table she found her pistol and made certain it was loaded. Tip toeing gingerly into the front room she crossed to the window and peered through the lace net curtains. The cul-de-sac was clear, only a fat tabby cat grooming itself by the kerb.

Satisfied, the pistol was returned to the drawer and she went to the bread bin and pulled out the top loaf. Taking a plate from a cupboard she put both the plate and the bread on the table and sat down with a knife. This was the loaf that Francois Leroux had made a point of patting.

Discarding the knife in favour of a more gentle approach, she took the bread in her fingers and prised it apart. The friable texture broke easily and there in the middle a glint of steel caught her eye. With a thumb and forefinger she eased out a small cylinder resembling a tube of lipstick. Unscrewing the cap she found a tightly rolled scrap of paper, unfurled it, and smoothed the creases on the table. A series of hieroglyphics were revealed, in blocks of five or six. She pulled a writing pad from the drawer and settled down to decipher the characters. Fifteen minutes later she read the decoded message. "FOXCUB-TO PROCEED TALON. AWAIT CONTACT. THREE DAYS.- EAGLE" It was brief and to the point. She was to leave Cherbourg for 'Talon' the hideout at Le Cavalaire, and wait to be contacted in three days time.

Tearing off the top sheet of the writing pad she burnt it in the stove with the original scrap of paper. Thinking of her options, she settled on the cover of darkness to make her move to the hideout. More importantly, she needed to unearth the map of Cherbourg which she had so meticulously updated. Gun emplacements, barracks, ships, headquarters, any and everything that she felt was of interest to the Allies.

Marianne sighed and walked slowly to the bottom of the stairs and stopped to glance down at her outfit. The light summer floral skirt and blouse, her round-toed leather sandals and ankle socks. Pretty, feminine clothing. Now it was time to dig out the jacket and trousers, and the boots of her farming days before the Boche arrived. Her stay in this house had come to an end, but she had no regrets, it had all just been part of the job. This was the fulfilment of four years working for the British Secret Operations Executive, and the French section of the 'underground'. Many of the others had been betrayed and tortured before being shot, but she'd been lucky and survived. She smiled ruefully and climbed slowly up the stairs to the bedroom.

In a large Nissen hut well within the secure confines of Plymouth Harbour, Major Paul Wingham, one time Sherwood Forester, and a former member of the Special Operations Executive, sat listening through a pair of headphones. He'd been sending grid co-ordinates via a standard infantry wireless set. Five miles north, at a temporary wireless station, a Royal Navy signalman acknowledged receipt of his message.

Wingham glanced down at his notepad and the book of codes and gently let out a breath of air. It had been his final day of practice, the culmination of a six week refresher. This had been his last two hours of instruction by a Petty Officer Telegraphist, a rigorous programme specifically designed to simulate battlefield conditions. He felt, all in all, things hadn't gone too badly, but he hesitated to ask. Finally he summoned the courage. 'And . . . ? What do you think?'

The Petty Officer, a man who could code and send messages in his sleep, pursed his lips in judgement. 'You'll do,' he said grudgingly. A faint smile softened his craggy face. 'Another month or so and you might get the hang of it. I might even manage to decipher some of it.'

Wingham grinned. 'In that case I'm off to the canteen. Cup of tea wouldn't go amiss.'

The Petty Officer stood and offered his hand. 'All the best for the future. You never know, sir, might be me taking down your messages.'

Wingham shook his head. 'Provided I remember all the dots and dashes.'

The man looked at him, held his eyes. 'And the Map Reference Codes. But I'm sure you'll remember,' he said simply, and turned back to his bank of wireless sets.

Major Paul Wingham made his way outside to stand and watch an American infantry squad scramble aboard an Assault boat. In the cockpit, a Royal Navy Sub-Lieutenant nodded to the Cox'n, and with a rumbling roar the boat pushed out into the bay.

Wingham's blue eyes narrowed as the boat headed away and then began to turn in a wide arc to the left. He gazed out beyond the harbour losing himself to the northern shores of France. He knew that stretch of countryside like the back of his hand. For two dangerous years, he'd fought with the Resistance using guerrilla warfare to disrupt the German occupation of the Cotentin Peninsula. Within days he'd be back in the same towns and villages. He wondered how much it had changed.

'Sir?' came a voice from behind.

Wingham, standing rigidly upright, looked round.

'Phone call for you, sir,' said the hard faced Sergeant Foster. 'Sounds important.'

Wingham turned back to watch the boat. 'And who would be calling with such importance?'

'A Vice-Admiral Sir Hugh Stanford, sir.'

Wingham met that with the prominence it deserved, swung round and strode purposefully towards the Nissen hut. Barging in through the door he grabbed the receiver off the desk and put it to his ear. 'Wingham, sir.'

'Ah, Wingham, Admiral Stanford here, we have something to discuss. I want you to report to me here at Southwick House.'

Wingham frowned into the mouthpiece, wondering where the hell Southwick House was. 'Of course, sir. When?'

'Yesterday?'

'Right, sir. On my way.'

'Good man. Tell that Sergeant of yours to stay on the phone, get all the details. By the way, you'll be meeting a chap called Thorburn.'

There was a click as the line went dead and Wingham carefully replaced the handset. He thought for a moment, memories flooding back. Richard Thorburn, eh? That was a blast from the past. A man after his own heart, but more than that, reliable, a good friend. He waited for Foster to take down the particulars. 'So where's this Southwick House?'

Foster unclipped a map case, pointed to Portsmouth and tapped his finger on the northern countryside. 'Just there, sir.'

Wingham sucked at a tooth. 'Sergeant, do we still have that motorbike?'

'Well. . , yes, sir. Somewhere.'

'Dig it out for me, there's a good chap. And find some petrol; I'm off to the land of the gentry.'

Sergeant Foster gave him an old fashioned look. 'Right, sir, but I'm not sure if that bike's reliable.'

Wingham was in no mood to argue. 'Just do as I ask, Sergeant, let me worry about the rest.'

Foster made a move for the door. 'Helmet and goggles, sir?'

'If you can,' Wingham agreed.

Foster walked out shaking his head. He'd known Wingham for a while now. Never a dull moment.

Wingham stepped back outside the hut and stood for a moment, waiting. Every conceivable type of Landing Craft jostled for space in what seemed like organised chaos. A few of the boats had berthed at purpose built ramps sloping down to meet the water. These Landing Craft for Infantry (LCI's) waited now, ramp-doors hinged down, for men to fill their holds. This was the embarkation area for the American 4th Infantry Division and with them, on one of the smaller Higgins Assault boats, would be Major Paul Wingham.

The door to the Nissen hut creaked open and banged shut behind him.

'Hi there, Major. How's it goin?'

Wingham turned to the sound of the American's drawl. He was a big man, loud, outspoken and generous, and over the last month Wingham had grown to enjoy his company. Sergeant Chuck Rivers had joined the Rangers during '42. More to the point he was Wingham's primary source of tactical information during the assault, and that made him almost indispensable.

'Hello, Chuck. Won't be long before your men start going aboard.'

'Yeah, I guess.' The Sergeant walked forward, hands on hips. 'About time it happened. They're ready; as good as we can make 'em.'

Wingham nodded to himself. He'd been training with the Americans for three weeks, and to his way of thinking, they certainly were ready.

Rivers swung round. 'You sure you're gonna hang on to that Sten gun of yours? You're more'n welcome to one of ours.'

Wingham smiled. 'Sorry, Sergeant, I like what I'm used to. Simple and reliable. That'll do me.'

'Have it your way, Major.' He grinned, a wide charitable show of teeth. 'Sure as hell ain't gonna keep asking.'

'I'm fine,' Wingham said, and changed the subject. 'Heard anything about when we go?'

'Well, for certain sure it won't be none too soon. It's gonna take a couple of days just to load the Division.'

Wingham thought the same, said as much. 'True, and that's if it all goes smoothly. You Yanks are sure to mess it up.' He closed one eye and smiled.

'Aw, go to hell. We only do what you Brits teach us, and that ain't much.' He nudged Wingham discreetly in the ribs then looked at his watch. 'Better go, there's a lot to do.' He turned away, the wide shoulders holding him tall. As he walked off he looked back and yelled. 'By the way, how's that radio of yours? Found out how to switch it on?' His laughter rang out loud and clear and he disappeared around the end of the Nissen hut.

Wingham ambled forward, the smile dying on his lips. Even now the harbour was busy; it was hard to imagine what would happen when the 4th Division arrived.

Wingham turned away in search of Sergeant Foster and found him pushing the 500cc motorbike out into the lorry park. 'Petrol?' he asked.

'Full, sir.'

The Major removed his beret and tucked it inside the blouse of his battledress. He grabbed the goggles and helmet and fired up the B.S.A in a cloud of blue smoke. There was a tap on his arm and he found Foster offering him a thick pair of gauntlets. Pulling them on with a nod of thanks he thumped the leather to settle his fingers. Waving a raised glove to Foster, he blipped the throttle, bounced over a kerb, and accelerated away. It might be a long road to Portsmouth.

In the sheltered water of Cherbourg's western docks, ten Schnellboats swayed and dipped at their moorings. The Command boat, under the captaincy of an experienced Oberleutnant, was warped up to a solid wooden jetty. At precisely 10.45 hours Werner von Holtzmann arrived in his staff car. He waited for the driver to open the door, and having dressed in his best uniform, and with the Iron Cross prominently displayed round his neck, made an exaggerated show of climbing out from the back seat. For a moment he stood tall, surveying the busy harbour. A cargo ship unloaded at the wharf, dockside cranes swinging heavily laden nets to the waiting flatbed lorries. Anti-aircraft ships hurried to and fro and the crew of a U-boat replenished supplies. Fixed harbour gun emplacements ringed the water's edge, the defences enhanced by a dozen mobile 88's strategically positioned on the breakwaters. A company of Wehrmacht infantry marched noisily out from the town and along the seafront. Holtzmann's eyes lit up with pride. This was the all conquering magnificence of the Fuhrer's Atlantic Wall, enough to dissuade even the most powerful of enemies.

He dismissed the driver and strutted out over the cobbled road, his damaged arm tucked across his chest, the epitome of a wounded officer who'd suffered for his Fatherland. He strode on down the dockside accompanied by the screeching call of seagulls, weak rays of sunlight glinting off the distant sea. At the jetty he stepped down tentatively to the greasy planks and a waiting seaman reached up to offer his support. He waved him off with his good arm. 'Leave me. Get out of it!'

The Oberleutnant saluted and Holtzmann stretched a foot onto the deck of the boat. He ducked inside the cockpit and made himself comfortable.

'Are we ready to proceed?' he asked abruptly.

'Jawohl, Herr Kapitän.'

'Then take us out.'

The roar of the engines hammered into life and the torpedo boat nosed clear of the jetty. The helmsman increased speed and the boat powered up to curve gracefully out of the harbour and meet the open sea.

Holtzmann leaned against the portside of the cockpit, pulled out one of his favourite cigars and lit the end. A mist of blue smoke drifted through the compartment and he smiled thinly. He was back at sea, how best to exploit this new opportunity? The bows thumped into a wave and the Schnellboat set course for Alderney.

Sergeant Chuck Rivers sat outside his tent in the forward United States Army transit camp on Dartmoor, a few miles east of Plymouth. His Thompson submachine-gun lay on an upturned wooden crate in front of him. With a quick glance at his wristwatch he closed his eyes and reached blindly for the weapon. Practised fingers stripped the gun, each disassembled part placed in order on the box, and then the whole weapon expertly reassembled. He finally felt for the empty magazine and clipped it in place. He cocked the weapon, squeezed the trigger and opened his eyes to the wristwatch. He was two seconds over his best. He sighed and prepared to repeat the process.

A tall loose limbed Ranger ambled over from the communications tent.

'Sarge? The C.O. wants you.'

Rivers squinted up at Corporal Joe Donavon's lean features and tightened his lips.

'Mmm . . . , he say where?' He wondered if the Colonel really had anything new to add. The Rangers had been here two weeks now, continually rehearsing assaults on makeshift targets, and taking part in long marches over the moors.

'Down at the chow tent,' Donavon said. 'Squad Leaders only.'

Rivers levered himself to his feet, slung the Thompson and nodded.

'Okay. Don't let the fellas stray too far. Might be something important.

Donavon chuckled sarcastically. 'Fat chance. They just like the sound of their own voices.'

'Could be,' Rivers acknowledged, and strode off along the bracken trampled path between the lines of tents. It was a small camp, just four platoons of Rangers split into specialised squads to fulfil vital missions during the D-Day assault. His own squad included Major Paul Wingham. And Chuck Rivers surmised the Major knew a thing or two about warfare, knew how to handle himself. Above all, the Englishman was proficient in radio communications, particularly the British Royal Navy procedure.

The Sergeant stepped over a pegged rope and joined a few of the other Squad Leaders queuing at the tent flap.

'Hey, Rivers. You heard anything?

It was a Texan drawl and he looked back to see the piercing gaze of Sergeant Dan Pitman with his eyebrows raised in query.

'Nah,' Rivers said, shaking his head. 'You?'

The Texan stuck his chin out towards the coast. 'Word has it that 4th Infantry are heading for the boats.'

Rivers eyed him for a long moment. Pitman wasn't prone to exaggeration, checked rumours before making a comment.

'Let's hope you're right, Dan. Might be we get to join 'em.'

The queue of men began to move through the tent flap and Rivers pushed inside. The eating tables had been stacked to one side and the slatted folding chairs lined up in rows. The interior reeked of canvas and cooking fat and at the far end of the tent he could see the Colonel waiting impatiently.

He squeezed along between the chairs and took a seat behind the front row, and when he peered between a pair of heads he could see British Naval officers and a U.S. Army General standing with the Colonel. An air of expectancy filled the tent before the Colonel took a pace forward and cleared his throat.

'I've called you together to tell you we're on the move.'

There was a restrained chorus of approval from the Squad Leaders and the Colonel held up a hand.

'You have four hours before we load up the trucks.' He half turned to acknowledge the uniforms behind him. 'These gentlemen will run you through the necessary details and allocate your squads to their Assault Boats. The infantry are moving down to their assembly points and you Rangers will join them at approximately 18.00 hours.' He paused and placed his hands on his hips.

'As soon as you're done with the Navy, General Stockman and I will show you the missions for each squad.' He looked behind, had a quiet word with the General and nodded. When he turned back, he glanced at his watch. 'Right, you have fifteen minutes to saddle up, and then I want all of you back here for that final briefing. Get to it.'

Rivers came to his feet, excited but contained. He jostled his way to the exit, ducked under the tent flap and collided with the Texan, Dan Pitman. The Sergeant looked at him and grinned.

'Guess somebody got the low-down right this time.'

Rivers nodded. 'Sure did.' He glanced up at the grey clouds, spitting with rain. 'Hope to hell the weather boys get the low-down on what's happening in their neck of the woods.'

They parted company and Sergeant Chuck Rivers, a veteran of Patton's campaign to take the island of Sicily, straightened his shoulders and headed back to the tents.

7 Secrets

Richard Thorburn lay on his bunk, half propped against the bulkhead. He turned to the next page of his orders and read from top to bottom. His forehead creased in concentration, storing away the important, discarding the extraneous. He was astonished by the amount of planning and detail, the numbers involved, the sheer scale of ambition. Eventually he came to the final page and sat up. Time to inform Armstrong. He called up the voice-pipe to the bridge. 'Is the First Lieutenant up there?'

'Yes, sir.'

'Have him come to my cabin.'

'Aye aye, sir.'

Thorburn went to his desk and dropped the papers in the middle, stood there pondering. He heard footsteps in the corridor and looked up.

Lieutenant Robert Armstrong peered in the door. 'You asked for me, sir?'

Thorburn nodded and indicated a chair. 'Come in, Number One. Take a seat.'

Armstrong sat down, eyes questioning.

Thorburn studied him for a moment, reflecting on their four year relationship. Eighteen months ago, on Thorburn's recommendation, Armstrong could have accepted promotion to a command of his own, but had turned it down in favour of remaining as First Lieutenant with H.M.S. *Brackendale*. Thorburn had accepted his loyalty with genuine pleasure and their partnership had continued much as before. The two executive officers, sharing a mutual respect and a quiet friendship had served the ship well and Thorburn took great satisfaction in the arrangement.

'I've just finished reading this lot,' he said, pointing to the stack of pages. 'We're going in with the Americans, part of what they're calling Force U. That's short for Utah, the codeword for the beach they're landing on. Believe me, that's the simple bit. From then on in it gets complicated. I'm already concerned about the crossing; there'll be a marked channel, critical for navigation.' He paused to collect his thoughts. Armstrong sat patiently, waited.

'I want to see all officers in the wardroom. Petty Officers too.' He glanced at the time. 'Let's say two o'clock. I still need to get my head round some of the detail.'

Armstrong nodded. 'What about ammunition? You mentioned extra rounds for the four inch.'

'Yes, we'll have to get that sorted. Should get a call from supply.'

Armstrong came to his feet. 'I'll let the officers know, sir.'

Thorburn stood back and rubbed his chin. 'Thank you, Number One. I take it you've secured ship, no comings and goings?'

'The Cox'n put two Leading Seamen on the gangway and had a word with the crew.' Armstrong grinned tightly. 'I don't think there were any arguments.'

Thorburn conjured up a picture of the Cox'n's briefing. There wouldn't have been many brave enough to disagree. 'Mmm . . . , in that case, I'll see you in the wardroom.'

'Aye aye, sir. Two o'clock,' and Armstrong quietly closed the door behind him.

Thorburn sat down and selected a cigarette. God, he thought, there was a lot to get through. And what was that about ship-to-shore signalling? He dug into the pages and pulled out a separate section entitled 'Close Support' and focused on the contents. The muted sounds of shipboard life receded into the background.

600 nautical miles west of Ireland, in the wide open reaches of the Atlantic Ocean, three Royal Navy warships maintained station on a predetermined area of watch keeping. On board the most southerly of the three ships, a recently commissioned heavily armed sloop, H.M.S. *Rosefinch*, the navigator was wholly occupied with piloting the ship. Every thirty minutes, while zigzagging to circumvent an attack by U-boats, the ship changed course and steamed at twenty-five knots in the opposite direction. Half an hour north, followed by half an hour south, a rhythmic repetition of course and speed.

Lieutenant-Commander Peter Willoughby R.N., D.S.O., controlled his urge to break away and alleviate the tedium. He of all people knew the importance of his mission. In his day cabin below were three members of a Metrological Survey team. It was their job to monitor the current weather conditions out here in the Atlantic. On the hour, every hour, they compiled a report which was then sent to England and immediately forwarded on to the Met Office for analysis. And Peter Willoughby knew he wasn't the only one. Four-hundred miles north, a brace of fleet destroyers were repeating the exercise; and beyond the horizon another pair of American warships patrolled west of the Azores. From Iceland, Scotland and Ireland the information flowed in. Peter Willoughby quelled his urge for action, sat himself in the bridge-chair and lit a cigarette. And just beyond the visible horizon the prevailing winds brought the threat of rain. Conditions began to deteriorate.

It was early afternoon when Werner von Holtzmann eyed up the approaches to Braye harbour. His Schnellboat pushed south round Alderney's northern headland, bristling with the heavy coastal artillery and their massive fortifications. There was a long breakwater to his right, the western arm of protection against the prevailing winds. In the calm waters of the harbour, two anti-aircraft vessels sat prominently near the entrance. A handful of men from the flack battalion could be seen manning the guns.

The boat throttled back and eased over to the high breakwater, the powerful engines burbling and grumbling in neutral. At the top of the stone steps a very young Wehrmacht officer saluted. 'Welcome to Alderney, Herr Kapitän.'

Holtzmann scowled. 'You make it sound like a holiday camp.'

The young man smiled. 'But it is, sir. Fine weather, much sunshine, and warm enough to swim.'

Holtzmann remained straight faced. 'I am not here for holidays. There is much work to do and I will inspect the flotilla. Now!'

The young officer dropped the smile and straightened to attention. 'Jawohl, Herr Kapitän, but there is not much to see. The Kriegsmarine only have a few personnel.' He spread his hands to the harbour. 'There is your navy. A couple of gunboats and three Schnellboats who are patrolling to the west. What is there to inspect?'

Holtzmann swallowed, taken off guard. He thought there would be more boats in the flotilla. Even so, his orders were clear. He was now in command and he'd reinforced the Alderney flotilla by a further ten boats. It was enough for now. He nodded to himself and smiled. Admiral Krause had saved him for a reason. This was obviously only the beginning.

'In that case, you may show me to my quarters. You can at least do that, can you not?'

'Jawohl, Herr Kapitän,' said the young officer. 'This way.' He turned and hurried off, and Holtzmann, bolstered by his own arrogant self belief, marched off behind him.

In the tented encampment east of Plymouth, Chuck Rivers left the Colonel's second briefing and felt for his pack of Lucky Strike. He tapped out a cigarette and headed for his squad of Rangers. They were bivouacked on the far side of the field and he arrived in the middle of a game of baseball.

'Okay, guys. Gather round,' Rivers ordered, and waved them over to the tents. 'C'mon, settle down.'

They came in dribs and drabs, wandering over with an assortment of bats and balls and bits of uniform. There were nine of them in total, and they were tough, fit and experienced. They'd all been in an assault landing before, in Sicily '43, and helped spearhead Patton's race to Messina.

Rivers waited for them to quiet down, reassessing their capabilities. Corporal Joe Donavon knelt down on one knee. He was a twenty-three year old from Pennsylvania and was born tough. Chewed a lot of gum and carried a Thompson machine-gun. Corporal Frank 'Doc' Bell sat cross-legged, squinting. Rivers had seen him tend the wounded under fire. Larry Vandenburg had volunteered from the Marines and fell in love with the Browning machine gun. Zach Carson, his Number Two, carried spare ammunition belts and an M1 Carbine. The man with the radio was Bill Tierman, and he too carried an M1. Hernandez worshipped his Remington Sniper rifle, and had fifteen 'kills' from Sicily. Belluci was the ace with a Grenade thrower. Raised in Chicago, he was a street wise kid before he was twelve. Ramone and Bradley were sharpshooters from the backwoods of Virginia. All in all, they commanded a lot of respect and Rivers was more than happy with the men under his command.

He hunkered down and pulled a map from his case. 'All of this goes no further.' He paused. 'Do I make myself clear?'

There was silence, a few nods. Donavon spoke for them all. 'We hear you, Sarge.'

Rivers unfolded the map and spread it on the ground. 'This is where we're headed. The top brass have called it 'Utah' beach and it ain't Normandy. The French call this the Cotentin Peninsula and 4th Infantry are goin' in to protect the right flank of the invasion before they take the port of Cherbourg, up here.' He jabbed his finger on the northwest tip. 'Our job is to get in behind the beach and locate a unit of mobile 88's.' Again he pointed, this time to a semi-circular area shaded in red. 'That was the last known position. The French resistance tell us it's protected by a slight rise.' He looked up from the map. 'You with me?'

There were nods and grunts of agreement.

'Well, you all know the Limey Major. It's our job to get him close. When we find those guns the Major's gonna call in one of them Royal Navy boats to knock 'em out. He'll send the right map co-ordinates and the Brits will send in their salvoes.' He stood up and folded the map. 'Our main objective is to get him there in one piece. We go in to 'Tare Green' on the right-hand side.' He looked them over. 'Any questions?'

Hernandez tapped his Remington. 'What do we do after we take out the guns?'

'Move inland and join up with the Airborne, a place called Sainte-Mère-Église.'

Hernandez spat from the corner of his mouth. 'So long as I get my sights on some Nazis.' He made an adjustment to the telescopic mount and trailed his fingers down the barrel.

Rivers laughed. 'I don't see a problem. There'll be more'n enough to go round. But just remember, you take out the officers and NCOs first.' He slung his Thompson and straightened his back. 'Anything else?'

Vandenburg raised a finger. 'I got one.'

'Shoot.'

'Why us, Sarge? We done our soldiering with Patton. What the hell we doin' fightin' over here?'

Rivers lowered his gaze, tight lipped. He wasn't surprised by the question, had always expected it to come. Not that he had a ready answer either.

'Well,' he said, digging a toe in the dirt. 'I can only tell it as I see it. I ain't here to fight for the Limeys. They been in this war a sight longer than us; towns and cities bombed, families killed, and they know what they're fightin' for.' He swung his gaze from one to the other. 'Me? I'm just a soldier, done alright too. Did my duty and they landed me with these.' He gestured at the stripes on his arm. 'We all think we ain't gonna die, and we've all seen it close up. None too pleasant, but we get over it.' He hesitated, cleared his throat.

'That was until we came up against them SS.' He stood for a moment looking over their heads. 'Remember that bridge over the gorge? We attacked and took it late in the day. The Krauts counterattacked the next night, and finally we won it back. That's when we found out what the SS did to prisoners-of-war. They slaughtered them. Lined 'em up and mowed 'em down, cold blooded murder.' He brought his gaze back to Vandenburg. 'I can't tell you why the top brass chose us. Maybe 'cause most of them guys in the infantry are just kids and they need some experience to lead the way. I dunno . . , but I tell you this. I'm glad I'm here. Now I get the chance to kill as many of

84

those SS bastards as I can get my hands on.' He dropped his eyes, embarrassed at having explained his personal feelings.

Vandenburg stuck out his chin, grinning. 'Jeeesus . . , but you sure make a fine speech. I'm sold.'

Rivers nodded, relieved. 'In that case, get your gear. And if we come up against the SS, blow 'em to hell, we ain't takin' no prisoners.' He turned to go. 'Talkin's done. Let's get some chow.' They gathered together and made for the mess tent. Unusually, Sergeant Chuck Rivers hung back from his squad of Rangers, thinking of the future, about the landings. Watching them file into the tent he wondered about their chances. How many of them would really make it through the day? Not many maybe. He kept his thoughts to himself and followed them in.

Commodore James Pendleton climbed out from the back of his staff car and looked up to the imposing entrance of Southwick House. Somewhere inside was Admiral Bertram Ramsey, overall naval commander of Operation Neptune. Pendleton glanced to his left, beyond the beautifully manicured front lawns, to a large wooded area, more than half-a-mile from where he stood. Three camouflaged trailers sat inside the fringes of the trees. They belonged to the Supreme Commander Allied Forces, General Dwight D. Eisenhower, and Field Marshal Bernard Montgomery, Operational Commander for Overlord. Conveniently the woods were also large enough to hide the enormous variety of Nissen huts, tents and trailers for the hundreds of ancillary staff involved.

Pendleton straightened his uniform and marched into the large foyer. A red-capped Military Policeman stepped into his path and saluted.

'Beg pardon, sir, can I ask where you're going?'

'Vice-Admiral Sir Hugh Stanford,' Pendleton said.

Pendleton nodded, not needing to be told, but bemused by the increase in security. He touched the peak of his cap in salute and walked into the corridor. He recognised the ante-room and a plaque marked 'Admiral Stanford', took off his cap, and knocked.

'Come,' he heard from inside, and entered to find the Admiral chalking notes on a blackboard. 'Have a seat James. Be right with you.' The chalk screeched on the board and Stanford stepped back to admire his handiwork.

'That's better,' he said, and walked back to his desk. 'So you found a replacement.'

'Yes, sir. *Brackendale*, 'Hunt' class, Lieutenant-Commander Richard Thorburn.'

Stanford looked at him and furrowed his brow. 'Thorburn? I've heard that name.' He stared at the ceiling in thought. 'I remember. Sank a destroyer north of Cherbourg. Got the DSO.'

Pendleton was surprised by the accuracy of his memory. In this war, four years was a long time. 'Yes, sir, same man.'

'Bit of a firebrand, eh? Just what we need right now.' He sat down and fumbled in a drawer. A sheaf of papers appeared on the desk and he checked his watch. 'Eisenhower's due another meeting with the Joint Chiefs of Staff about now, an update on the weather forecast. It's still not looking good.' He selected a piece of paper. 'Assuming things go as planned this ship of yours has a specific role to play.' He stood up and paced the floor. 'Every assault, on every beach, will be accompanied by Rangers tasked to neutralise specific targets. Utah is no different. When 4th Infantry hit the beaches one of the landing craft will have a squad of Rangers on board. In our case they'll have a special guest, a chap called Wingham.'

Pendleton blinked. 'Paul Wingham?'

Stanford stopped pacing. 'You know him?'

'Most definitely. We worked together for about two years. He was part of Special Operations in France, in the Cherbourg area. Commander Thorburn had rescued Wingham off a beach when they ran into that destroyer he sank.'

Stanford smiled tersely. 'Well well, small world. Thorburn will be helping him again.' He swivelled the chair and sat down. 'Major Wingham's task is to pinpoint a mobile battery of 88's between the flooded pastureland and Sainte-Mère-Église. The Rangers are there to protect him until he can use the radio to call *Brackendale* with the map reference. Commander Thorburn will then close with the shore and bombard the guns.'

Pendleton leaned back and stroked his beard. It all seemed so straightforward sitting here in the quiet office. The most recent aerial reconnaissance had revealed seventy-seven guns overlooking those waters, not the best place to be sitting around firing at a fixed position. He wondered what would happen if the squad didn't make it. 'And if the Rangers fail, sir?'

The Admiral gave him a solemn look. 'That's a chance we're willing to take. If they succeed, the 4th Infantry will have a lot less casualties and the Airborne might hold out in Sainte-Mère-Église.' He looked away to the blackboard. 'So much hinges on being able to expand the bridgehead.'

'Exactly how many men are going in with the first wave?'

Stanford rubbed his forehead. 'Six-hundred infantry, plus our Rangers. 26,000 by the end of the day. That's not including the air drop, they make up another 15,000.'

Pendleton pursed his lips. 'And once *Brackendale*'s done, sir?'

'She'll remain off the beaches in close support of 4th Infantry.' Stanford glanced down at his notes. 'If all goes to plan, Thorburn will then redeploy to screen the right flank for the follow up convoys. We have information, confirmed, that shows reinforcement of E-boats at Cherbourg, Alderney and Brest.'

'But that's all dependant on the assault moving inland?'

Stanford nodded. 'It is indeed.' He inclined his head towards the window. 'And the bloody weather. I hope to God the weather boys get it right.' He tugged at an ear. 'Now, there's one other thing. Where possible, all communication officers embedded with the Rangers have met with the captains of the close support vessels. The American's insisted on it, they like the idea of personal contact, makes for better co-operation.' He rose from his chair and stepped round the desk. 'Major Wingham should be here by three this afternoon, and if you bring along this Thorburn chap, it'll give me a chance to meet him too.'

Pendleton stood. 'If that's all, sir?'

Stanford walked over and opened the door. 'I think that wraps it up for now. I'll expect you here for three.'

Pendleton headed out for the manicured lawns to gather his thoughts. Thorburn and Wingham, it had been a long time. They'd been a good partnership.

8 False Dawn

At 14.00 hours Lieutenant-Commander Richard Thorburn stepped into *Brackendale*'s wardroom amidst a respectful hush. The area was crowded, almost standing room only, but Armstrong had reserved him a small space underneath the starboard scuttle. Thorburn squeezed through and stretched tall enough to see most of their faces.

'Gentlemen,' he began. 'As you've no doubt guessed, we've become part of the invasion. I've opened a set of sealed orders and you can take my word as to how many pages there are. Having said that, I'm only telling you the basics, our role in it.' He craned his head sideways to take in some of those at the back. 'I hope you can all hear me?'

Chief Petty Officer Barry Falconer, standing in the far corner, answered. 'Yes, sir, we can.'

Thorburn nodded. 'Right then, I'll continue. At the moment we're in Portsmouth with the British assault forces, but it's the Americans, sailing from Dorset and Cornwall, that we'll be joining. And our job is fairly straightforward. We escort them across the Channel, and when we arrive, the landing craft go in and we bombard enemy positions in support.' By the look on some of their faces he could see he'd made an impression. 'It will mean close support, moving into shallow waters, probably under enemy fire. Assuming that we accomplish all that in good order, we'll move out to screen the right flank of the convoys, at least for the rest of the day.'

A subdued murmuring followed, and he gave it time to die away. 'Mr Martin?'

'Sir?'

'There's an entire folder of navigation stuff you need to look at.' He looked inquiringly round the room. 'And W/T have a file of new codes to sort.'

Chief Petty Officer Telegraphist Glen Baxter acknowledged. 'Aye aye, sir.'

Thorburn gave them a moment to settle. 'The First Lieutenant will be available to answer any specific questions regarding anything irregular because of this deployment. Other than that, are there any questions I can answer in the general scheme of things?'

There was a movement to his left and the Welshman, Lieutenant Bryn Dawkins, pushed forward. 'Not so much a question, sir, but just a reminder. We're due a boiler clean and the turbines need an overhaul.'

'Point taken, Chief, but that just might have to wait for a slightly more opportune moment.'

Dawkins smiled and nodded. 'I appreciate that, sir, it's just that we're down on power, one or two knots.'

'Understood,' Thorburn said, and looked round. 'Anyone else?'

Sub-Lieutenant George Labatt spoke up. 'When does it start, sir?'

Thorburn grinned at his show of exuberance. 'I wish I could answer that, Sub, but I have a feeling it won't be too long. There's enough shipping down here to walk across the Channel.'

The room dissolved with laughter and Thorburn made a move. 'Carry on, Number One.' They came to attention, and as he walked into the corridor, the general hubbub of voices increased in volume. He entered his cabin hoping that *Brackendale*'s reduced lack of speed wouldn't make too much difference. He called for his steward and ordered a coffee. Reluctantly he picked up the orders and again sat down to read. Why did everything come down to so much paperwork?

There was a knock on the door.

'Come in.'

A Telegraphist appeared. 'Message from Commodore Pendleton, sir. You're to attend a meeting. His car will be here at 14.45 hours.'

Thorburn checked his watch and nodded over the top of the papers. 'Very well, acknowledge.' The door closed as he gave the meeting a disrespectful thought, and then buried himself in the next paragraph.

Jennifer Farbrace checked her appearance in the mirror, refreshed her lipstick and patted her hair into shape, then made doubly sure the hat pin was secure. Back in the outer office, she pulled on her coat and grabbed the gas mask bag. She tapped Pendleton's door and popped her head round.

'Time we were off, sir.'

Pendleton looked up from the desk, phone to his ear, obviously distracted by the call. He nodded, waved a hand. 'Be right there.'

She pulled the door closed and waited by her desk. A moment later he came out patting his cap in place.

'I get the feeling Eisenhower might have to postpone the invasion. There's a storm coming in.' He opened the door for her and they quickly made there way out to the car. The driver had the doors open and they ducked onto the back seat out of the wind. She watched him from the corner of her eye. He was agitated, unusually so, and recently she'd noticed the bags under his eyes, the obvious signs of greying hair. His responsibilities had begun to take their toll and all the decisions and sleepless nights were on show. She looked away at the crowded quayside, men and equipment, landing craft and warships. If they postponed the invasion, could they really keep all these men cooped up in the boats?

Pendleton interrupted her thoughts. '*Brackendale*, driver, you'll find her on number twelve.'

'Aye aye, sir,' the man said, and eased the car out between a line of parked lorries.

At a snail's pace they drove on through the never ending rows of equipment, but eventually found themselves parked alongside the small destroyer at Loading Berth Twelve.

Jennifer's heart jumped as she saw Richard Thorburn take the piped salute and start down the gangplank. She'd seldom seen him on board his ship and she thought how grand he looked in his best uniform. The driver hopped out and opened the front passenger door and she watched him slide effortlessly into the seat.

'Afternoon, sir,' he said, turning his head to Pendleton.

'Want you on your best behaviour today, m'boy. Off to see Sir Hugh Stanford up at Battle Headquarters.'

The driver started up and began to find his way out of the dockyard.

Jennifer noticed Richard push out his lower lip and raise his right eyebrow. 'I'm impressed, sir. What does he want with me?'

Pendleton smirked secretively. 'You'll find out when we get there,' was all he said, and Jennifer smiled to herself. He was being particularly truculent today. She sat back and smoothed her skirt. She was excited by Richard's close proximity; there would surely be a few minutes when they could be alone.

Thorburn followed Pendleton up the outside steps and into the large foyer of Southwick House. They each showed their I.D. cards, for the third time in as many minutes, and Pendleton led the way down a corridor. He walked along to a door on the left and stood back for them to enter. Thorburn glanced at Jennifer but she was too far back to go first so he pushed inside. He took two paces into the ante-room and stopped in surprise. 'Good God, I didn't expect to see you!'

Paul Wingham stepped forward with a broad grin. 'Hello, Richard. It's been a long time.'

Thorburn laughed and took the offered hand in both of his own. 'What the hell brings you here?'

'Not sure, just following orders.'

Thorburn stared at him, hardly able to comprehend the turn of events. Wingham looked older somehow, a lot more weathered. And of course, it wasn't the single 'pip' of a Lieutenant on his shoulder, but a crown. 'Major Wingham, no less. I approve.'

They both laughed in unison, and then Thorburn turned to look at Pendleton. 'You knew all about this, didn't you?'

It was Pendleton's turn to grin. 'Of course, but I wasn't going to spoil the fun.'

Jennifer reached through to Wingham and shook hands. 'Hello, Paul,' she said softly.

Thorburn stood back with genuine pleasure. These were some of the few people he trusted, thought of as friends. In Jennifer's case, more than just a friend. It was good to be back together, however briefly. They found seats and Thorburn continued to stare in amazement. 'I thought you'd be dead by now,' he blurted out.

Wingham looked embarrassed. 'Well, for a couple of years, it wasn't for the lack of trying.'

Pendleton roared with laughter, slapped his thigh. 'True, all true! I never expected you back.'

Thorburn sat back feeling a warm glow of contentment wash over him. The conversation turned to times gone by, to the summer of '40 and how naïve they'd all been. And how quickly they'd grown from innocent newcomers to hardened veterans. The buzz of nostalgic banter filled the room.

Vice-Admiral Sir Hugh Stanford glanced at the time and called through to his duty officer. 'Are we ready for this meeting?'

'Yes, sir. They're waiting outside.'

'Well, bring them in, man. I don't have all day.'

The officer, immune to his superior's brusque mannerisms, made a quick note of the time, and went to open the door.

Stanford stood up as the four officers came in, and moved round to meet them. Pendleton made the introductions. 'Lieutenant-Commander Thorburn, of *Brackendale*, sir.'

Stanford took his first good look at the man in front of him. Tanned, alert, easy smile, and Stanford immediately appreciated why people put their trust in him. He reached out and shook the firm grip, and nodded. 'Welcome to Neptune, Commander. Sorry to bounce you in at such short notice.' He grinned. 'It's the war you know.'

Thorburn smiled in return. 'Yes, sir. Of course.'

Stanford released his handshake and turned to the Major.

Pendleton cleared his throat. 'Major Paul Wingham, Commando, attached to the Rangers for Utah, sir.'

Stanford shook hands and squinted at the weather-beaten face, clear blue eyes. 'Major,' he acknowledged. 'How was the trip up?'

'Interesting, sir. There's a lot of security out there.'

'Glad to hear it. Wouldn't want just any old chaps wandering around now, would we?'

Pendleton gestured to Jennifer. 'And you know First Officer Farbrace, sir.'

Stanford had a soft spot for Jennifer Farbrace. From what he'd seen of her, she was a wonderfully efficient, cheerful young lady, and he'd even thought of transferring her to his own staff. He smiled and nodded. 'Yes, I do, and it's always my pleasure. Sit down, sit down,' he insisted, and strode back to his chair, paused while they found a seat.

He used the moment to take another, more considered look at Thorburn. Since Pendleton had nominated him for Neptune, Stanford had taken the opportunity to take a look at the man's service record, reminding himself why Thorburn's name had sounded familiar. It was all there in the file; the first evidence of leadership as a Midshipman in the China Station, fast tracked for promotion, Mentioned in Despatches and awarded the Distinguished Service Order for a gallant action against superior forces. A few caustic comments had been scribbled in the margins. They all referenced the man's rebellious nature.

'I understand the two of you have worked together before,' he said.

Wingham grinned widely. 'Owe this man my life, sir. Nobody I'd rather have at my back.'

Thorburn looked sheepish, the ghost of a smile playing across his lips.

Stanford liked that. No bravado, no blustering, just a quiet uncomfortable acceptance. He rubbed his chin. 'I take it you're both aware of what we've got you into?'

Thorburn took the lead. 'Yes, sir. After an initial bombardment under the Flagship's orders, I'm to give close targeted support when the Major calls for it.'

Stanford nodded. 'That's it in a nutshell, couldn't have put it better. You happy with things at your end, Major?'

Wingham looked from Pendleton to Thorburn, and then met Stanford's gaze. 'The Rangers know what they're about, and I've been put through the wringer by a Chief

Petty Officer Telegraphist. A 'refresher' course they called it. I didn't know there were so many ways of saying the same thing.'

Stanford glanced over at Pendleton and they both smiled knowingly. They'd all been there. 'Good,' he said gravely. 'As long as you understand the importance that's attached to it. All the beach heads have the same procedure, and each of the designated units has a nominated destroyer to work with. The hope is that the navy will be able to manoeuvre close to the shore and back you up. If we can do that then this kind of close liaison will make the task of the second and third waves that much easier.'

Wingham and Thorburn both nodded, and Thorburn leaned forward to emphasize the point. 'We do understand, sir.'

Stanford felt they'd recognised the significance of their mission. For the first time since losing the original destroyer for repair, he began to see that Utah might actually go according to plan. At least now he had everything back in place, and from what he'd seen of these two, they both had the gumption to get it done. Utah, and all the planning that went with it, had been a late addition to Overlord. It was Montgomery who'd insisted on this right flank protection. It was the major port of Cherbourg and what it offered to the American landings, that was key to a successful outcome.

He was nothing if not perceptive and he got the impression they'd had enough of this old Admiral, so he stood up to let them go. 'I'm glad we met, gentlemen. From my aspect, there are often too many names I can't put a face to. At least this time I'll know who's carrying out some of the orders.'

Chairs scraped as they stood and he shook the hand of each of them in turn. He wondered whether they'd all make it back. 'Good luck,' he called as they left the room. And then to himself, 'good luck to us all.'

It was precisely five o'clock on that Friday evening when Sergeant Dave Cooper heard the unexpected Morse code signature from Cherbourg. It broke through the hiss of static in his earphones. He touched the key and sent a standard acknowledgement. He waited for the brief message, signed off and decoded the letters. Two minutes later he reached for the phone and rang through for the General. 'Bainbridge speaking.'

'Urgent from Cherbourg, sir.'

'Go ahead, Sergeant.'

Cooper cleared his throat. 'Message passed, sir. That's all.'

Far to the south, on the island of Alderney, the first of the rising winds began to be felt. FlotillaKapitän Werner von Holtzmann finished putting on his sea-going uniform and stepped outside. Grey scudding clouds darkened the horizon and short waves sprayed the breakwater. The late evening light was failing fast and Holtzmann squinted into the wind. Provided the weather didn't deteriorate too much more he might use the darkness to his advantage. It was common knowledge the Allies must mount their invasion soon, even Hitler had said it was imminent, and Holtzmann had been ordered to step up his patrols.

This evening he would personally take three of his twelve Schnellboats and head north. If he managed to penetrate the Englander's defences he might be the first to send a warning.

The Flotilla leader had tied up to the main breakwater, the remainder were strategically dispersed through the harbour to minimise damage from an aerial attack.

An anti-aircraft gunner was on the quarterdeck checking the twin machine guns. 'Good evening, Herr Kapitän.'

'It is not,' Holtzmann said, 'but it suits our purpose very well. Where is the Lieutnant?'

A head appeared on the far side of the cockpit. 'Herr Kapitän. We are ready for sea, as you ordered.'

Holtzmann smiled thinly, not with his eyes, just the hard lines of his mouth. 'Good,' he said softly. 'Very good. Let us get under way.' He stepped aboard and swung into the cockpit. 'Start the engines, Lieutnant. Tonight we go north.'

'Jawohl, Herr Kapitän.' The motors throttled into life, they cast off and the boat grumbled out from the side towards the harbour entrance. Two of the other boats peeled away from their moorings, and one by one the three vessels nosed out into the open water. Holtzmann decided on a more circumspect approach to the English coast. He would swing in from the west along with the driving winds. 'Steer to the west. We will come in towards Plymouth.'

'Jawohl, Herr Kapitän.' With a steady increase of power the boat met the darkening waves and accelerated clear of the island.

In the gloom of Cherbourg's unlit harbour, Kapitänleutnant Kurt Schneider slammed his fist into the unyielding door of his room and swore in frustration. He was disappointed by the torpedo reload. The designated shipment of acoustic torpedoes allocated to Cherbourg had failed to arrive. The continued heavy bombing of the French interior, the devastation inflicted on the bridges and railways, to the stations and adjoining roads had totally disrupted the flow of supplies to the U-boat pens. So Schneider had accepted the inevitable, the limited offering of old technology and the good wishes of the shore staff.

He rubbed the soreness from his knuckles and cursed again. The bedside clock showed it was time to leave and he began to collect the few belongings he needed.

There was a knock at the door. 'Come!' he demanded, irritably.

A junior Officer of the Headquarters Staff poked his head in. 'The Commander wishes to see you, sir.'

'Now?'

'Yes, sir.'

Schneider took a last look round the room and shrugged. He had all he required. 'If I must, so be it. Lead on.'

The man led him to the office of Kapitän Johann Freidricks, Deputy Commander of U-boats, La Manche, now located in the cellar of Kriegsmarine Headquarters. Schneider entered, saluted and remained standing to attention.

A tired looking Kapitän Freidricks came out from behind the desk, solemn faced, serious.

'Welcome, Kurt. Take a seat. I have news.'

Schneider sat while Freidricks settled himself behind his desk. He picked up a typewritten form.

'This is an order from Admiral Dönitz to all U-boat commanders.' He looked up to emphasise the point. 'This applies to the entire fleet, from Norway to Biscay, and we are included. That is a total of sixty-three boats.'

Schneider nodded, attentive.

'Headquarters' directive is as follows. The boats in Norway are to form a hunting line across the North Sea stretching as far as Wilhelmshaven. Sainte Nazaire and Brest will put to sea and patrol west of the Channel Islands and wait for orders. Bordeaux and Lorient are to hold until the invasion begins.' He discarded the paperwork, ran a thumb and forefinger over his eyes and leaned back in the chair. 'Your mission is to guard the approaches to this harbour. We do not anticipate an invasion here, but the Allies might use Normandy as a diversion. If so, it is reasonable to argue that Cherbourg would be a useful port to acquire, a deep water harbour for troop transports. Your task is twofold. To give us early warning and to attack and sink as many ships as possible.'

Schneider had listened in silence, partly from respect, but also in bewilderment. Sixty-three U-boats, all that was left to counter the Allied strength. Last year there had been hundreds, and even though he knew many had perished with their boats, it was hard to believe so few remained.

Tentatively, he raised a query. 'There are no other commanders in port. Am I on my own?'

Freidricks nodded, slowly. 'We believe Ackermann was caught on the surface and bombed, and Griesbaum reported being attacked by a destroyer to the west of Ireland. We have heard nothing from either of them since.'

Schneider dipped his head. If that was what Dönitz had ordered, then so be it. 'When do I leave?'

'As soon as possible. A minesweeper will check the harbour approaches whenever you give the word.' Freidricks stood and held out his hand. 'I wish you luck, Schneider. Remember, as much warning as you can give us. If this part of Normandy is attacked we must be ready.'

Schneider saluted and made his way back to the harbour. At the very least, his Grey Shark would be more than ready.

On the other side of the English Channel, thousands of men began to board their ships.

9   Grey Skies

Late evening on England's southwest coast and the harbour town of Plymouth braced itself against the strengthening breeze. A silver haired old man limped down towards the waterfront, a small dog bouncing by his side. Inland, beyond the town's rooftops, the green, undulating countryside faded into the grey distance. A far-off church steeple, tall against the sky, overlooked an old village hidden inside an ancient wood, and isolated farm houses straddled the quiet road from Tavistock. High overhead a Peregrine Falcon circled in the wind and far below the outstretched feathers, camouflaged to conceal their presence, a Regiment of Sherman tanks sat waiting for orders. To the east, a temporary aerodrome vibrated to the throb of fighter bombers preparing for take off.

The old man hobbled out of Pier Street and turned for the docks. With an excited bark the dog ran off along the quayside and then skidded to a halt. Tail wagging furiously he began to yap noisily until his master whistled and called him back. Twenty-five uniformed soldiers wearing the khaki battledress of the British Army occupied the adjoining space. Three anti-aircraft guns pointed at the sky; a heavy calibre long barrelled 3.7inch, and two trailer mounted Bofors. Each gun sat behind a high wall of sandbags, and nearby, closely guarded, a separate compound for the ammunition. With the animal under control the old man leant on his walking stick and shook his head. Twenty-six years ago he'd come through the trenches of the Great War, the war that was supposed to end all wars, or so they'd said. Now the Nazis, the old enemy, were at it again, and had been since '39. With his failing eyesight he looked out beyond the quayside, past the ancient landmarks and the southern breakwater. A great armada of warships filled the bay, from the smallest of ship's boats to the destroyers and cruisers escorting a vast assembly of troopships. And then the old veteran caught the distinctive flash of a White Ensign flapping in the breeze. Thank God, he thought, thank God for all those sailors and the ships of the Royal Navy. He half smiled and turned his back on the sea. His dog barked at a pair of seagulls, and ran to join him. Hobbling away from the harbour, the old man paused and sniffed the air, looked west to a veil of low cloud. Storm coming, he thought, and walked on. That would freshen things up.

Major Paul Wingham, after three hours of hard riding, made it back to the Nissen hut, abandoned the motor bike and went in search of Sergeant Foster.

'Everything in order?' he asked, poking around at his equipment.

'Yes, sir,' Foster said, looking at his watch. 'The last of the boats are being loaded now.'

Wingham went through his pack, stripped and reassembled the Stengun and checked the time. Gathering everything he needed, and stuffing the map and signal codes safely inside his thigh pocket, he reached out with one hand. 'Thank you, Sergeant.' He gave him a lopsided grin. 'Sorry you couldn't come along, but that leg of yours . . . .'

Foster solemnly shook hands. 'Never mind, sir. It's all down to you now.'

Wingham nodded, winked, and moved outside. The orders had come through for embarkation to commence, and the final wave of the American 4th Infantry began to file down towards the boats. Despite the wind and grey skies, and the landing craft rocking in the swell, the GI's appeared to be in good spirits. Wingham guessed they were glad to be on the move, all the training behind them, ready to go. On a concrete ramp at an adjacent hard, a column of Sherman tanks rumbled and smoked their way down to a Landing Craft for Tanks (LCT), the big gull wing doors wide open to swallow the armoured cargo. Each tank ground to a halt fifty yards from the bows. The driver then swung round through 180 degrees and a guide reversed him jerkily back into the hold. Wingham recognised the old adage, last in first out. Some of the boats were waiting four or five abreast and beyond them three destroyers made way for a troop transport. Shouted orders made him look round and a file of American half-tracks growled into view, white stars prominently painted against the dull green camouflage. A line of Jeeps towing small field guns jostled for space and a company of infantry moved into single file, avoiding their wheels.

Wingham slackened off the weight of his pack and eased the Sten gun from his shoulder. Somewhere in amongst this chaos was Sergeant Chuck Rivers. He strained to look through the throng of men and machines. The deafening noise of the vehicles intensified, blue exhaust fumes filling the air, the taste of diesel sharp on the tongue. The tracks of the armoured units squeaked and groaned as the drivers inched forward and made their turns. And then Wingham saw what he was looking for. A row of men in distinctive uniforms slowly making their way along the sea front, their round helmets misshapen with foliage. They wore an unusual battle dress of olive-green and brown. Long gaiters protected their ankles, firmly secured by a strap under the boot. Wingham was suitably impressed. They looked as if they were ready for war, and he strode off in their direction.

Sergeant Chuck Rivers stopped as Wingham approached. 'Hi, Major. Y'all ready for this?'

'I am,' Wingham said, 'and it looks like I've found the right team.'

'You hear that boys? He reckons we're the right team.'

The reaction was noisy, good humoured, and Wingham grinned in response. He picked out Tierman with the swaying antenna. 'Anything on that piece of junk they call a radio yet?'

'Nah,' Tierman pouted. 'Only some Brit radio station.'

Wingham feigned surprise. 'Well, it's a start, better than I hoped for.' He turned and fell in step with Rivers.

The Sergeant pointed down the slipway. 'That assault boat is ours and once we're aboard they take us out to that ship.' He pointed again. 'When the time comes, the skipper puts the boats back in the sea and we make the assault.' He glanced sideways at Wingham. 'Easy ain't it.'

Wingham half nodded. 'Let us hope the waves aren't too big.'

'Amen to that,' Rivers said, and they walked to the water's edge and stepped up the boat's ramp. A young Sub-Lieutenant stood watching them board and find their places. He ordered the ramp to be raised and they reversed cautiously, turned around and headed out to a waiting ship, the four thousand ton, Empire Richmond.

From the west, the wind rose and rattled the guy ropes of the empty bivouacs. The first spits of rain darkened the bare earth.

Kapitänleutnant Kurt Schneider leaned back against the periscope housing and studied the U-boat's depth gauge with a critical eye. The dial showed seventy meters and the seabed varied between ninety and one hundred meters below the surface. What he didn't know was whether there were British mines in the area. If the boat snagged a moored mine at this shallow depth it was imperative they stop quickly and then reverse out of it. Out of necessity he had ordered a speed of four knots, enough to give them good warning if they hit a cable. The control room was quiet, the boat maintained a listening watch, and every now and then, the men stole a surreptitious glance at the wireless operator. He sat very still, eyes down, headphones on, and slowly turned the small wheel as he searched for that distant acoustic signal.

Schneider relaxed a little and crossed to the chart. There was really nothing to see, just the line of travel, a couple of way points, and their predicted position in forty-five minutes.

In the wide expanse of the North Atlantic, a Leading Telegraphist in the wireless room aboard H.M.S. *Rosefinch* scribbled a message on his pad. He tapped out an acknowledgement and called for the Petty Officer in charge.

A short while later the Chief Yeoman reported to the bridge, found the captain in his chair and saluted. 'Urgent signal, sir.'

Peter Willoughby took the slip, visibly brightened as he read it through and came to his feet.

He turned in the chair. 'Pilot?'

'Sir?'

'Put her on a course for Lands End. We've been recalled.'

The Navigating Officer grinned. 'Aye aye, sir.'

A few minutes later the ship was steaming for England via the Western Approaches. On the bridge Willoughby rubbed his hands in anticipation. A few hours and he'd know why.

In a field in northern France, to the south of a town called Montebourg, a twelve man section of Panzergrenadiers set up a forward Observation Post. The Lieutnant was in command of a sergeant, two corporals and eight privates. Their means of communication with the rear echelon was by means of a field telephone via a landline they had laid out as they moved forward. It was a straightforward job, one to which they were well drilled. Their detachment would last a week and after that the OP would either be moved or a second patrol take over.

The officer in charge decided on the best location, in this case a raised bank at the base of a hedge overlooking an approach road, and settled on a long, deep ditch as their main base. Easy access was by means of a gated entrance.

They were trained to be the eyes and ears of their battalion, but if attacked, were more than capable of defending themselves. The squad mounted two heavy machine-guns, three Panzerfausts, rifles and submachine-guns. They had a well stocked supply of grenades and enough ammunition to see off all but the most determined of attacks.

Satisfied with his arrangements, and with the first watch keepers already posted, the officer relaxed under the cover of a camouflaged tarpaulin. It might be a long boring week. The entire German army knew the threatened Allied invasion would take place round the Pas de Calais. With that comforting thought in mind, he settled down to sleep.

10 Spitfire

At 04.35 hours on Saturday the 3rd 0f June, Battle Headquarters at Southwick House buzzed with anticipation. Sir Hugh Stanford, buried in an all consuming pile of paperwork, gratefully reached to answer the securely scrambled telephone.

'Admiral Stanford speaking.'

A staff officer came on the line. 'Lieutenant Davidson, sir. General Eisenhower confirms the decision for the US task force to take passage as planned.'

Stanford glanced at the time. The convoys for 'Utah' and 'Omaha' had the greatest distance to travel, coming up from the ports of Devon and Dorset. The battleships and cruisers of the bombardment fleet were already at sea, having departed Northern Ireland a few hours before. 'So,' he said, 'we're sticking to schedule, Monday the 5th for D-Day.'

'Yes, sir, only the weather can stop us now.'

Stanford turned to look out of the big Georgian windows, at the blue skies and warm sunshine. He was well aware the meteorologists were having trouble with their forecasts, a bit unpredictable apparently. 'Right, I'll pass the word, get them under way.'

'Thank you, sir,' Davidson said, and rang off.

Stanford sat for a moment, letting it all sink in. He thought back to the previous year, those early months at the Admiralty, when he'd first joined Admiral Ramsey's planning team for Operation Neptune. It had been an enormous challenge to overcome the problems given to them by the Chiefs of Staff. The number of vessels involved, the logistics of transporting 160,000 men and their armoured reinforcement to the beaches of Normandy, seemed insurmountable. And yet, after all the arguments, the innumerable changes to the plans, he was about to order the start of the biggest amphibious assault ever undertaken.

He tentatively reached for the receiver and dialled the number for Plymouth command.

The answer from the American was brusque, impatient. 'Hallam speaking. How can I help?'

'Hello, Brandon, Sir Hugh Stanford here. We're on. You can get them under way.'

The man from Long Island whistled softly. 'About time. Sure as hell been a long time coming'

Stanford grinned into the mouthpiece. 'Into the valley of death . . . .'

The American finished with his own interpretation. 'Sandy beaches more like. Alright, thanks, Hugh. I'll pass on the order.'

Stanford hesitated, a minimal pause. 'Good luck, Brandon.'

'Luck favours the brave,' said the American, and the line went dead.

Mid-morning and Flight Commander Chris Johnson dropped the Spitfire out of the cloud base, side-slipped down to three thousand feet, levelled off, and yanked open the Perspex hood. A welcome blast of fresh air buffeted the inside of the cockpit. He unclipped the dank oxygen mask, took a lungful of cool air and wriggled his goggles onto the flying helmet. Ahead of him lay the great curve of Lyme Regis Bay and beyond that the familiar landmarks of England's Dorset countryside. He checked the fuel gauge. Thirty gallons, more than enough. Goggles down, oxygen and microphone clipped back in place, he pulled the stick to the rear and rolled right. Eyes everywhere now; up, down, rear mirror, right shoulder, left shoulder.

No sign of enemy aircraft. Bank left, nose down, ease the stick and check altitude. Twelve thousand feet.

He flew over the coast and watched the pretty little cottages of Lyme Regis slide beneath the starboard wing. He glanced left at the port wing tip. There were a cluster of bullet holes in the skin where the Spit had been hit from below, leaving the upper surface marred by jagged punctures. It had been a close call, the first time he'd been hit by ground based machine-guns. And the old girl had taken more damage when he took his revenge, this time to the fuselage. Then it seemed as if the whole of the northern coast of France had marked him as a target. So he flew! That wonderful Rolls Royce Griffon engine powering him up through 12,000 feet, and beyond, up into the clouds. At 22,000 feet, bright blue sky came to his rescue. A gentle turn to the north, a precautionary drop in altitude to the top of the white clouds and a very relieved fighter pilot set course for home. Now, with friendly ground below, Johnson banked left for Exeter, and Dartmoor's rugged upland plateau.

His airfield was southeast of Tavistock with enough well known landmarks to give even a novice the confidence to find his way home. Time to concentrate; get the old girl down in one piece. He dropped to 1,100 feet, eased the nose up over Exeter and throttled back. The new American army base appeared ahead of the port wing, thirty or more tents camped on the south side of Dartmoor's wilderness. He reduced throttle, altimeter showing eight-hundred feet. Soon be time to try the undercarriage and he hoped to God it was still working. Airspeed at 160 miles an hour. Remove a bit more speed. Heart in mouth he initiated wheels down and waited for the mechanical thump. No thud, no sign of a green light on the instrument panel. He tried again. This time there was one thump as a wheel dropped down. Still no green light.

Awkward, one down, one up. He wondered if he could jolt the other one into position, shake it down? Either that or retract the good one and attempt a belly landing. Better to have a go at shaking it loose.

Opening the throttle to gain height, Johnson climbed to a 1,000 feet, levelled out and waggled the wings, violently. There was no response. He banked right, moving away from the airfield until he was on the reverse heading. He immediately found himself having to correct to starboard. He began to sweat. Everything seemed to indicate the port wheel was down and he was compensating for drag on that side. Convinced by the theory he took a gamble. He flipped the fighter onto the left wing, held it port side to the ground, then whipped viciously to starboard and back to horizontal. He felt more than heard a satisfying metallic thump, stared hard at the display, and finally saw the green light switch on. Constant, no flicker. But could he trust the wheels to stay locked in place? Only one way to find out, get down on the deck. At least the uneven drag had disappeared.

With a determined grimace he commenced a flat smooth turn to the right, watching his bearing, holding height. On a bearing of 270 degrees the runway appeared dead ahead.

The nose was a touch too high. Throttle back into the approach. Airspeed, 150. Too fast, decelerate, speed coming off to 110, then down to ninety miles an hour. Flaps down, would the undercarriage hold? He braced himself. The Spitfire's wheels hit the ground, hard, and the aircraft bounced horribly. Johnson fought the stick for control, fed in port rudder against the cross wind, straightened her up, elevators trimmed. Then the wheels met the ground again, evenly this time, locked rigid, holding up, and he let the Spit run out on the grass strip before gently applying the brakes. Wouldn't do to upend her onto the nose. He unclenched his teeth and breathed out. He laughed aloud in the cockpit, a trifle embarrassed. For those watching, that must have looked like a trainee at the end of his first solo, not an experienced Flight Commander with years of flying under his belt.

The Spitfire trundled on down the runway and at a signal from the ground crew, turned left for dispersal and he allowed himself to be waved to a halt.

Corporal Lassiter jumped up on the wing root and leaned in to help him with the straps. 'Alright, sir?'

Johnson gave him a sideways glance and grinned self-consciously. 'I think so, not so sure about the old Spit.'

'No, I can see that, sir. Bit knocked about.'

Johnson hauled himself out, stepped down on the wing and dropped to the ground. He walked a few paces and turned to inspect the damage, raising his eyebrows in surprise. A neat row of holes angled up along the fuselage and the tail plane had a chunk of the rudder missing. He walked round the prop to the far side and bent to check the landing gear. A thin residue of hydraulic oil dripped down the strut and onto the tyre, no obvious sign of damage.

'Can you take a look at the old hydraulics? I had to shake this one down. Lucky it held up when I touched.'

Lassiter squatted by the wheel, rubbed the oil and sniffed his fingers. 'Yes, sir, definitely hydraulic. We'll see to it.' He backed out from under the wing. 'Any other particular issues?'

'Port aileron. Seemed a bit sticky.'

The NCO wiped his oily hands onto a piece of rag. 'Right, sir, we'll sort it.' He walked back behind the port wing and picked up Johnson's parachute. 'Better get this checked too, sir. It's been a while.'

Johnson nodded, slung it over his shoulder and took a last look at the Spitfire. 'It didn't feel like anything major got hit, the power was just fine.'

At that moment the familiar growl of a Merlin engine made them look up. An unidentified Spitfire flew low across the airstrip, banked to the east and circled round for a final approach. Nose into the westerly breeze, slipping off the speed, the aircraft touched down without a bounce, turned, and taxied back towards the Squadron HQ. The prop spluttered to a stop and the pilot clambered to the ground.

'Not one of ours, sir,' Lassiter volunteered, stating the obvious.

Johnson nodded. 'Mmm . . . , let me know what you find,' and curiosity getting the better of him, wandered off after the stranger.

In the office, Flight Sergeant Carter looked up from his desk, eyes narrowed in warning. 'Wing Commander Sutton, sir,' he said softly. 'He's in with the CO.'

Johnson tugged at his right ear. Must be a flap on, Wing Commanders rarely flew themselves around to visit operational aerodromes. He ambled over to the window and picked up a flight roster to familiarise himself with the day's next sortie. It was scheduled for 14.00 hours; a patrol from Lands End to the Isle of Wight.

An indistinct murmur of voices could be heard coming from behind the office door, incomprehensible. Through the window he watched a petrol bowser trundle out to dispersal and a flatbed trailer of ammunition boxes stopping at each Spitfire to be unloaded. The armourers jumped down to feed the belts into the magazines, secured the flaps, and moved on. Only the mechanics busied themselves around his Spitfire. She wouldn't be back in the air today.

Johnson glanced up at the large oval clock above the blackboard. It was ten minutes to midday. 'I'm off for a bite to eat.' He inclined his head towards the CO's door. 'They might be there forever.'

The Flight Sergeant grinned. 'Might be days, sir.'

Johnson stepped out into the fresh air and breathed in. Halfway to the Mess hall he heard voices behind him and turned to see the Wing Commander heading for his cockpit. A ground crew had mysteriously appeared as if out of nowhere and a minute later the airscrew spun into life. The CO saluted the Perspex canopy, and after the Spitfire weaved out to the end of the strip, it powered up and flew off.

Johnson frowned. There didn't appear to be any sense of panic, nobody dashing about shouting orders, so what was that all about? Time to find out, he thought, and marched back to the office.

The CO saw him coming and waited. He had a big grin on his face. 'Hello, Chris. Got back alright then?'

'Yes, sir, but some nasty Jerries had the cheek to fire some old muskets at me. Won't be fixed today.'

The CO chuckled.' Ah well, they'll be able to finish her off with a fine new coat of paint.'

Johnson tilted his head. 'Sir?'

'Starting tomorrow, every aircraft flying anywhere near occupied territory will be painted in black and white stripes.'

Johnson stared at him.

'Aircraft recognition, old boy. If it has the new paint job don't shoot it. More for the trigger happy navy types; they left it till the last minute so the Jerries won't pick up on it.'

Johnson grinned. 'Is that why the Wing Commander graced us with his presence?'

'Precisely,' said the CO. 'The first stocks of paint are due to arrive at 05.00 hours tomorrow. No more sorties after today, not until we're given the green light.' He looked over to dispersal, a wicked smile on his face. 'I think I might take a stroll over to the ground crews and tell them the good news. I'm sure they'll be delighted.'

Johnson took a pace back and saluted. 'I'm sure they will, sir.'

The CO walked away whistling, and Johnson resumed his trip to the Mess hall. There'd be a lot of muttering and mumbling over in dispersal, mutiny maybe. He laughed and entered the room full of tables and chairs. At least, just for once, he'd be able to have a leisurely meal and enjoy what was left of the day.

That same afternoon Empire Richmond cleared Plymouth's headland and turned east for the Isle of Wight. Sergeant Chuck Rivers sat uncomfortably on the upper boat deck. Six feet away Hernandez leaned on the rail watching the convoy assemble, dozens of ships jostling for position and forming up in long columns. A Tank Landing Craft with four Shermans packed inside, butted headlong into the choppy seas, and Hernandez watched with amusement as the tank crews dodged the windswept spray. In comparison, the Empire Richmond sailed majestically on, big and stable, a slow rise and fall.

Hernandez called over his shoulder. 'Hey, Sarge, I reckon we got ourselves the best seat in the house.'

Rivers pursed his lips. 'Sure thing . . . , for now. Wait till we're headed for the beach. See if you still feel the same.'

Hernandez saw the LCT corkscrew through a long roller, another drift of heavy spray washing inboard. He grinned as the men hid behind a tank, one of them leaping onto the turret and disappearing inside the hatch. But the Sergeant's words had struck a chord and it was hard to shake them off. This would be his second landing and it was hard to describe how he felt. Excitement at being involved, the rush of blood when he was caught up in the action. The other side of the coin, apprehension. Not so much fear but the risk of embarrassment. That first time he'd gone in, landing in North Africa, the seas had been flat calm, but he'd vomited all over the place. Looking back, he knew it had been a combination of nerves and fear, nothing to do with being in a boat. As soon as his feet touched dry land and he got to shooting at the enemy, all that retching and weakness had vanished. Waiting is what he didn't like and he hoped it wouldn't happen again. Just let him get on with the war.

In the evening light he caught sight of another convoy angling out from the south coast. Fast destroyers led the way, dashing about the flanks, throwing up a glistening curl of bow waves. The ships made up of a similar mix of vessels to his own convoy; troopships and warships, landing craft and tugs, big and small. He began to count them, everything he could see. When he reached fifty-six he lost interest and gave up. Either way, it was a hell of a lot of ships. The two convoys gradually merged into one and a blanket of rain descended to obscure his view.

Hernandez turned away from the rail and decided to get some sleep. It might be a long while before any of them slept again.

On *Brackendale*'s quarterdeck, Thorburn paced slowly from one side of the ship to the other. Deep in thought, he ignored the noise and activity in the harbour surrounding his warship. His head was full of 'ifs and buts' and wrestling with solutions, the hundred and one different scenarios he might be faced with. Chief amongst his concerns was the close support needed to ensure Paul could make the best use of *Brackendale*'s guns. He wondered how deep the water was against the theory of the charts. Exactly where would they be against a rising

115

tide? A thousand yards out from the shoreline? Could he risk eight hundred?

'Sir?'

He stopped pacing and turned to the Yeoman.

'Sir, message from headquarters.'

Thorburn raised his eyebrows. 'You can read it.'

'*Brackendale* will depart Portsmouth for Convoy U1A at 02.00 hours on Sunday 4th. Rendezvous eight miles southwest of Needles. End of message, sir.'

'Very well. Acknowledge.'

'Aye aye, sir.' The Yeoman gave a quick salute and turned away.

Thorburn moved to the port rail, staring down at the ripples of oily flotsam lapping at the side plates. He felt the tension leave him, the worry over close support forgotten. There was relief in knowing that in a few short hours the ship would be under way.

He straightened up from his ponderings and strode off past the rear gun turret, swung by the bridge and up onto the fo'c'sle. Stepping gingerly between the anchor chains and capstans he reached the bows and paused to look out over the harbour. Beyond the narrow entrance bounded by Gosport and Southsea the waters of the Solent divided east and west round the Isle of Wight. It would be the western arm and out past Southampton's estuary to the Needles and then the tricky waters of the open sea. He clasped his hands behind his back and straightened his shoulders. A new beginning. *Brackendale* would be amongst the first to leave the anchorage, only the minesweepers leaving harbour earlier.

It was time to prepare and he turned aft for the bridge, a fresh spring in his step.

At exactly 02.00 hours on Sunday 4th of June, Thorburn cast off and eased the destroyer cautiously out between the lines of assault craft. A moored up fleet destroyer appeared in the darkness and Thorburn brought *Brackendale* to starboard. Navigating carefully through the crowded basin the ship eventually found clear water and headed for the Solent.

At yet another meeting in the library of Southwick house, the Supreme Commander, having listened to the prediction for rising winds, poor visibility, and waves of up to six feet in height, reluctantly postponed the landings for twenty-four hours.

As the ship crept past Gosport's prominent headland, from out of the dark night a signal lamp began to flash.

There was an acknowledgement from *Brackendale*'s starboard lamp. The land based lamp flickered again, beaming out a rhythmic pulse of light. The signaller read the letters, mouthing them to himself. He clattered the shutter in response and turned to face the bridge. 'Signal, sir. Reads, "Operation postponed. Abort mission." End of message, sir.'

Thorburn stood stock still, disbelieving. There must be some kind of mistake. An entire Fleet was at sea, the whole of the US First Army, had been for hours, and now he was being ordered to turn round and go home. With a blanket ban on all wireless transmissions during the amphibious operation he was restricted to a visual confirmation. 'Ask them to repeat the signal.'

'Aye aye, sir.' The lamp clattered, briefly.

Once again the distant signal lamp beamed out its message and Thorburn's signaller confirmed the original communication, the operation was postponed.

Thorburn swore, loudly, venting his frustration at whoever was in earshot. There was an embarrassed silence from those around him and he swore again, angry. Finally, knowing that he'd been given a direct order, he reluctantly gave a nod. 'Acknowledge.'

A brief exchange of lights followed and Thorburn bent to the voice-pipe. 'Starboard twenty.' Bitterly frustrated he bowed to the inevitable and waited for the bows to come round. 'Midships.'

'Midships, aye aye, sir.' It was the Cox'n on the wheel, calm, unhurried, the consummate professional, and Thorburn took a moment to master his emotions. 'Slow ahead, steer three-five-oh.'

'Slow ahead both, steer three-five-oh, aye aye, sir.'

Thorburn smiled to himself, well done the Cox'n. All was well. He straightened from the voice-pipe and squinted through the gloom, alert to the crowded waters. 'Number One,' he said. 'I think someone in the bows would be useful.'

'I'll go myself, sir.' Armstrong replied, and slid down the ladder before Thorburn had a chance to argue.

With a good deal of caution and Armstrong's diligent guidance, *Brackendale* returned quietly to her berth. In the western approaches a storm gathered, high winds and eight foot waves. Not a night to be out at sea.

11 Terror

In Cherbourg, as the clock pointed at 02.45 hours, Oberleutnant Gerhardt Ziegler was summoned to the headquarters of the Intelligence Section, and more specifically, to the Signal Detachment stationed in the top floor of the Hotel Le Castel. The old Parisian style building, six stories in height, had the added advantage of a long wide roof span which housed the complex array of electronic surveillance equipment used to intercept French underground transmissions.

Ziegler marched into the room, clicked his heels and saluted. The layout was much the same as his last appointment, a few more radios and desks, and a much larger map of Cherbourg itself. But since that previous visit the Intelligence people had contacted him direct, at the chateau, and he'd taken it upon himself to deal with any issues. This was different. Glancing discreetly about the room he recognised a dozen senior officers, some in quiet conversation, others excitedly gesticulating with a radio operator.

'Ziegler! What took you so long?' The call came from the far end of the room. He strained to see who it was and then spotted Major Dietrich Weisbaum sat slouched on a pink and gold couch. The Major waved him over and offered him a cigarette.

Gerhardt Ziegler was well aware of this man's reputation. Twice wounded by the Russians during the campaign to take the oil fields of the Caucasus, he'd eventually been sent to Paris for rest and recuperation. His right leg had refused to mend leaving him with a crippling limp, and Ziegler could see the fingers of his left hand were permanently frozen into a twisted claw. In revenge

119

for his sufferings, and before he left the battlefield, Weisbaum had ordered his SS Panzergrenadiers to butcher two hundred Russian prisoners. This was not a man to be trifled with and his arrival in Cherbourg last summer had coincided with the introduction of a much harsher regime against the civilian population.

'Now then, Ziegler, I hear you have a new hobby. I am informed that you have a certain flair for such things.' He looked up with cold eyes, a thoughtful appraisal.

Ziegler found himself caught off guard. 'Sir?'

Weisbaum laughed, a short explosive grunt. 'You kill enemy agents, do you not?'

'Ahh . . . , only when there is no alternative, Herr Major.'

'Do not apologise, young man. It is good to find such attention to detail in our new breed of officers. And you've been very thorough by all accounts. No one left to tell the tale.' The Major paused, inhaled on his cigarette, blew a haze of smoke. 'Our colleagues here,' he gestured at the signals section, 'have pinpointed an operation within the streets of Cherbourg.' He smiled, thin lipped. 'Can you believe that? Under our very noses.' He shook his head in wonder, and then straightened to sit forward. 'But not for much longer, Ziegler. You are to raid this place, no stone unturned. I want everything you find and you bring it here, to me. And unless you are fired on, no killing. We very much want them alive.'

He handed over a slip of paper. 'This is the address, a patisserie. Do you know where that is?'

Ziegler read it and nodded.

Weisbaum looked at his watch. 'I want this timed for 06.00 hours this morning. During the night our surveillance people managed to triangulate their precise location, but on other days we have heard regular transmissions between six and seven o'clock. Never enough to identify the spot. Understood?'

Again Ziegler nodded.

'Then I leave it with you. Report back as soon as you are done.'

Ziegler clicked his heels, came to attention. 'Jawohl, Herr Major!' He turned smartly away and headed for the ornate staircase, pleased with himself.

By 04.00 hours, Thorburn lay on his bunk and fidgeted in the darkness of his cabin, wide awake. Sleep had eluded him and he gave up trying. He sat upright and came to his feet, found the chair by his desk and slumped onto it. He felt for his cigarettes, extracted one and lit it behind the shield of his cupped hands. He inhaled deeply and as he breathed out, let the smoke roll slowly over his tongue, forcing himself to relax. Like everyone involved, from the highest ranking officers to the thousands of men who would land on the beaches, he waited for news of Eisenhower's decision. He understood that the Joint Chiefs of Staff were due to meet in the next hour or so to make a final decision.

By rights, the invasion would already have been halfway to France, and as he now knew, had in fact begun yesterday, when Force Utah, with the furthest to travel from the west coast, had sailed for the Isle of Wight rendezvous. But then, with the forecast predicted at force five to six, and with no moon and low cloud, Eisenhower had been forced to issue a recall. That was why *Brackendale*'s mission had been aborted, and why he now kicked his heels in the shelter of Portsmouth harbour. The last he'd heard, the American task force had made it back to the sanctuary of Lyme Regis bay, there to reform and await instructions.

Thorburn cursed in frustration, stubbed out the cigarette, grabbed his duffle coat and made his way topside to the bridge. If he couldn't sleep, the least he could do was expend his energies on the bridge.

Sub-Lieutenant George Labatt, hunched inside the protection of the bridge-screen, heard him arrive, realised who it was and stiffened to attention.

'Morning, sir.'

Thorburn turned his face away from the lashing rain. 'Morning,' he said curtly. 'Anything?'

'Nothing, sir. No messages.'

Thorburn nodded in the gloom, instinctively rubbing his hands together against the wind. 'Very well. See if you can get the galley to rustle up some hot drinks.'

'Aye aye, sir,' Labatt said, moving past.

'For everyone on watch, Mister Labatt.'

'Yes, sir.'

Thorburn heard him descend the ladder, and stepped over to the forebridge. Out there in the darkness thousands of men remained cooped up inside a multitude of vessels. Conditions couldn't be worse for the land lubbers; there wouldn't be much respite from the gales. He hunched into a corner of the bridge, anxiously awaiting the signal which would set them on their way.

Kurt Schneider opened the hatch to the torpedo room and stepped inside. The door to Number Two tube was open and the torpedo withdrawn for maintenance. The routine of mechanical and electrical inspection was rigorously applied and even now, in close proximity to the enemy, the men laboured over the lethal cylinder.

Stripped to the waist, glistening with sweat, the Petty Officer in charge saw the Old Man enter the compartment, and straightened to attention.

'Is all in good order, Schmidt?'

'Jawohl, Herr Kapitän. This is the last one in the tubes. Then we will check two of the electrics.'

Schneider looked round for a moment, meeting their eyes as they stopped to stare at him. 'Well done,' he said, making a point of including them all. He stretched out a hand and stroked a spare torpedo secured in the bottom rack. 'Your work is never wasted and I trust you do a good job. Our future depends on these 'eels', they will give us many victims.'

The men nudged one another, teeth smiling through the grime.

'And when this patrol is over, there will be two weeks in Paris.'

They cheered the news and made lewd gestures, instantly dreaming of Parisian night life.

Schneider interrupted. 'But first we use these 'eels', then we will see how the ladies love the men of the U-boats.'

A chorus of ribald shouts followed him out of the hatch and he slammed it shut behind. The smile disappeared and he looked at his watch. In a few hours they might be in action. No harm in giving them something to raise their spirits. They would work all the harder.

He moved through the officers compartment to his curtained off bunk on the port side and stopped opposite the sonar/ radio room. The operator looked up and shook his head. Schneider nodded and ducked into the control room. He crossed to the navigating table and picked up the dividers, deep in thought. Soon he would turn the boat to the east, close to the seabed, pass through the last of the minefields, and then work into the designated patrol line. He doubted the Allies would launch their invasion in Normandy. Too far from the English ports, it would definitely be the Pas de Calais. But with luck he might even find an unsuspecting destroyer.

The deserted Sunday morning streets of Cherbourg awoke to the low rumble of military vehicles driving out from the fortified harbour and heading south to the cobbled suburbs. A gleaming black Mercedes led the way, two truckloads of Waffen SS in close company. The soldiers were well armed and warned to expect determined opposition. In the grey light of dawn the Mercedes stopped outside a disused warehouse and Oberleutnant Gerhardt Ziegler stepped out. He gave an order for the troops to dismount. The quiet road turned noisy with the guttural commands of German NCOs.

Twenty men formed ranks in two units and Ziegler checked his watch. A signal to the second squad sent them off down an alleyway, a wide circle to cover any possible means of escape. He gave it five minutes and turned to Corporal Adler. 'Time,' he said simply, and marched them off down the cobbled street. The turning he wanted appeared on his left and he checked the name of the street. Adler and three men moved up to join him.

'Ready? He warned.

Adler nodded.

'Follow me.' He turned into the side street and walked to the entrance of the patisserie. Standing to one side he nodded to Adler. 'Break it down.'

Adler squared up in front of the glazed door, raised his boot and kicked hard. The flimsy lock burst inward under the shock and the Corporal lunged in beneath the tinkling bell.

Ziegler strode inside and waved for the others to enter.

Adler dived round behind the counter and pushed through into the back room with the two large ovens. A set of stairs ran up from the far corner and he covered them with his machine-gun.

Ziegler called out in his impeccable French. 'You up there. I would advise you to come down, very slowly.'

A floorboard creaked and a pair of blue carpet slippers under striped pyjamas stepped cautiously down the stairs.

Adler raised the gun and Ziegler smiled at the sight of the bespectacled, wide eyed Frenchman.

'Name?' he snapped.

The Frenchman fumbled with tying the belt round his robe, and looked up in defiance. 'My name is Monsieur Francois Toussaint.'

Ziegler beckoned him closer, grabbed him by the robe and pushed him roughly to one side with his back against the ovens. 'Adler, go check upstairs.'

The Corporal stuck out his bottom lip and edged up the first few steps.

The Oberleutnant carelessly inspected his Luger, twisting it nonchalantly round his finger. 'So, Monsignor Francois Toussaint, tell me, where do you keep the radio? In the attic, or under the floorboards?'

Toussaint declined to answer, lips compressed into a tight line.

Ziegler sighed. 'It would save us all so much trouble if you were to tell me. We know there is one on these premises, Sooner or later . . . ,' he left the threat hanging in the air.

From the room above came the sound of a disturbance, heavy footsteps, and then a woman screamed.

'Adler? What's up?

A middle aged woman in a pink nightdress walked down in front of Adler's gun, saw Toussaint, and ran to his side.

Ziegler half nodded to himself. Perfect, he thought. Now I will make the baker talk. He stared at Toussaint, deliberately holding him with his eyes. The man glanced up from above his glasses, desperate to avoid the confrontation. Ziegler could see from his expression that he wished his wife were not involved.

A floorboard creaked. It came from the bedroom. Adler swung round in alarm and went for the stairs, gun poised. Too late. A pistol banged and Adler crashed backwards. Blood spurted from a hole in his neck. The woman screamed.

Ziegler waved another soldier forward and he jumped up the stairway, machine-gun firing on the move. The magazine was half empty when he stopped, and was followed by the distinct thump of a body falling to the floor. Silence, smoke drifting, and then an old revolver bounced aimlessly down the steps. The soldier kicked it away and moved up out of sight.

From somewhere outside came the strident shouts of a warning. The rattle of gunfire rang out, a fusillade of shots, echoing in the streets. Then once again, silence settled over the suburbs.

Gerhardt Ziegler's patience snapped. He dragged the woman away from her husband and pressed the muzzle of the pistol against her throat.

'Monsieur . . . , either you tell me where the radio is or your wife dies.' He raised his voice, shouted in the man's face. 'Make up your mind!' The terrified woman started to scream, her body convulsed in shock.

Toussaint looked up, staring from one to the other, then hung his head in defeat. Stepping away from the cast iron ovens he pointed to the one nearest the stairs. 'In there,' he muttered.

Ziegler let go of the woman in surprise, wrenched the weight of door open and peered into the dark interior. He hesitated, straightened up, and waved for the Frenchman to step away. Satisfied, he reached in and carefully dislodged a metal box. Pulling it forward into the light he briefly examined what appeared to be the main control panel of a radio, traced a wire to a set of headphones, stood back and relaxed. Major Weisbaum would soon have his information. A crunching of broken glass from overhead made him look towards the stairs. 'What's going on up there?'

'We have one dead, and we think one escaped through the window.'

'Alright, I'm sending these two up to get dressed. Watch them.' He motioned with his pistol. 'Go and get some clothes on. You are invited to attend SS Headquarters. Need to look your best.'

The pair shuffled to the stairs and slowly trudged up to the bedroom. Ziegler grinned, perched himself on the counter. Time was not so critical; he could afford to wait while his men searched the property. One of the soldiers came back downstairs. Ziegler waited.

In the room upstairs Francois Toussaint pulled on his shirt and reached for his shoes. His wife was dressing in the corner, modestly facing away from the German soldier. She slipped the dress down over her shoulders and bent for her ankle socks. Toussaint stared at the back of her greying hair. He loved this woman; they had become sweethearts in school, engaged and married, brought up two fine sons. Now one at least was dead, and there was no telling what had happened to the other. And she would never be strong enough to stand up to the Nazis. Their lives were over. For himself it no longer mattered, but he could not let her suffer.

He finished tying his shoes and reached for his jacket. Behind the jacket, in the pocket of a coat hanging on the hook, was his old revolver. He deliberately fumbled as he retrieved the jacket, and pulled the gun from the inside coat pocket. With the jacket in front of his chest he turned towards the soldier. The man was watching his wife, a big mistake. Francois Toussaint squeezed on the trigger. The hammer went back, snapped forward and the bullet slammed into the soldier's chest, driving him backwards.

Without hesitating, Toussaint swung round to his wide eyed wife and pulled her close. With a hand gently steadying the back of her head he looked sorrowfully into her eyes. In that moment she understood, he saw it through the tears in her eyes, and she nodded, very faintly. 'I love you,' he said, kissed her soft lips and pressed the muzzle against her temple. She was dead before he lowered her gently to the floor. With the semblance of a smile, and knowing he'd beaten the Gestapo, Monsignor Francois Toussaint pulled the trigger.

Even as Ziegler got to the bedroom, his glasses hit the floor, and the finest baker in all of Cherbourg passed away.

Admiral Sir Hugh Stanford looked up over the brim of his tea cup and eyed his companion with a thoughtful frown. His fellow officer was a lean, wiry, middle-aged American, and right now he stood with his back to the room looking out through the large bay window at the well manicured lawns. He was a three star General by the name of George 'Willow' Solomon Jnr., and held the post of Assistant Deputy Commander to Overlord's Strategic Planning Group. He'd been part of the Staff since joining the team in September the previous year, and along with more than forty officers of Allied command, had eventually managed to have the stratagem approved. Over time, Stanford and 'Willow' Solomon had become genuine comrades, able to freely share their concerns as they arose.

Stanford placed the cup gently into the saucer and leaned back, chin on his intertwined fingers. 'What can I do for you, George?'

'It's not me, it's Ike. He's worried about Utah beach,' the General explained, bouncing on the balls of his feet.

'Well it seems a bit bloody late to start having doubts now.' Stanford shook his head in disbelief. 'Forgive me for saying so, but I thought you might have persuaded him otherwise by this point in the proceedings.'

'Yeah, well he thinks the Germans are pulling a double-bluff. They flooded the ground behind the beach to make it impassable. End result, they don't need so many troops to defend that area.'

Stanford sighed. 'I'm listening.'

The General thrust his hands in his pockets. 'So, their assumption is that we won't go for drowning half the assault force to get inland, a waste of good resources. Or so we thought.'

'So?'

'Well, since Rommel took over the reins it seems they've changed their minds. The latest reconnaissance shows a build up of reinforcements, a whole heap of guns and mines.'

The Admiral pulled at his ear. 'Oh, come on, George, we know all that. Seventy-seven pieces of heavy artillery. Aerial reconnaissance have it all plotted.'

The General squared his shoulders and turned from the window. 'And last night a Waffen SS unit of mobile field artillery moved up close to the floodwaters.'

Stanford smiled sarcastically. 'One unit? The battleships will slaughter them.'

'Mobile Panzergrenadiers, a crack unit, and mobile, Hugh. Mobile! On top of that the French Resistance report that at least two battalions of infantry were deployed north of Sainte-Mère-Église.'

Stanford hesitated, working out what it might mean. 'So you think they've called our bluff. Sucked us in to what we thought was a soft underbelly, assumed we'd go for it.'

The General grimaced. 'Exactly, and now they're sending in reinforcements.'

The Admiral glanced up at his small map of northwest France. 'But we obviously have contingencies to fall back on, revising our plans to suit?'

'Nope. We ain't got a snowball in hell's chance of changing tactics at such short notice. Gotta bite the bullet and prey.'

Stanford climbed wearily to his feet and wandered over to the window, staring out at the peaceful grounds.

George 'Willow' Soloman stepped over and joined him. 'Casualties, Hugh, that's what worries the top brass. The troops are young, fresh; don't know much about real war. Just how many casualties can those guys take before the bridgeheads crumble? Too many and we'll be back in the sea.'

Stanford inclined his head in thought. For all the expertise amongst the top brass, for all the weapons and might of the US army, it always came down to the men on the ground. Did they have what it takes to prosecute a war, to advance when it mattered and stand when it was needed. 'I don't know where we go with that, General. As I say, bit bloody late for Eisenhower to start worrying now.'

Gephardt Ziegler feared for his life. He was standing rigidly to attention in front of Major Weisbaum's desk and the Major was in a foul mood. He sat studying his fingernails, peering at them in minute detail and turning them slowly in the light from the window.

'You failed me, Ziegler.' His voice was cold, menacing.

'Not I, Herr Major. Corporal Adler did not search the room.'

'Do not argue with me! There are no excuses, Ziegler. This was your operation.' Weisbaum stood up and pointed an immaculately manicured finger at Ziegler's head. He shouted. 'You are incompetent, totally and utterly incompetent. But for you I would now have all the names of an entire underground network. Idiot!'

'But we weren't to know he had the gun,' Ziegler protested, stunned by Weisbaum's furious outburst.

'And how exactly did you think he might defend himself? Throw buns at you?'

Ziegler winced. This was not going well. He expected Weisbaum to give him the benefit of the doubt; after all, the baker was just a radio operator, not the head of the resistance.

Weisbaum fumed. 'Gross dereliction of duty! I could have you shot for this. I told you I wanted them alive, now the whole of the underground are in hiding.' He cursed and shook his head. 'You are not worthy of the SS uniform.' He marched to the door and wrenched it open. 'Hans! This so called officer is relieved of all duties. He will be placed under house arrest until I have a chance to speak with his commanding officer.' He spun on his heel and came to stand at Ziegler's side. 'Now, get him out of my sight.'

Gerhardt Ziegler couldn't believe his luck, he was still alive. As he was returned to the château he began to relax. He was certain the Colonel would sort it all out. No more raids, he thought, leave it to the Gestapo.

Sunday dragged on. For the men cramped together in the ships of the American task force, conditions deteriorated rapidly. In Lyme Regis bay, relatively sheltered from the worst of the winds, it was still a bad beginning for anyone who'd never experienced stormy weather at sea. Cramped together in the limited space of the landing craft, with little in the way of protection from the squalls, even the anti-seasickness pills didn't seem to offer much in the way of warding off the agonising bouts of nausea.

The Rangers aboard the Empire Richmond and the infantry in the other troopships were not immune to the feeling of sickness. The bigger vessels behaved differently, taking the waves by riding in long tortuous corkscrews, slowly rolling as they dragged anchor. The stomach reacted just as strongly and it wasn't long before they ran out of sick bags.

For Chuck Rivers, unable to eat or hold down a drink, it was all he could do to stay focused. He knew the Rangers would look to him for leadership, but just at that moment, waiting for the storm to abate, he felt too weak to care.

The day wore on amidst the buffeting wind and rain, undiminished in the vicious ferocity unleashed. A tank landing craft swung broadside to the high waves, shipped water and wallowed dangerously. The skipper managed to regain control, fighting to get the craft facing into the wind. Night came and the Americans waited. Surely it must blow itself out soon.

12 Choppy Seas

It was precisely twelve minutes past four in the morning of Monday the 5th when Thorburn received the long awaited signal to say the invasion was under way. By the indistinct light of predawn he called the ship to readiness. Within a remarkably short space of time, the men appeared at their stations; so swiftly in fact, that Thorburn guessed the majority had been just as wide awake as he had. He smiled at the thought and pushed the hood of his duffle coat over the back of his head, settled his cap in place.

'Number One,' he called quietly.

Armstrong stepped forward from the back of the bridge. 'Sir?'

'Ask the Chief to join me.'

'Aye aye, sir.'

Thorburn gripped the bridge rail and looked intently at the growing number of vessels already beginning to raise steam, the tell tale sign of smoke rising from their funnels. A large flotilla of minesweepers began to emerge from the inner harbour, forming up to nose out towards the Solent.

A movement made him turn.

'You wanted me, sir?' The Welshman was wiping his hands on a piece of cotton waste.

'Yes, Chief, sorry to drag you away. What's your guesstimate of our best speed?'

'Well, sir, if my last readings are anything to go by, we should get about twenty-four knots.' He shook his head slightly, a look of resignation on his face. 'Can't really guarantee any more than that.'

Thorburn rubbed his chin. His Chief Engineer knew *Brackendale* better than anyone aboard. Those grimy fingers had explored the inner workings of just about every piece of mechanical equipment on the ship. The engines were his life's work, and if he reluctantly admitted to a lack of horsepower, then the captain wasn't about to criticise the man's integrity.

'Not to worry, I doubt we'll be doing much dashing about. Convoys tend to dawdle along in their own good time.'

Dawkins dabbed oil from the back of his hands. 'I'll do what I can, sir. She's never let us down yet.'

'Very true,' Thorburn smiled. 'We have a lot to thank you for.'

The Welshman shook his head, embarrassed. 'Just doing my job. Is that all, sir?'

Thorburn wasn't about to detain him any longer. The Chief was happier in the humid confines below decks than up on the bridge fending off stupid questions to which he'd already given the answers. 'Yes, that's all. Thank you, Chief.'

'Aye aye, sir,' Dawkins mumbled, and retreated down the ladder, a lot quicker than when he'd come up.

Thorburn turned for the bridge-screen. The crew were busy tending to their duties and the Cox'n's bark echoed around the decks. Time to check the charts and ensure Lieutenant Martin knew where they were going, diplomatically, of course.

As night gave way to day, 'Operation Neptune' swung into action. From England's southern shores, thousands of vessels put to sea from a multitude of ports. The Americans, coming in from the west, sailed early. From Falmouth, Plymouth, Dartmoor and Poole, and from all the tiny tributaries in-between. And for those that had sheltered in the waters off Lyme Regis, the ponderous advance to the Isle of Wight began all over again.

Then came the British, French and Canadians in their convoys from Southampton, Portsmouth, Spithead and Harwich, their destination, Area Z. Centred twenty-five miles to the south of Portsmouth, and with a theoretical diameter of eight to ten miles, this would be the jumping off point for the greatest amphibious task force ever assembled.

'Hands to stations for leaving harbour. Special sea duty men close up.' Thorburn slipped *Brackendale*'s mooring and left harbour slightly ahead of schedule. Now in the clear light of day, he pushed out beyond Gosport's headland and turned for the western arm of the Solent. Cowes slipped past the port bridge-wing, and then Yarmouth drifted astern.

The narrows between Hurst Castle to starboard and Fort Albert to port, 1,500 yards of turbulent waters, not helped by the freshening wind.

'Port ten.'

'Port ten, aye aye, sir.'

'Midships . . . , steady.'

The ship ran on, and made the tricky turn south beyond the Needles light house, breaking waters crashing in a windswept mist on the rocks below. And now they met the full force of the driving waves, broadside on to the worst of the weather.

Eight miles southwest of the Needles, *Brackendale* found the convoy and took station off the starboard side, protecting the right flank.

The worst of the storm had passed, but the winds blew strong, five to six foot waves threatening to swamp the vulnerable tank landing craft.

Thorburn, standing in the port bridge-wing, could only watch in admiration as the strung out miles of transport managed to maintain strict adherence to their line astern progress.

'What's our course, Pilot?'

'One-one-oh degrees, sir, but it's really a case of follow my leader. The Americans are homing in on marker buoys. Until night falls, we just hold station behind their lead.'

Thorburn glanced astern, at the great phalanx of assorted warships. 'Very well, carry on.' Certainly no-one would be going astray in daylight, nightime might be an altogether different proposition.

Armstrong returned from an inspection of the main magazines.

Thorburn smiled thinly. 'Remember that signal ordering us to report to Pendleton? Who'd of thought it would lead to this.'

Armstrong leaned against the bridge-screen and stared at the ships ahead. Far out over the port bow the main fleet were beginning to congregate. 'Quite honestly, sir, I don't think I ever imagined there'd be this many ships, not even in my wildest dreams.'

Thorburn grinned. 'That's not difficult; your dreams have never amounted to very much.'

Armstrong gave him a narrow-eyed sideways glance, spoke with an exaggerated seriousness. 'That, sir, was entirely uncalled for. It is only my deference to the authority of your rank that prevents me from making an offensive remark.'

'Naturally,' Thorburn agreed, and with a good-natured silence, the two men settled down for the voyage ahead.

In the graveyard of the Chapelle de la Croix, seventeen mourners joined the procession to witness the burial of Jacques and Lucille Fuberge. Beneath the wind driven ragged clouds they gathered round the deep dug holes and listened to the Priest give his final blessing over the plain wooden coffins.

Some of those who knew them well, cast a few crumbling handfuls of freshly dug soil on the unmarked lids. A small bouquet of wild flowers, picked from Lucille's favourite meadow, were gently dropped on each of the caskets. The men held silent vigil; the women shed tears behind black veils.

When the simple service ended and the mourners filed away, the two men who'd dug the graves began to fill them in.

The Priest hung back for a moment as the earth clattered on the coffins. He caught the eyes of the older man, who paused, resting on the spade. Mathieu Picard, the Miller, looked up at Claude Theroux, a sadness in his eyes, and the Priest bent forward slightly and spoke in a quiet voice. 'He was a brave man, served us well. Their deaths will not be in vain.'

Mathieu Picard nodded and shovelled more dirt, and the Priest, head lowered, walked solemnly away.

It began to rain.

General Scott Bainbridge sat at his desk in the Victorian town house, turned on the wireless, and waited for the BBC's evening news broadcast. Across the channel hidden within the depths of the French countryside, many men and women of the underground resistance were doing the same. Those clandestine forces were about to receive a variety of messages, disguised in passages of poetry, that would begin the systematic, well planned sabotage of the network of hidden telephone cables used by the German high command.

For some years now, the code breakers of British Intelligence had successfully cracked the supposedly impenetrable German Enigma codes. More often than not, they were able to read the signal before the German operators deciphered it. But if the landline between varying HQ's remained intact, the Allies would be deaf to the deployment of reserve forces being sent to Normandy. With the telephone cables cut, communications between Paris and Cherbourg and the Fuhrer's headquarters in Berchesgarten, could only be conducted by wireless

That would enable the Allies to monitor the airwaves and gain important access to the German military command.

From experience, Bainbridge knew that listening for the announcements took time, there were a long list of messages, and it was almost fifteen minutes before the short, apparently meaningless rhyme was read out. Subterfuge was vitally important. In order not to give the Germans any help in isolating a probable landing site, the entire network of French resistance had to be activated at the same time, including the more obvious Pas de Calais.

The General sat back with half a smile on his scarred face. Maybe now Churchill's famous 'Set Europe Ablaze!' would become reality and the unheralded men and women of occupied France would have their moment.

Sergeant Kunz Gruber took a motorbike and sidecar and rode a few kilometres southeast of Cherbourg. In the last light of a dull windswept day he pulled up outside a dairy farm and reached down into the sidecar's foot well. Lifting out a bulging canvas holdall he dismounted into a puddle and checked the contents. There was a large bottle of Cognac from the Hotel Chavalerie, four red wines, a pretty little gold necklace, and, folded carefully inside a cardboard box, several pairs of the finest silk stockings. With the bag in one hand and machine pistol in the other he lumbered up to the front door.

It opened before he knocked, the farmer's lined face smiling a welcome. 'Such a filthy evening, Kunz. Come in, get out of the rain.'

Gruber squeezed through and walked into the big warm kitchen. The farmer's greying wife sat knitting in a cushioned chair. She glanced disdainfully over the top of her spectacles, muttered something unintelligible and ignored him.

The thick set Sergeant chuckled at her obvious distaste and carefully lowered the holdall on the stout table. He grinned at the farmer, winked and pulled out the bottle of Cognac.

The farmer sighed, but managed to maintain the semblance of a smile. It was almost eighteen months since he'd first set eyes on the SS Sergeant. An unheralded search of his premises had ended with a demand for food and something to quench his thirst. Unfortunately, Kunz Gruber then met the farmer's nineteen year old daughter. Members of the SS usually got their way and under pressure to keep his family in one piece, the farmer had reluctantly accepted the Sergeants unwelcome attentions. His daughter, Anne-Marie, afraid for her father's safety, had allowed herself to be seduced by the clumsy oaf's brutal love making.

Disguising his loathing for Gruber's presence the farmer produced two large tumblers from the sideboard.

'Aha,' Gruber grunted. 'Wunderbar!' He splashed out the fiery liquid until the glasses were full and raised his in a toast.

'Your good health.' Then he drained the tumbler and poured himself another. 'And where is the lovely Anne-Marie?'

A movement at the door caught his eye and the dark, auburn haired young woman stepped quietly into the room. 'I am here, Kunz. But am I not worthy of a Cognac too?'

Gruber lost the smile. He prided himself on showing off his manners, never realising how pathetic his attempts to emulate the upper classes were.

'Another glass!' he snapped at the farmer. He scraped a seat back from the table and gestured for her to sit. Spilling the Cognac as he poured, Gruber watched her take a mouthful, and then delved inside the holdall. 'I have a present for you, ma Cherie.'

She took the cardboard box, prised open the lid and shook out a pair of flesh coloured stockings. 'They are very nice,' she lied.

Gruber gulped more Cognac, wiped his mouth with the back of his hand and smirked. 'You must try them on for me.'

She shrugged in resignation, topped up the glass and drank deeply. It was one way to dull the senses, to make life bearable over the coming hours. She hated these times when he came, disgusted by his lust for pleasure. One day, she thought, one day I will kill this pig.

He pushed the remaining Cognac across to the farmer. 'For you, old man.' He turned to acknowledge the mother, clicking away with her needles. 'Good night, madam.'

She snorted, chose to ignore him and concentrated on her knitting.

Gruber shrugged his shoulders at the snub, lit a used white candle and thrust a bottle of red wine into the daughter's hand. 'Come, Anne-Marie.' He led her out to the stairs and then waited behind for her to take the first step, enjoying the sight of her shapely legs climbing up to her bedroom. He smirked; they always looked so good in silk stockings.

Outside, the rain lashed in on a driving wind, but to the north, in the middle of the English Channel, the stormy conditions had eased, and thousands of ships closed in on Hitler's Atlantic Wall

Not far from Anne-Marie's farmhouse, in the Chapelle de la Croix, Claude Theroux heard the message from the BBC and crossed himself. He turned off the radio, hid it in the wooden chest of alter sacraments, and walked to the entrance. His footsteps echoed loudly within the ancient walls. Slamming the heavy oak door firmly shut he hurried to the house and unearthed his bicycle. Pausing only to bid farewell to his wife he mounted the saddle and rode off to find the Miller.

Within an hour, by the light of a flickering candle, the pair were huddled together inside Mathieu Picard's storeroom. Hidden beneath his freshly ground sacks of flour, a small trapdoor revealed a cache of explosives, neatly stacked in their waterproof wrappings. One by one they were lifted to the surface and Theroux packed the plastic explosive gingerly into three large carpetbags.

Picard watched him and smiled. 'There is no need for such care. You cannot make it blow with your hands.'

The Priest looked at him with narrowed eyes. 'No, my friend. It might not blow up in your hands, but I assure you, anything is possible with mine.'

Picard solemnly bowed his head. 'If you say so, Father. But you could hit this with a hammer, it will not explode.' He dropped the trap door back into the recess and they both replaced the sacks of flour.

'Will you start tonight?' asked the Priest.

Mathieu Picard, still on his knees, peered up at the churchman's eyes. 'Oui, no time like the present. The culvert first, on the main road. Difficult to repair.'

'And the lines between the gun emplacements?'

Picard hesitated, tightened his mouth. 'Yes . . . , it would have been a job for Jacques Fuberge. But the others will manage, they know what to do.'

Theroux looked around the floor. 'Where are the detonators?'

Picard grinned. 'I have them in the vegetable garden.' He shrugged, spread his hands. 'I know, they are not so good to eat.'

The Priest smiled in turn, held out his hand. 'God go with you, Mathieu. Be careful.'

Picard blew out the candle and Theroux found his bike leaning against the shed.

Forty miles south of Lands End, H.M.S. *Rosefinch* butted her way into the westerly seas. As the last light of day dwindled and darkness cloaked the ship, the lookout in the crows nest lost visual contact with the Flotilla Leader to the north, and Willoughby ordered him down from the masthead. The luminous dial of the radar screen now became their primary means of contact.

Willoughby turned to his navigating officer. 'What next, Pilot?'

Lieutenant Ian Dixon consulted his chart. 'A turn to port, sir, on a heading of one-seven-five degrees.'

'Very well,' Willoughby muttered. It had been a long spell of watch keeping and so far as he was aware there'd been no attempt by the enemy to break through their lines.

Night came and the rain stopped. Under the cloak of darkness, two shadowy figures of the French resistance paused to take a breather. Mathieu Picard and his son crouched in a sodden ditch by the side of the road leading south from Cherbourg. They were seven kilometres north of Sainte-Mère-Église. Very deliberately they unpacked four parcels of plastic explosive and placed them on a square of canvas sacking.

Picard turned to his son. 'The detonators?'

His lad reached inside his leather overcoat and extracted the small metal tubes. Each cylinder ended in a pair of short wires for attaching to the main run of cable, enough to ensure they were far enough away when the charge exploded. This in turn would be wound onto the terminals of the magneto box, initiated by plunging down on the 'T' shaped handle.

The Miller moved forward in the ditch until he came to a large hole leading under the road. Searching through the trickle of water with his bare hands his fingers located a thick strand of cable. It was the German telephone line which ran from Command Headquarters in Cherbourg to General Gerd von Runstedt's Army Group West HQ in Paris. Laid in secrecy during the first year of occupation, mostly at night, the majority of its length was buried in the countryside. Over time, local farmers had unearthed poorly hidden sections of the network and informed the resistance. Having informed the British led SOE, the French underground had eventually been persuaded not to disrupt these lines of communications until given clearance to do so.

But now was the time to destroy what they could, and the Miller knew of five other locations across seven kilometres of farmland ready for demolition. His primary target was this culvert which diverted a small watercourse between ditches either side of the road. The job itself was simple. Blow up the culvert and destroy the road. Two for the price of one; cut the line and disrupt the flow of traffic. His only concern was to achieve all this in a fairly narrow time slot. From just after dark to no later than midnight when Allied aircraft would begin their raids.

Having found the armoured cable he returned for the first of the plastic explosive and crawling into the brick tunnel, packed it firmly into the central span. The British agent had shown him how to shape the charge to achieve

143

maximum affect and with a few old discarded bricks he managed to fashion a temporary shield. Crawling back to the square of canvas he picked up two of the pencil detonators and the drum of twin core wire.

Back inside the culvert he twisted the short lengths to the main line, pressed the slim tubes into the explosive, then felt along the wires to make sure all was tight. Satisfied with his efforts he clambered out from the cramped interior and allowed the wire to wind off the small drum. Fifty metres from the culvert, he and his son made the connections to the terminals and raised the plunger.

In the pale light of an intermittent moon he looked at his boy and grimaced. 'Now we get to play our part.' With both hands he drove down the handle and ducked his head.

The surface of the road erupted in a thunderous explosion. Huge chunks of tarmac cart wheeled into air. Rocks and pebbles flew in all directions, scything through bushes and flaying the ditch with bouncing missiles. It rained dirt. Picard spat to clear his mouth, shrugging his shoulders to clear the loose soil. As the blanket of smoke cleared he peered cautiously over the side of the ditch, eyes wide with disbelief. An enormous crater had been blown in the road, four or five metres wide.

His son stepped out shaking his head. He looked at his father, bewildered. 'Just how much did you need?'

Picard chuckled. 'Not quite as much as I thought.' He grabbed the spool of wire and retrieved the magneto box. 'Come on, lad, we can't hang around.' With one last look at their smoking handiwork they moved back down the road. Two hundred metres from the blown culvert they took a right turn through a gap in the hedge, and treading carefully along the well worn sheep track, set out for the adjoining field.

In Cherbourg's German headquarters, the main switchboard operator suddenly lost his telephone link to Paris and cursed. He guessed at the cause of failure, it had been expected. The Pas de Calais had suffered similar disruption. He logged the time and reported to the duty officer. A senior Telegraphist switched the wireless transmitter-receiver from standby to live, set up the encoding machine, and quickly re-established contact with Army Group West.

A hundred and fifty miles northeast, in a secret location to the south of London, a signalman tensed, sat forward and scribbled on his message pad. His duty as middle watch wireless interceptor had just paid off; a Wehrmacht transmission emanating from the Cotentin Peninsula. It was a recognised frequency, one of three he was tasked with monitoring. A runner took the message to central office and a short while later, in a large estate in the Buckinghamshire countryside, a well established unit of code breakers began to systematically apply the complex rules of 'traffic analysis'.

Lieutenant-Commander Richard Thorburn stood in the port wing of *Brackendale*'s bridge and squinted through the moonlit darkness. Vaguely seen to the east, the leading squadron of battleships and cruisers, all with their attendant escort of destroyers, moved steadily towards the French coast. Beyond those nearest warships of Force Utah, the invisible ships of Omaha, and then the even greater flotillas for Sword, Juno and Gold. *Brackendale*, riding the right flank of the task force, found herself bearing the brunt of the north-westerly gales raging in from off the starboard quarter. Thorburn estimated the gusts were still at force four; at times the waves hit them at five or six feet in height. For a small destroyer it was uncomfortable, but for some of the landing craft following along in their wake, life must be miserable.

Midnight came and Thorburn stopped his worrying and realised that D-Day had actually arrived, and this convoy headed for the Cotentin Peninsula, would be the first to begin the offensive. 'Well, Number One,' he said, 'I do believe the hour has come.'

Armstrong took a pace closer. He made an exaggerated pretence of looking around and grinned. 'Yes, sir, I concur.'

Thorburn caught the sarcasm and grinned in spite of himself. 'Sorry, I wasn't trying to sound dramatic. It's just that the day we've all talked about, the most important day in recent history, well . . . , here it is. Dark, windswept, quiet,' he copied Armstrong, looking into the emptiness, 'where are the trumpets, the fanfare? Nothing so grand, just a cautious, stealthy advance into the unknown. And when the daylight comes, there'll be a lot of dying. Them and us.' He smiled, sheepishly. 'Enough of the oratory, I just thought it was worth mentioning.'

Armstrong pursed his lips, nodded, serious. 'It was, sir. History in the making.'

The ship corkscrewed uneasily in the following sea and Thorburn steadied himself to the roll.

Armstrong called a sharp reminder to the wheelhouse. 'Watch your heading.'

Thorburn crossed to the forebridge and peered ahead, thankful for the protection of his duffle coat. At times the wind whistled venomously out of the black night and it was then that the sea thumped the bow plates with extra malice. God knows what it was like in the tank landing craft. He lifted the binoculars and tried to find a visible horizon but only agitated waves and white tossed foam swam across the dark void.

A brilliant flash lit the far horizon, a blaze of white and orange, burning into balls of fire. Rumbling detonations reached his ears and he stared in wonder at the devastating bomb runs being unleashed on the enemy coast. This was the beginning of the air bombardment designed to soften German resistance. The enemy anti-aircraft guns began to reply, tracer and searchlights probing the sky. The unseen Flying Fortresses, holding their formations, savaged the targets. In the far distance, where the left flank of British and Canadians forces would land, Avro Lancasters of the Royal Air Force pummelled their sector in the same destructive pattern.

Thorburn felt Armstrong's presence at his side. He was staring out beyond the bows. 'That's a lot of explosive going in over there, sir.'

Thorburn nodded inside his hood. 'Let's hope it's on target. There are too many guns on that shoreline. How's the radar performing, Number One?'

'Last time I looked, sir, there were more dots than I could count.'

Despite everything, Thorburn chuckled. 'I take it that means it's working well.'

'Yes, sir. Top notch.' The ship lurched to port then swayed to starboard, riding a long roller.

'And the Asdic?'

'Not so good, sir. There's a lot of interference.'

Thorburn grimaced, knowing there were too many propellers thrashing the waters. 'I guessed as much.'

Brackendale thumped into another wave then dipped her bows to a trough. The huge armada sailed on, under the cloak of darkness, in the windswept choppy seas.

Two miles astern of Thorburn's small destroyer, a former peacetime coastal steamer, now a troopship renamed the *Empire Richmond*, pushed steadily on

147

towards her rendezvous off the French coast. Her decks were crammed full of the American 4th Infantry Division, and in place of her peacetime compliment of lifeboats, ten Assault Landing Craft waited to be hoisted out to sea.

Major Paul Wingham had managed to find himself a relatively sheltered spot behind a life raft on the port side, and sat with his legs drawn up under his chin. The squad of Rangers huddled together close by. They too snatched what rest they could in the cold night wind, few bothered to speak. The rank smell of men's vomit wafted through the confined spaces, while others still did their best to hold it together.

Wingham raised his head for a moment, wriggled to get more comfortable, and hunched up against the swirling wind. The voice of General Douglas Carlswright, Combined Operations, echoed in his memory. "Find those guns, Major. A lot of men's lives depend on it." And Wingham closed his eyes and remembered the aerial photographs of the inland terrain. There was a time when he'd walked the same place, in the early days of the French resistance. He cleared his mind and pulled up his collar. Not long now. The *Empire Richmond* ploughed on and the men of 4th Infantry endured.

A Tank Landing Craft off their port side, carrying a full load of four Sherman tanks and their personnel, was hit broadside on by a large wave. The boat rolled wickedly and dropped her stern. Tons of seawater surged over the gunwales and she staggered under the weight. The pumps dealt with some of it, but the boat settled lower and struggled to maintain speed. Another three and a half hours before they would arrive off the Normandy coast.

Colonel Otto Reinhardt had decided to stay the night in Fresville, somewhat more sheltered from the storms whipping in from the northwest. He'd managed to aquire a room on the south side of the old house, but even so the wind rattled the glass windows, and at midnight he was still awake. The distant sound of the first bombs exploding towards the port of Cherbourg brought him to his feet and he hurried through to the first floor landing. He looked out of the window from the gable end and cursed. He cursed the bombers and he cursed the war, and most of all he cursed in frustration. He'd been posted to the Atlantic Wall from the Russian Front, ostensibly for rest and recuperation. For a while, after the rigours of the Russian winter, the comparative warmth of the French coast had made for a very pleasant interlude. But then the ever growing threat of an Allied invasion loomed large and in the intervening months nobody, from the lowest minion to Hitler himself had any doubts as to the veracity.of those claims.

So Reinhardt cursed and clenched his fists and swore at the Gods for bringing all this on him. This was the fifth consecutive night of bombing, from Calais in the east, and down as far as Brest in the west. Only this time the bombing seemed more intense, and it was getting nearer. He turned away and called loudly for his driver. He dressed quickly, checked his Luger and ran downstairs. His intuition warned him that tonight was different, that this might be a prelude to something more. His driver stumbled down the stairs behind him, struggling to fasten the buttons on his uniform.

'Take me to the Command bunker. Schnell!' Reinhardt shouted, and they ran outside to the small Kübelwagen. He jumped in and they raced off towards the underground shelter, five kilometres from the western arm of the Seine Bay. The bombing multiplied, ever closer, huge erupting fireballs lighting the sky in all directions. With gritted teeth they found the farm track leading through the hedgerows. The driver swung the Kübelwagen into the gap, skidded on the wet soil, and braked to a standstill at the rear entrance of the bunker.

Reinhardt jumped out and waved him off, just as a stick of bombs found the far side of the field. Violent detonations rocked the ground. A bomb exploded mid-field, a second erupted twenty paces closer, forcing Reinhardt to duck from the blast. A third bomb exploded and destroyed the Kübelwagen. When he looked again what remained of his driver was a bloody carcass hanging upside down on the hedge, and the engine smouldered on the edge of the crater. A wheel bounced off across the field and toppled on its side. More bombs fell, moving away over the hedgerows, a rolling pattern of destruction.

Coughing violently, Reinhardt slapped the dirt off his uniform. He dropped down the concrete steps and banged on the door, shouting to be let in. A call from inside and the heavy steel door swung out of the way. A single, dim wall light showed him the interior. He ignored their salutes and crossed to the field telephone.

'There is no connection, Herr Oberst. The line is dead.'

Reinhardt swore, but tried it for himself anyway, and threw it down in disgust. He strode over to the forward observation slit and looked out across the invisible pastureland. Nothing to be seen in the dark night. Another flurry of bombs away to his right, over towards Ouistreham, and the receding throb of aircraft engines. Wind and rain drove in from the bay, gusting over the headland. A filthy night, he thought, too rough for an invasion, and yet that worrying premonition stayed with him.

'Coffee!' he demanded. He glanced round the bunker and found what he was looking for. 'You there in the corner. See to the remains of my driver,' he ordered, and sat down at the plain wooden table. 'When daylight comes we will repair the telephone cables. We must have a line to the guns.'

Outside the bunker, the wind eased and it stopped raining. The Allied bombers completed their missions and turned for home. Unknown to Oberst Otto Reinhardt, most of his guns had been disabled, and only a few, well protected canon remained to repel any assault on the beaches below.

Inexorably, the ships of Force 'U' pushed on through the dark night, ever closer to the hostile shore. On *Brackendale*'s bridge, Thorburn sat in the chair with a worried frown. At any minute he expected them to be discovered. How could the biggest amphibious assault ever mounted go undetected for so long. Where were the U-boats? Night patrols by the E-boats? A stray low-flying night fighter? Somehow their luck was holding, but for how much longer? He rose to his feet and paced the forebridge, sensing a slackening of the weather. Certainly the gusts had decreased in intensity, the waves moderating.

'Time?' he asked.

'One-fifteen, sir,' Martin answered from the chart table.

'Thank you, Pilot,' Thorburn said, and went back to the chair. Only quarter past one. Like so many others in that windswept darkness, he waited impatiently for the first signs of dawn.

Thirty kilometres north of Alderney, Werner von Holtzmann's small flotilla of E-boats struggled to maintain progress in the heavy seas. Speed was necessarily reduced to avoid damage to the vulnerable craft, and he reluctantly made the decision to abandon the patrol and turn back for Braye harbour. Given the prevailing conditions he couldn't believe Eisenhower could possibly order the invasion until the weather improved. He made a wide turn to the east, brought the boats round for the southern run to the islands, and settled down to enjoy a large Cuban cigar.

Flying high overhead, the C-47 Douglas Skytrains, carrying over 6,000 parachutists of the 101st and 82nd American Airborne Divisions, throbbed through the all enveloping clouds. Their drop zones were the inland sectors behind Utah beach, and their main aim was to prevent the German forces from bringing up reinforcements to disrupt the amphibious assault.

On the sea below, his boat's engines, coupled with the wind and waves, drowned out the sound of the aircraft. Von Holtzmann relaxed with his cigar, oblivious to the thousands of men winging their way towards German occupied territory.

In Southwick House, Vice-Admiral Sir Hugh Stanford, stood to the left of the main door in the downstairs drawing room, and watched the Wrens plot the advance of the invasion fleet. The enormous map covered the entire area, from England's southern coast, all the way down to Normandy including the French hinterland. The markers farthest to the south showed the deployment of three-hundred minesweepers clearing the ten channels through which the fleet followed. From what he could see, they were well within range of the German guns, and yet there had been no reports of enemy action.

'Won't be long now, sir,' Pendleton said, indicating the map. 'The battleships are almost on station.'

Stanford nodded thoughtfully. 'I find it hard to believe they've made it without being discovered. It seems we've achieved total surprise, absolute secrecy.' He shook his head in wonder. 'For all the planning, I didn't really think it would go unnoticed.' He turned to Pendleton, uncertain as to whether the Commodore should be taken into his confidence. 'I honestly thought 'Ike' had made the wrong decision. The forecast was so unpredictable, and then the storm came in. Glad it wasn't our decision.'

Pendleton grinned, stroked his beard. 'Goes with the territory, sir. Supreme Commander, the responsibility was his.'

'Even so,' Stanford said, 'it was a tough call to make.' He reflected on the overall plan. The landings were yet to take place. 'Let's hope the next phase works as well.'

A sliding step-ladder was pushed across the map and he watched as a Wren reached up to place a blue parachute marker near the town of Sainte-Mère-Église. The American airborne were landing. Behind his back, out of sight, he crossed his fingers and then forced a smile. 'Well, James, looks like battle's commenced.'

Pendleton inclined his head. 'Yes, sir. It's half-past-one. On schedule.'

Stanford pursed his lips, about to answer, but he saw a movement of personnel beneath the large map. He straightened in an effort to get a clearer view, and then caught a brief glimpse of an American officer's uniform at a small table. He might have been mistaken, but he thought he saw a small ring of five silver stars glinting on the man's collar. It was enough. Good to know the Commander-in-Chief had his finger on the pulse.

Kapitänleutnant Kurt Schneider ordered the U-boat to be brought up to periscope depth. It was not done without difficulties. As they rose from the depths they began to encounter severe oscillation and the boat was twenty meters below the surface. For the men on the diving planes, the job of stabilising the boat was proving as much as they could cope with. The power of the waves disrupted the trim and the Chief Engineer needed all his skills to maintain the horizontal. The conning tower was acting as a keel in reverse, forcing the boat through an uncontrollable arc.

Schneider's patience snapped. 'What are you doing?' he shouted. 'Can it be so difficult? It's not the Atlantic, this is just a puddle!'

His First Officer was used to the tantrums. 'If we could turn into the weather it would be better. We are broadside on to the waves.'

Schneider made as if to argue, anger welling inside, but he recognised the truth when he heard it, and changed his mind. 'So,' he hissed, 'come to west-north-west. At once!' he ordered raising his voice.

The First Officer glanced at the Chief, who nodded to the man on the steering, and with the rudder hard over, the U-boat took a long turn to port. When Schneider finally called for the steering to be centred the boat was riding to a controllable pitch.

'Bring the motors up to six knots.' It helped smooth the last of the undulations. He turned to his First Officer. 'Periscope depth?'

The man eyed the depth gauge and nodded. 'Twelve meters. Not steady, but it is all we can do.'

Schneider grimaced, tight lipped. 'Periscope,' he ordered.

The tube came up and he pushed his cap back from his forehead. He settled himself at the eyepiece looking for clear vision. Bubbles raced past the scope, swirling foam and darkness. He waited for the next trough, the periscope in clear air, a half-seen expanse of breaking waves, sheets of spray. The U-boat rolled and dipped, his vision gone, then lifting clear, another wave. He knew it was all a wasted effort, worse still, the boat might break the surface. The Englanders had excellent radar, too much of a risk.

He winced as the waves slammed into the tower, jolted his eye in the viewing glass. Settling himself for one more look he rotated the periscope to starboard, straining to focus across the turbulent sea. A subtle brightening of the eastern sky, the faintest hint of pre-dawn grey. The boat surged down a valley, the periscope engulfed, and he backed away from the eyepiece.

The First Officer raised an eyebrow.

Schneider shook his head in exasperation. 'Take us down. Sixty metres, four knots.' The boat sank away from the confusion above, and steadied in the hidden depths.

Twenty kilometres to the east, fine off the U-boat's starboard quarter, a small 'Hunt' class destroyer pushed on, headed south for the French coast.

The first Americans to touch enemy occupied territory unclipped their parachutes and began moving towards their target areas. The men from the sky were scattered, some already under fire, searching for their 'buddies' and cursing the dark. Many were dead before they hit the ground. Slowly but surely they gathered into functioning squads, grew to platoon strength and formed companies. They became a fragile fighting force, deep behind enemy lines, and although very few in number, creating utter confusion in the German chain of command.

13 Causeway

Just before dawn, four miles from the enemy coast, H.M.S. *Brackendale* made a final turn to starboard. She had arrived on station to commence bombardment of the hostile shore. Thorburn leaned against the port screen and focused his binoculars to scan the rising ground beyond the beach. In the faint eerie light that accompanies the pre-dawn grey, he found the darker remnants of thinning smoke from the overnight bombing. There was little or no evidence of the German army making any effort to counter the invasion.

'Slow ahead together, Number One' he called. 'Hold her head to the wind.'

The ship was parallel to the shore, pointing north-north-west and riding the oncoming waves. The engine room giving just enough power to give *Brackendale* steerage way against the current. Not perfect, Thorburn concluded, but stable enough for 'Guns' to achieve an accurate broadside. In the waters between the warships, the assault boats of the 4th Infantry Division began to concentrate, forming up into their allocated start lines. The larger tank landing craft detached themselves from the convoy and made their way forward to the assembly area. Rocket firing assault craft lined up alongside boats carrying heavy mortars, and all the while, troopships continued to disembark hundreds of men into the boats.

Thorburn moved to the forebridge and looked down at the pair of four-inch gun barrels, trained out over the portside. The gunners had closed up for action, clearly visible in their light coloured anti-flash capes and helmets. 'Guns' had assured him everything was in order. Thorburn's greatest concern was in *Brackendale*'s forthcoming role to support Wingham's mission. If the

Rangers got in too close to their objectives the risk of 'friendly fire' could not be discounted. He pulled back his sleeve and peered at his watch. It was 05.50 hours and daylight came, a stealthy lifting of the gloom, as if a curtain had been drawn aside.

On the *Empire Richmond* eleven miles from the sands of Utah beach, Major Paul Wingham gathered his gear, moved to the portside guardrail, and waited in line to board the assault boat. The Rangers stood quietly with the other two squads of infantry that would fill the boat to capacity. In the pale light of the moon, the crew of the troopship began the job of swinging out the boats and lowering them on the derricks. When the gunwales reached the level of the main deck, the order was given to climb aboard.

Wingham shuffled forward, clambered over the rail and squeezed down into the bottom, hemmed in by an infantryman one side and Hernandez the other.

Sub-Lieutenant David Galbraith R.N., called out to the soldiers. 'Are all you gentlemen sitting comfortably?'

'Like the bloody Waldorf Astoria,' came a sarcastic reply.

'Lovely,' said Galbraith in the same vein. 'Hang on now, here we go.' His face turned inboard. 'Lower away!'

Wingham felt the boat drop and tensed in readiness. A rising wave caught the boat and swept it high, then passed away beneath, and the boat plunged down hard. It hit the water with a heavy jolt, a jarring impact through his feet. The engines came to life and the boat shimmied away from the troopship's hull and Wingham winced as a deluge of cold water spilled over the side. He wiped his eyes and looked up at the troopship. Engines rumbling, the assault boat moved out towards the overhanging bows before circling round to the opposite side.

Seawater poured over the gunwales and surged over their boots. A wave slapped the ramp, shot into the air and splashed down on unprotected necks and shoulders. The boat rocked and pitched, yawing from side to side. Someone retched and threw up, his vomit slopping round their feet, giving off its own putrid stench.

Wingham caught sight of other boats rising and falling to the waves, and still they circled, waiting.

'How much longer for Christ sake?' a hidden voice queried.

'Shut your noise, Collins. You know the drill.' It was a voice of authority, and there was no reply.

A change in the boat's behaviour made Wingham look up. They were moving away from the troopship into clear water and forming up for the ride in. The boat lifted on a long roller and he spotted the silhouette of the two huge American warships, their big guns swinging round towards the shore. Major Paul Wingham screwed up his eyes and bowed his head. No turning back now.

Sub-Lieutenant Galbraith caught the flagged signal from the command boat and called out a warning. 'Sit tight, lads, we're off! Full ahead, Cox'n!' The note of the big diesel engines lifted in response and the flat bottomed assault boat bucketed into the waves. As the engine increased to a subdued roar the square bows lifted, and from what had been an ungainly pitch and roll, she steadied into a powerful push towards the enemy coast. Below him the packed helmets of the soldiers swayed in unison, drenched in spray, glistening with water. To their left the main body of Landing Craft stretched out in a long line, an impressive phalanx of amphibious weaponry.

He watched a Landing Craft Rocket manoeuvre towards the centre of the line, pushing on through a wall of foaming sea. He took a look astern, at the Empire Richmond receding into the distance, just one of the many troopships about to weigh anchor and return to England. He made a quick check on their position in the line and glanced at his watch. They were an estimated ninety-five minutes from the beach.

An enormous thunder of gunfire caught him by surprise. The battleship opened up with a broadside and the first salvo stunned the men under the muzzles. His ears blocked and he swallowed hard, opened his mouth to relieve the pressure. The shockwave kicked him in the back and the boat yawed in the water. The Cox'n wrestled with the wheel, fighting the boat back on course. A large wave thumped the square bow, blue-green seas cascading into the boat, swilling down through the men behind the ramp. Galbraith held his breath. This was rougher than anything they'd encountered before, dangerous. There was no option but to reduce speed.

'Ease the throttle, Cox'n. Try her at ten knots.'

The Cox'n reached for the control. 'Ten knots, aye, sir.'

Galbraith felt an immediate improvement in the boat's behaviour, riding over, rather than through the waves.

In the chateau on the outskirts of Cherbourg, Gerhardt Ziegler awoke to the sound of heavy gunfire. He opened his eyes and stared at the ceiling trying to place the direction. There were distant rumbles, hard to define. It seemed to be coming from the east. The woman's arm lay across his chest, her bare leg pinning his thigh. In the dim light of the window he turned his head on the pillow and studied her sleeping profile. The makeup was smudged, the red lipstick faded, and the lines on her face showed clearly. He looked down the body at her naked breasts, the swell of her stomach, running to fat. Still, she'd served her purpose for the night, but in the sober light of dawn he might have thought twice.

He pushed her arm to one side and slid his leg away from under hers, and swung his feet to the floor. She moaned slightly, turned over and settled. He padded quietly over to the window. Out there to the north the sea was angry, less than it had been, but still with breaking crests and scudding grey clouds. So why the gunfire? The Allies would surely not have chosen to attack in this weather.

The telephone in the hall downstairs began to ring, stopped, and he heard a man answer. Ziegler had a premonition and began to dress. He was pulling on his boots when he heard footsteps and a knock on the door.

'Ja?'

His new driver put his head round. His eyes went to the naked woman before he managed to speak. 'That was headquarters, Herr Lieutnant. You are to report immediately.'

Ziegler reached for his jacket. 'Then fetch the car. I will be down shortly.'

The driver snatched a last glance at the woman's long legs, 'Jawohl, Herr Lieutnant.'

A black leather briefcase held Ziegler's maps of Cherbourg with the dispositions of all major units on the Peninsula. His own command was a company of the 198th Panzergrenadier Reconnaissance Battalion, stationed on the south-eastern approaches to the port. He screwed his face up in concentration. That gunfire was definitely coming from that direction.

By the time the Mercedes pulled up outside, Ziegler was waiting on the steps. The driver opened the front passenger door for his officer and jumped in behind the wheel. The noise from the guns was louder, constant.

Ziegler nodded to himself, convinced it was the invasion. 'The day has come. Time to fight.'

His driver said nothing. If the rumours were true, he might not live long enough to care.

Seven minutes later the car drew up alongside Battalion Headquarters, previously the mayor's office block. Ziegler looked about in surprise. There was a distinct lack of mobilisation; there appeared to be no obvious response to the invasion.

Nodded through by the guards he strode briskly down the hall and presented himself to the duty officer.

'This way, Herr Lieutnant.'

Entering the sparsely furnished interior he found the Battalion Commander leaning over a map.

The duty officer saluted. 'Oberleutnant Ziegler, Herr Oberst.'

Colonel Weimar looked up. 'Ah, the man who has upset Major Weimar. Well, as of this moment you are no longer under his jurisdiction.' He nodded to the duty officer. 'Thank you, Hans.' He turned back to the map. 'See this, Ziegler?' he asked, pointing to the coast. 'It seems the Allies have launched a diversionary raid between Le Havre and us. I have tried to get confirmation but the lines are down.' He straightened from the map and strode to the window. 'As far as we are aware the main invasion will be at the Pas de Calais, but . . . ,' he swung round raising a hand in thought, 'it would be foolish to assume the Intelligence people are always right.' Back at the map, he ran a finger from the coastline to Cherbourg and down towards Sainte-Mère-Église. 'You will reconnoitre the approach roads to Cherbourg. I want troop numbers and vehicles, if they have any. We have heard of airborne drops overnight, quite large numbers I am informed. But the Panzers are not far away. Without armoured support, paratroopers could not hold out for long.'

Ziegler nodded in agreement. Von Runstedt's Army Group West would annihilate such lightly armed troops, well before they could advance. And his own reconnaissance would prove vital in providing the latest information to High Command.

'My company is on standby, Herr Oberst.'

The Colonel scrutinized the map for a moment longer. 'Then make haste, Lieutnant. Time is not on our side.'

Ziegler threw up a salute. 'Jawohl, Herr Oberst,' he barked, and hurried out to find his driver.

Back in the front seat he eagerly banged the dashboard. 'We have a job to do, Corporal. Company HQ, go!'

The Mercedes came to life and the man put his foot down. Ziegler narrowed his eyes in anticipation. They would soon be in the thick of things.

Twenty miles southeast of the speeding Mercedes, the American soldiers of 4th Infantry Division began their final approach to the beach.

For Lieutenant-Commander Richard Thorburn, the deafening crash of the fourteen-inch guns, the battleship's full broadside, shattered the tense wait, and that salvo marked the beginning of the navy's bombardment. *Brackendale* exploded into action, the crash of her guns vibrating the decks, blinding flashes in the dawn light. Each battleship, each, cruiser, every destroyer, joined the onslaught of the invasion coastline. The distant ground lit up with explosions, brilliant flashes, a myriad colours, and heavy, drifting smoke.

Thorburn caught a brief glimpse of the first wave of assault boats, well on their way to shore. He wondered where Wingham might be, which boat; surely towards the right flank, close to their objective. Amidst the intense blast of noise from the American battleships, he stepped up to the compass platform, glanced at their bearing. All was well so he moved to look aft down the portside guardrail. The quarterdeck guns fired in tandem, a constant reliable stream of shells pouring onto the pre-designated targets. He swallowed a drift of acrid smoke and coughed, eyes watering. And still the guns hammered on, round after round of high explosive.

The Higgins boat was four hundred yards from shore when a red smoke marker hit the beach and the shelling stopped. A fast flying squadron of B26 Marauders tore in over their heads, steadied into formation, and released their bomb loads a half mile inland. A long line of explosions rolled over the countryside, an enormous column of dirty smoke coiling into the wind.

Wingham's feet shuddered as the assault boat hit the beach. The ramp dropped, grinding on the coarse sand, and someone yelled. 'Go!' He heard bullets zipping overhead, ricochets whining, flinched as glowing tracer flashed by. He ran, down the ramp and through the surf, onto solid sand. A mortar hit, ten paces to the left, amongst 4th Infantry. A man staggered, half-fell, came to his feet and stumbled on. Anti-personnel mine blew up and a soldier lost his foot, screaming.

The buzz of an MG42 from up the beach, the sand jumping and spitting, leaving a pock marked trail.

Rivers shouted at his squad. 'Move right!'

Wingham's boot snagged on an entanglement of barbed wire. In the blinding smoke he tripped and hit the sand, hard. It knocked the wind out of him. A hand dragged him over. 'You all right?' It was Belluci, chewing gum.

Wingham nodded, fighting for breath.

The big hand pulled him up by the arm, patted sand from his battle dress.

Belluci grinned at him. 'Come on, this way.'

Wingham stumbled behind him, and then Belluci stopped abruptly, turned and pulled him to one knee. Machine gun fire chased over their heads.

Chuck Rivers appeared through the smoke. 'We gotta move right. We landed too far to the left; we need the west exit over there.' He pointed along the beach in the smoke. 'The Infantry are attacking from where they landed, straight in.' The smoke cleared and they found themselves in the open, exposed. A mortar thumped sand into the air, muffled.

Wingham realised the Rangers had spread out around him, kneeling or lying prone. Sixty or seventy yards ahead, beyond a low wall, a German pill-box flickered with gunfire. There was the distinctive buzzing of that MG and he saw rifles firing from the slits. Bullets hissed close.

Rivers swore, eying up the opposition. 'Right, we're on our own. We have to take out that pill-box. Smoke grenades in and then we move, left and right.' He paused, nodded. 'Go!'

Three grenades arced out up the beach, the white smoke billowed, spread, began to drift.

'Now!'

They rose as one, sprinting forward, crouched low. Wingham hit the swirling smoke and surged out the other side, Sten gun up. The muzzle of the MG moved and a Thompson submachine-gun fired from his left. Wingham fired a burst from the Sten gun, aimed, spaced. From the right a grenade went in but missed the opening, bounced and exploded.

Rivers appeared, running in from the left, grenade in hand. He lobbed it through the slit and dived to the side.

A bullet grazed Wingham's right shoulder, with enough force to twist him, burning, a painful gash.

The grenade detonated inside the pill-box, a stabbing flame of smoke. In seconds the Rangers followed, the rear entrance kicked in followed by a sustained burst of gunfire to finish the job. Donavon stuck his head over the concrete. 'Clear.' They paused to catch their breath, fanning out in the sand dunes.

Wingham took the opportunity to glance back over his left shoulder to the water's edge. Sherman tanks were driving up the sand, following 4th Infantry, firing on the move. The second wave of assault boats pushed in on the surf, ramps dropping, men weaving out on the run. Out in the waves an LCI burned fiercely, thick black smoke curling down wind.

'Major!'

He heard the call and looked round.

It was Tierman with the radio. 'You hit?' He was looking over, concerned.

Wingham looked down, surprised by what he saw. His right arm and chest were red with blood, some of it congealing, dark. The arm moved freely so he looked up and grinned. 'Flesh wound, top of the shoulder. I'm okay.'

Rivers interrupted, called across. 'Check your weapons.'

Wingham unclipped his magazine, pressed his thumb down on the next cartridge. There was plenty of resistance, more than half full, and he snapped the mag back in place.

The sound of heavy gunfire erupted to their left, choking off the lighter noise of mortars and machine guns. The first of the Sherman tanks were moving up.

Rivers bellied up to the top of the rise and cautiously peered over. He stayed that way for a long moment, then looked back and waved the Major up to join him.

Sten gun leading the way, Wingham crawled up and raised his eyes over the top. An expanse of wind-swept water met his gaze. To the right, rising out of the flood, was the causeway, a rough embankment flattened on top by a makeshift road.

Rivers nudged him and gestured with his chin, at the far side of the flooded ground.

Wingham thought he recognised a small field gun behind a rubble strewn wall. The gun was trained on the causeway. He fumbled for his binoculars and carefully brought them up to get a better view. He found the movement of German soldiers and the muzzle of the gun projecting through the wall. It appeared to be a PAK 38 anti-tank. He swung the glasses to the left, to a wooden gate, passed on and spotted a machine-gun nest tucked under a low hanging tree. Beyond that a hedgerow and he gave an involuntary intake of breath. A tracked vehicle, he could clearly see the tracks and bogey wheels. He searched for the gun barrel, and then it dawned on him. It was a German troop carrier, a half-track. He relaxed the binoculars and sank down out of sight. However you looked at it, that was a tough proposition.

He leaned in to Rivers. 'That's an anti-tank gun with a machine-gun nest, and a half-track. Must be at least platoon strength up there.'

Rivers stared at him, thinking. 'Can you get your Navy guys involved?'

Wingham thought on it, frowning. 'Nice theory,' he said, 'but if they drop short we might lose the causeway.' Sporadic mortar rounds crunched into the sands, searching for the Rangers.

Rivers squinted, wriggled up for another look. Wingham watched him, trying to think of a solution. It was too far for the grenade launcher, and if they tried an assault across the embankment one well aimed round from that gun and it might be all over.

The Sergeant slithered down the bank. 'We need a tank.' He turned away searching along the line of Rangers.

'Hernandez, there's an anti-tank gun behind a wall, at two o'clock. See what you can do.' With that, he came to his feet and sprinted back down the beach. A Tank Landing Craft was off-loading Shermans and he made straight for them.

Hernandez crouched and loped along the dunes to the far right of the incline. He flopped down and crawled up the slope into a patch of wispy long grass. The sniper rifle eased forward and Wingham saw him settle behind the scope. There was a pause, and he lifted his head, then settled again. The rifle kicked as a shot rang out, and Hernandez slowly turned his head and grinned. He held up a single finger and mouthed the word, 'one'.

A Spandau opened up above Wingham's head, raking the ridge, seeking a target. He spat sand, ducked away and checked his watch. Thirty minutes since they'd hit the beach. Time was slipping, they had to get forward, inland, and find those 88's.

Faintly heard through the noise of battle, Rivers shouted from the beach. He was trotting up alongside a Sherman, the gun pointed upwards, traversing the slopes. The tank grumbled to the wall and stopped, and Rivers weaved over to Wingham. 'The tank's gonna take the exit for the causeway. When his turret's up he'll put a couple of shells on the gun and then send in some smoke. Soon as that's laid we go in.' He reached for Wingham's lapel and pulled him close. 'You hang back on this one. This is our job.'

Wingham protested but Rivers wasn't listening.

'I'm not hearing you, Major. You're precious cargo. Stay back.' He called to the Rangers and they gathered on one knee, Hernandez last to arrive. They took the briefing and moved out, making up two separate files. Rivers walked to the front of the tank and gave a thumbs up, then strode off leading the way.

Wingham walked after them, bent forward by instinct, avoiding the bullets hunting in from over the rise. The tank reached the turning point and slewed left, came to a stop. Rivers indicated the German gun, to the right of twelve o'clock, and then jumped out of the way.

The Sherman started up the rise and Wingham crawled to the nearest bank. He heard the engine growl and the tank lurched forward, no more than hull down, and cracked a shell off. The barrel moved a fraction, traversed away, and another shell banged out at the target. The wall collapsed and a man cart wheeled through the air.

A heavy machine gun began to pump shells at the tank, and Wingham saw the German half-track swing wide. The tank changed to smoke, fired again, and then thumped one right in front of the machine gun nest.

As the white smoke billowed, Rivers and Donavon took off on the run, either side of the causeway's road. The Germans fired blind, the tracer punching through the smoke. The tank came to life, squealing after them, banging off a shell between the men. Zach Carson with the bandoliers went down backwards yelling he'd been hit, turned on his stomach and brought the rifle up to his shoulder. A breeze cleared most of the smoke and the tank fired again. Vandenburg found a hollow in the verge, dived in with the Browning machine-gun and set up harassing fire. The rate of fire coming in from the Germans continued to increase.

Wingham had seen enough, they needed every man possible. Scrambling to his feet, he made for the causeway, reached the rise and weaved up the road to the back of the Sherman. In front of the tank, to the right, Donavon whistled to Rivers and signalled he was going forward.

'Covering fire!' Rivers yelled. The squad opened up, firing blind towards the half track. The tank inched forward and the hull mounted machine gun sprayed the last of the smoke. It fired the 75 mm over their heads and something went up in flames. Donavon reached the end of the causeway, came to his feet in the open and hurled two grenades beyond the smoke. The machine guns stopped firing and the tank accelerated up the road. The barrel swung left and fired two shells at the wall near the half-track. It slewed hard right and ran over the remains of the anti-tank gun, blazing away at fleeing Germans. Donavon saw Wingham walking up and grinned. 'Beautiful,' he said. 'Just beautiful.'

Wingham nodded, knowing it took guts to get in so close. Frank Bell staggered up half carrying Zach Carson and sat him down near the wall. The others ran past to the wall and found some safety behind it. Wingham crouched and moved to join Rivers. Behind him Donavon gave a muffled grunt and Wingham heard him fall, saw him on the ground. The right side of his head was a mess of red blood.

'Sniper!' Hernandez shouted, and they dived for cover. 'Doc' Bell, ignoring the danger, crawled over to Donavon and began to work on him.

Wingham glanced to his right. The tank had stopped and the barrel slowly swung round to the twelve o'clock. He turned to Rivers. 'What's he waiting for?'

'Us,' the Sergeant said. 'He won't advance without ground support. Could be Panzerfausts out there.'

Wingham understood immediately. 'I'll tell him we're pinned down, see if he can find the sniper.' Without waiting for an argument he crawled and scrambled his way along behind the wall until he reached the gap where the German gun had been destroyed. The tank had stopped thirty paces into the last parcel of high ground. That would leave Wingham exposed to the sniper when he crossed. Struggling to his feet but crouched on his haunches, he prepared to launch himself across the opening. He took one more deep breath and leaped into the open, running as fast as the ground allowed. He sensed a bullet zip past his head and threw himself in a heap at the protected side of the tank. Keeping the bulk of armour between himself and the enemy, he climbed up on a bogey wheel, and then the track, to the safe side of the turret. He banged the butt of the Sten gun on the hatch and shouted to gain attention. A ricochet whined off the steel and he ducked back down. The hatch opened a fraction.

'What's all the hollering?' came a voice from inside.

'There's a sniper out there. We hoped you might see him off.'

'Who're you? You sound like a Limey.'

'I'm with Sergeant Rivers.'

There was a moment's silence. 'Okay, Mac. We're on it.' The hatch banged shut, and Wingham jumped clear. He scampered back to the section of wall immediately behind him, staying within the tank's silhouette. Diving over the top of the wall, he landed safely, checked the Sten gun and began to make his way along to the Rangers. He heard the Sherman move, engines growl, tracks squeak. It banged off a shell, and Wingham dashed over the last bit of ground to cover. As he straightened his back against the bricks, he saw a man lying with a helmet over his face. He looked at Rivers, who shook his head. Donavon hadn't made it. The tank fired again, cracked a shell into the distance. Carson had a bandage round his forearm. Back along the coast where 4th Infantry had gone in, the battle continued, small arms fire, the occasional mortar. In the meantime here they were held up by a lone sniper.

Anne-Marie had lain awake in the darkness for an hour, listening to the raucous snores of the fat man in her bed. With the coming of dawn she turned away from his ugly profile and stared at the grey clouds rushing by the partly drawn curtains. She watched for a while, encompassed by the vibration of Gruber's heavy wheezing, loud in the quiet bedroom.

The sound of thunder rolled across the heavens and she hunched into the pillow, eyes closed against the expected lightning. Another rumble, more prolonged, but no bright flash. Raising her head from the pillow she tried to distinguish the noise over Gruber's persistent snoring. It pulsed in strength, fluctuating in the wind. She closed her eyes again. Was it gunfire? It wasn't a bombing raid, there was no anti-aircraft guns firing. And if that was gunfire, she'd never heard such deep rumbles. The barrels must be enormous.

Gruber flinched in his drunken stupor, slack mouthed, momentarily silent. Again there was the sound of rolling thunder and she was becoming convinced it was big guns. Maybe it was the invasion, but right here in Normandy? Her bedroom window faced south. All she could see were a maze of fields and hedges, so long a major part of her life.

The Sergeant slept on, oblivious to the guns, snoring with his dreams.

Anne-Marie slipped very stealthily from her side of the bed and padded across to the tiny window. She shivered. It might be early summer but it was a cold morning and her nightdress felt flimsy. She gathered up her woollen robe and draped it round her shoulders, careful not to disturb his drunken sleep. Pressing her face to the pane of glass she looked as far right as she could, but to no avail. Only the outskirts of the farm met her gaze. Then, faintly on the wind, came the sound of machine-guns, a distant rattle. The noise was familiar, long forgotten, from when the Germans had first conquered this stretch of her homeland. She smiled as a wave of happiness surged through her

171

veins. It was the first time she'd felt such emotion since the French army had surrendered. She trembled with excitement. Had her mother and father heard? Did they realise what was happening?

Gruber gargled on his own saliva, snorted, and she froze. Looking round she could see all his nakedness, his fat white gut resting on the bed. She grimaced at the sight. If only they could be rid of him. Maybe if she told him what was happening he would go, join up with his unit? The problem would be his foul mood. He was always the same in the morning, hung-over and irritable. She wondered what time it was, and guessed at seven o'clock.

The volume of gunfire suddenly increased, a continuous succession of explosions. She would have to wake him. Walking round to his side of the bed she reached down and shook his fleshy shoulder.

'Klaus! Klaus, wake up!' She detested the name but he liked her to use it, and it was no good antagonising him for no valid reason.

The small bloodshot eyes opened a fraction, saw who it was, and closed. He mumbled something which she couldn't understand.

'Klaus, wake up. Can you not hear the guns?'

Gruber's eyes popped open, wider. He coughed. 'Guns? What guns?'

'Listen,' she said, 'they are very big.'

He pulled his weight up the pillow, half upright. He heard the resounding crash of distant artillery and sat bolt upright, scowling.

'My uniform, woman!' He stabbed a finger at his clothes.

Inwardly, Anne-Marie breathed a sigh of relief. It had worked; he would be gone, off to fight the war. She piled the clothes on the foot of the bed and watched while he struggled to dress. Lastly, he stamped into the boots and

172

picked up his Maschinenpistole, unclipped and checked the magazine and snapped it back to the chamber. At the door he paused and turned to face her.

Her heart sank; he had that look in his eye. He took a pace closer. 'It was a good night, eh? I will have a kiss before I go.'

She shrank inside. God, how she hated this pig of a man. He forced his mouth on hers, roughly grabbed her breast, and then slapped her backside.

'We are good together, no?' He laughed obscenely, moved to the door and clumped down the stairs.

14 Confusion

Oberleutnant Gerhardt Ziegler clambered into the front seat of the half-track and waved for the unit to advance. The two armoured scout cars were up front, closely followed by his own half-track, then a motorbike and sidecar with heavy machine-gun, and bringing up the rear, a pair of open trucks carrying his company of Waffen SS.

With a grinding jolt the half-track rumbled forward and Ziegler stood up to balance himself against the windshield. A short while later the armoured column had cleared Cherbourg's outlying dwellings and turned onto the paved highway running south towards Sainte-Mère-Église via the crossroads at Valognes. At a familiar fork in the road the scout cars took the bend to the right and Ziegler glanced down the rutted track behind the apple orchard. He caught a fleeting glimpse of the red tiled farmhouse and smiled grimly. It had been a good raid. A radio confiscated and the young couple wiped out. And more to the point, congratulations from the Intelligence Section.

But now he frowned in concern at the billowing clouds of smoke drifting inland from the coast. The distant shoreline, hidden beyond the low lying hills, bore vivid evidence of a major engagement. The sound of heavy artillery bellowed across the fields and as he stared at the smoke a dozen Allied fighter-bombers swept in from the sea. He scanned the sky to the south. Where were the Luftwaffe? Without air cover this recce might be suicidal.

He leaned down and unclipped the radio handset. 'All call signs, halt!'

One by one he watched them pull up, heads turning in his direction.

He depressed the button on the mouthpiece. 'All units will maintain one-hundred metres between vehicles. Attack by enemy aircraft is almost certain. Keep your distance.'

He waited for confirmation that they understood.

'Good,' he said. 'All in order. Move out.'

The lead scout car drove off and at regular intervals the remainder followed. Ziegler looked behind, saw they had complied with the order and concentrated on watching the skies. After twelve kilometres the scout cars entered the outskirts of Volagnes, to be greeted by empty streets, not a soul to be seen. The civilian population had melted away, afraid of reprisals. The small town of Montebourg came next with the same deserted streets, just the odd frightened face peering from an upstairs window. Ziegler ignored them and ordered the lead vehicle to push on for Sainte-Mère-Église. What the SS officer did not discover were a straggling assortment of 82nd Airborne gathering on the northwest side of town. They began to infiltrate the outskirts and secure the streets.

Ziegler drove out and left the relative safety of the buildings behind, once again hemmed in by the tall hedgerows. A few kilometres further on the road veered left, bounded on one side by a line of poplar trees and to the right, by dense thickets of tangled shrub, limiting his view of the sky. Near the middle of the line of poplars the lead car halted and he heard a call in his headphones. 'Achtung! The road is blown, too deep to cross.'

Ziegler frowned. This was the only decent road in the area. They would have to fix it somehow. He glanced round at the trees and then at the hedges. No chance of a detour just here, maybe back up the road.

The leading scout car revved hard, smoked its tyres in reverse, and machine-gunned an invisible target.

'Achtung!' came a call in his headphones. 'Enemy infantry.'

He shouted to his driver. 'Move up. Schnell!'

The scout car took a hit and exploded. Ziegler grimaced. What was that, anti-tank weapons? He turned and called up the troops behind him. His driver slammed on the anchors and the half-track rattled to a halt behind the blazing car, and Ziegler hesitated. This was a reconnaissance mission and he was supposed to report enemy contact. But what exactly had they encountered, as yet there was nothing to see. The infantry ran past his position and the 80mm Granatwerfer mortar team went into action, the first shell lobbing out beyond the hedgerow. A smoke grenade came in from the enemy, wobbled along the road, machine-gun bullets whipping through the haze.

Submachine-guns fired through the smoke. Grenades bounced and exploded, shrapnel flying. Men cried out, shouted orders, confusion reigned.

Ziegler looked around in desperation. A soldier dropped, hit in the face. An explosion tore apart his mortar team, two men writhing in pain. It sounded like enemy mortar fire coming down; what was he up against? He shouted at an SS Sergeant.

'Attack up the right side. We will give you covering fire.' The man turned away, shouting commands, and Ziegler called to the gunners. 'Covering fire!'

Otto Reinhardt crouched below the observation slit and cowered in numbed silence as the bombardment blasted the countryside into scorched earth. He wasn't certain what size shells were being fired but he did know they were big, big enough to cause extensive damage. One of the shells had struck the bunker in the opening salvo. The explosion had knocked everyone to the floor, destroyed

176

the light and covered the room in concrete dust. When the smoke cleared a large section of the roof hung in tatters, reinforcing bars exposed to the elements. He'd ordered the soldiers into the underground sleeping quarters while he maintained a lookout with two men manning the MG.

Contact with his outside forces had never been regained, he wasn't even aware if any had survived the bombing let alone this latest storm of gunfire. The second shell to hit them had come in on a low trajectory and detonated against the right hand front parapet. It blew away the outside skin and left a ragged hole at ground level, leaving a thin veil of light to filter through.

He opened his eyes to a lull in the shelling and called across to the machine-gunners. 'Neuman! Are you okay?'

'Ja, Herr Oberst, all is in order.'

'What do you see?'

'Much smoke, and I think I saw ships.'

Reinhardt twisted round and raised his eyes to the slit. Drifts of black smoke obscured his view, orange-red flames licking along the dunes in the far distance. A strange silence fell across the landscape. The shelling had stopped. And then he heard small arms fire, well away from his position. Thick and black though the smoke was, daylight had arrived. He climbed to his feet, grabbed his binoculars and walked to the rear armoured door.

'Neuman. Get the men out. Defence places. Schnell!' Not without difficulty he prised the door open and stepped up into the acrid air outside. He climbed up to what remained of the concrete roof and stopped in astonishment. The bay to his front was covered in ships, as far as he could see. There were huge battleships and many destroyers and what looked like thousands of little boats all headed for his beaches. Many of the ships were firing their guns, not at him now, but over to the east and beyond.

My God, he thought, this is the invasion. The Allies would never commit so many ships as a diversion. He turned to look around him, at the ploughed up fields and the uprooted hedgerows. He wondered if the senior command knew what was happening, if the Panzers were moving up. Where were the reserves? He raised the glasses and scanned the beaches. Far off to his right some larger boats had made it to the shore and he could see tanks landing. Tanks! They fired on the move, rapidly moving towards the dunes. And the amount of soldiers running up the beach, a thousand or more, and nothing seemed to be stopping them. He took a last look to satisfy himself as to the direction of advance and scrambled down to the rear entrance.

He stumbled inside and found the map of the defences. The 112th Mobile Regiment should be near enough to reach, but he was trying to remember their last location. They were not under his command, but General Orders dictated he had to be aware of their disposition. Each night they changed position, he was struggling to find their orders. Then under the cement dust he found the file. He ran a finger down the itinery to the night of 5th through to the 6th of June. He checked it against the map reference and felt a momentary sense of elation. Four kilometres to the north in a field near Saint-Floxel.

'Brandt!' he called.

'Herr Oberst?'

'You will take a message to the 112th. Tell them the invasion has begun but the shore batteries are destroyed. Tell them to hold the road to Cherbourg.' He looked at the man's face covered in chalk-white dust. 'Do you understand, Brandt? Tell them to hold until the reserves arrive.'

'The Cherbourg road, they must hold the road. Jawohl, Herr Oberst.'

'Good luck,' Reinhardt said, and slapped him on the shoulder. 'Now get going, there is not much time.'

Brandt picked up a submachine-gun and made for the exit. As he cleared the outside steps he glanced back at the coast. Mesmerised by what he saw, he stood for a minute, almost unable to comprehend the magnitude of what he was seeing. With a shake of the head he ran off across the bomb craters and escaped through the damaged hedgerow. He knew Saint-Floxel, had been stationed there for six months. That was before Reinhardt came and issued new orders. He felt certain he'd be better off in the village than trapped in the bunker. He set off at a fast trot, a pace he knew he could sustain, and found the road leading west, and thankfully, away from the war.

Major Paul Wingham, hidden behind the old wall, watched Hernandez slide over to Sergeant Rivers. He pointed to his left where the remains of a damaged tree overhung the brickwork. They held a quick conversation and Hernandez set off on his hands and knees towards the tangle of branches. The Sergeant waited for the sniper to find himself a comfortable hide, and when Hernandez signalled he was ready to fire, shuffled awkwardly along to the gap and the Sherman.

The tank's engines revved into life and thirty tons of armour edged forward. The hull mounted machine-gun rattled, hammering bullets at the hedgerow, and a 75 mm shell streaked towards the enemy emplacement. Rivers went down on his belly and peered cautiously round the broken wall. A bullet splintered a brick above his head and he ducked away.

A single shot rang out from the left and after a brief pause Hernandez called from the branches. 'Scratch one!' He grinned wickedly as he backed out of harms way and then crept back behind the wall. Rivers scrambled to join him and Wingham moved closer.

Rivers reached into his combat jacket and pulled out his folded map. He showed it to Wingham and circled their position. 'We gotta follow this road west, to higher ground; see if we can spot those 88's. The tank'll have to come with us, it's his only clear route.'

Wingham thought it was time to assert his authority and shook his head. 'They'll have that road zeroed in. Probably mined as well. We wouldn't get far.'

Rivers tilted his head, raised an eyebrow. 'Chance we'll have to take. Time's running out, Major.'

Wingham studied the road. They might not have mined it, how else did they bring up the half track and field gun, not across all that water. Reluctantly, he conceded. 'Alright Chuck, have it your way. But the tank follows and we stay well spread, either side of the road.'

Rivers gave a wry smile and looked round at the Rangers. 'Okay. Belluci, you take point. Carson, go with him, stay left flank. Tierman, keep the radio with the Major.' He glanced at 'Doc'. 'You're with me, we'll lead the tank.' He hesitated. 'That alright with you, sir?'

Wingham showed his teeth. 'Good enough.'

Rivers half smiled and nodded. 'Let's move out.'

The unexpected roar of aero-engines made them flinch, and five, white striped P57 Mustangs swept low overhead, powering their way inland.

Rivers took advantage of the distraction to gain the attention of the tank commander. A few hurried words and he beckoned for the squad to move up, waited for Belluci and Carson to walk ahead, and then stood waiting for the tank. The Sherman growled blue smoke and reversed out of the gap in the wall, shuddered round on one track, engaged forward drive with a jolt, and squealed forward in their footsteps.

Wingham pushed on, aware of the time. From the beach behind, came the sound of heavy explosions. He stole a quick glance. Thick, black smoke spiralled skywards, and he looked away up the road. Inland to his left, the distant sporadic rattle of small arms. He checked the Sten gun, took a firm grip. Marching up this quiet piece of road the war seemed a long way off.

The news reaching Southwick House was being received with a certain amount of trepidation. In the confusion of reports coming out of the beach heads, Sir Hugh Stanford, immersed in conflicting information, found it difficult to make an accurate assessment of the battle's progress. The second phase of Operation Neptune, the convoys backing up the original assault, had swung into action and appeared to be operating to schedule. That was Stanford's area of expertise, the continued transportation of thousands of men and machines to the shores of France. His concerns centred round the ability of the Beach Masters to clear the landing zones and hasten the flow of traffic inland. And that all hinged on 4th Infantry clearing the way ahead.

As the day wore on and the seas subsided, the men of von Holtzmann's Flotilla prepared to strike against the Allied invasion fleet. Daylight would have been suicidal and Holtzmann anticipated leaving Braye harbour as dusk added to the enemy's difficulties.

Sergeant Chuck Rivers held up a hand and stopped. Up ahead, Hernandez had dropped to one knee. The tank rumbled to a halt, the engine ticking over, muted. Weapons at the ready, the Rangers paused, watchful.

Wingham crouched and ran left across the road to the hedge. He stood against the tall mass of tangled thicket, solid, uninviting. To his right, Rivers crept slowly towards the sniper's low profile, the road ahead hidden to everyone but Hernandez. He saw Rivers and motioned with his hand, indicating something round the corner. The Sergeant stooped low, covered the last few yards to the rifleman, and knelt just short of his position. They talked quietly, at length, and then Rivers edged backwards and crawled over to Wingham.

'Hernandez says he saw a Kraut run down the road into cover. Disappeared behind the hedge on the right. Says he was carrying a Panzerfaust.'

Wingham glanced back at the tank, isolated on the road. He frowned. If there was one German, there'd be others, if so, what was there strength? He turned to Rivers. 'Maybe just an OP. Any ideas?'

'Oh, sure,' he grinned. 'We sound the bugle and charge in there like there's no tomorrow. Krauts don't do half strength observations.'

Wingham bit his bottom lip, thinking. 'Grenade launcher?'

Rivers nodded. 'Yep . . . , then smoke, and go in hard.'

'And the tank?'

'Yeah, we'll need him too, fire support.'

Wingham craned his neck in an attempt to look around. The hedges were impenetrable, the road their only way forward. The Germans were well positioned. Even with the tank's support, this might not end well. But the 88's were down there somewhere, it had to be done.

'I'll tell the tankies,' he said, and turned to go, but as he looked at the Sherman and took in the weight of armoured steel, he hesitated.

'Chuck,' he said over his shoulder. 'What if the tank ignored the turn of the road and went straight on into that hedge. Could it get through that?' He expanded his theory.

'If it broke through it would be on the enemy flank. We become a diversion and the tank hits 'em from the side.'

Rivers rubbed his nose, studied the hedges, and Wingham could see he was weighing up the odds.

'It's a gamble, Major, but we sure ain't got much to lose.' He tightened his mouth, eyeing up the tank. 'See what they say.'

Wingham took off at a run. The tank commander must have seen him coming, and popped the hatch. 'Where we at, Mac?'

Explaining the situation as best as he could, Wingham queried their hedge busting capability.

The commander slapped the top of the turret and chuckled. 'Hell, this baby'll make that hedge look like cotton wool.'

'Right,' Wingham said, a half smile playing round his lips. It was easy to get caught up by the American's enthusiasm. 'Wait for the smoke.'

'Gotchya,' he said, and reached over the hatch for the Browning machine-gun.

Returning to the hedge, Wingham nodded at Rivers.

'He reckons it'll be a piece of cake.' He unclipped a smoke grenade and waited.

Rivers signalled for the Rangers to join him and made clear the plan. He singled out Belluci with the grenade thrower, told him where to drop his eggs, and checked for questions. There were none, just a few grunts of understanding followed by an exchange of glances, and Wingham guessed they'd known what was coming. The Sergeant lifted his head. 'All yours, sir.'

Wingham glanced at the grenade in his hand. 'Let's get this done.'

The Rangers split up, grenades primed, guns cocked, the tension of imminent combat coursing through their veins.

Chuck Rivers stepped sideways from the hedge and hurled his grenade. Hernandez lobbed his, high and long. Wingham tugged the pin and threw it hard, a fast forearm. Three sharp bangs and smoke billowed, white and dense. Belluci began sending in fragmentation grenades. A German Spandau opened up beyond the smoke, firing blind, tracer fizzing wildly through the haze.

The Sherman tank roared and lurched forward, revved up and gained momentum, charging headlong down the road at the hedge. The Rangers made their move, running at the whiteness, firing from the waist. Wingham gritted his teeth and weaved forward. The tank stormed past behind them, smashed into the hedge and surged upwards, tracks scrabbling for bite, crushing and snapping at the dense thicket. It broke through in a rush, accelerated, and swung to the left.

The Commander caught a glimpse of movement. 'Mortar! Nine o'clock! Fire!'

The gun roared, spitting flame.

'Again!'

A second round streaked across the field, impacted, detonated, on target.

'Driver, hard left!'

The Sherman swerved violently, left track stopped, the right track digging a furrowed scar. The Commander dropped inside, urging the driver forward. He found another target. The muzzle trained left, steadied, barked.

Wingham emptied his Sten gun at the smoke, yelled at the top of his lungs and charged in. He ran blind, heart pounding, breathing hard. A German appeared, rifle pointing, and Wingham jerked the trigger, self preservation. The soldier screamed and slammed backwards. He heard the tank blast another shell, out of sight over the hedge. Fifty yards ahead on the right, previously hidden by the hedgerow, was a gated entrance off the road.

Vandenburg sped past to the left of the road, dived to ground with the Browning, and a fusillade of bullets sprayed the opening. A dozen Germans scattered for cover.

Chuck Rivers burst out of the smoke firing from the hip. To his right a Kraut retaliated with two grenades. He swung the Thompson and cut him down. Tracer fizzed past his jaw. A blur of movement and a German rose with a rifle, aiming at a Ranger. Rivers gave him two shots, saw the bullets strike watched him tumble. Hernandez ran past the gate and Rivers went sideways to cover him, kneeling by the bottom rail.

A tank shell detonated, high explosive, a numbing concussion. A ragged torso spun out of the flames and dropped to the ground, charred and smoking. A Kraut NCO appeared above the ditch aiming at Hernandez. Rivers snapped off a few rounds, saw him stagger. Hernandez turned his head, nodded.

Rivers felt the shock of a bullet smash his left elbow. The bone shattered, splintered, and he gasped in agony. A second bullet tore through his ribcage, slammed him into the gate and left him hanging over the bottom rail. With his right arm he raised the machine-gun, lifted his head and pulled the trigger. The gun shuddered and sprayed a high arc of bullets into the air. A grenade exploded, close. His strength failed and he dropped the gun. Blood spurted from his chest and his head lowered with pain. His helmet fell forward, snagged on the strap, hung there, swaying.

Sergeant Chuck Rivers frothed blood through his teeth and knew he was finished. He stared at the grass in front of his eyes, the hint of a faint smile on the bloodied face. He'd never thought of his own death, but knew it was near. He'd made it over the beach only to collect one in this Godforsaken hole in Normandy. The trace of a smile froze on his lips and the blood stopped pumping.

Wingham flew past the entrance, hurled his own grenade over the hedge. He looked through the opening to the tank grinding closer, hull mounted machine-gun hammering.

From behind the hedge, a rocket streaked past. The Panzerfaust slammed into the tank between the tracks. It exploded on impact, ripped apart the steel and a fireball flashed.

The commander's hatch was thrown open and Wingham saw an arm appear, then a jet of flames erupted from the turret. A scorched hand scrabbled at the hatch cover, blackened, and sank inside. He watched squinting, waiting for the crew to emerge. As the fire took hold nobody came out.

Romero darted through the entrance, snapped off a couple of shots and dived to earth.

There was a moments respite as grenades exploded and Wingham felt the anger of battle wash over him. He blinked sweat from his eyes and turned to face the enemy. A bullet fanned his cheek, another tugged his sleeve, but he raised the Sten gun and took a pace forward. Breaking into a run he screamed wildly. A German jumped from a ditch, bayonet pointed. Wingham pulled the trigger, three rounds; chest, neck and the left eye. Blood spurted from the neck wound and he folded in a tangle. An officer aimed a Luger. Wingham sidestepped and fired in one movement. The man's right leg collapsed and he yelled in agony, falling. He looked up, pleading for mercy. Wingham glanced round at the burning tank, turned slowly back to the man on the ground, and without the slightest compunction, shot him in the head.

Vandenburg came up on Wingham's shoulder, the Browning at his waist, thumping rounds at anything that moved. A soldier carrying a Panzerfaust took a burst in the stomach, spewed blood and died. Another, with a submachine-gun, twisted away as a bullet smashed his jaw, and Vandenburg gave him a burst for good measure.

The rattle of gunfire stopped, an eerie silence, broken only by the crackle of flames from the blazing tank.

Wingham looked round, breathing hard, chest heaving. Hernandez sat slumped against a dirt bank holding his left arm, blood trickling through his fingers. Romero was dead, a bayonet wedged in his ribs, his fighting knife buried in a German's chest. Bradley winced with pain, a red mess oozing from his right thigh. Doc Bell finished wrapping a bandage and gave him a shot of morphine.

'Major!' It was Tierman, pointing a bloodied hand at the gate.

Sergeant Chuck Rivers lay sprawled over the bottom rail, helmet hanging, suspended by the strap.

Wingham walked heavily across the scorched earth and knelt. He reached out and gently pulled the body to the ground. The face and chest were covered in dark blood, the lethal fragments of a German grenade.

'Major!'

Wingham snapped. 'What!' He remained motionless, staring down at the lifeless eyes.

'Listen,' Hernandez called quietly.

In the distance, faint but distinctive, Wingham heard the sound of motors, engines of trucks, rising and falling as they manoeuvred. With an effort, he rose to his feet, head held to one side. Reinforcements? He strained to locate the direction. Inland, definitely. Southwest, in the same direction he wanted to go.

He paused to take stock. Chuck Rivers, dead. Romero dead. Donavon dead. Bradley out of it, Hernandez, walking wounded. Carson still losing blood, but managing. That left Vandenburg, Belluci, Tierman, Doc

Bell and himself to carry the fight. But as long as he had Tierman and the radio they could carry out the mission.

Again he heard the sound of engines. Trucks? Might be just what they were looking for. Trucks towed guns. He reached up for a rail on the gate and pulled himself to his feet. Beyond the ditch of dead Germans, the hedge that screened the next field appeared thinly woven, easily penetrated. He found his pack of cigarettes and lit one, dragged deeply, giving himself time. If those engines were part of the Mobile 88's, he needed to be certain, and the only way was to see for himself. Better for the wounded to rest up while they could, take advantage of the lull. That would give Doc a chance to do his stuff.

Mind made up he walked over to the ditch and dropped into the bottom. Avoiding two bodies, he stepped on a third and slowly raised himself up to peer through the tangle of leaves. He was looking at a much smaller field than the one they'd attacked, at a guess, no more than a hundred yards across. A large stone drinking trough was located centrally, but the grass lay undisturbed with no sign of livestock.

In the opposite hedge, on the far side of the field, an old dilapidated gate hung from a wrought iron hinge, twisted and broken. He studied the ground for a full minute then called over his shoulder, a shouted whisper.

'Hernandez!'

The bloodied marksman looked up, grimacing.

'I'm taking a recce up ahead. Don't get trigger happy when I come back.'

The sniper nodded, staggered to his feet and found a hide from which to watch.

Wingham nodded his thanks, took a swallow from his canteen, and clipped a fresh magazine into the Sten. He pushed aside a tangle of bushes, took a deep breath, and launched himself out to the open ground. He concentrated on the stone drinking trough, running swiftly, and finally slithered feet first into its protection. He waited before peering cautiously around one end. Nothing stirred, and steeling himself for the next sprint, he came up to one knee. Again he took off at a crouching run, veering to the left of the broken gate. Heart pounding, he threw himself down at the hinge post and listened. The growing noise of engines being revved made him stiffen and he risked a quick look through the opening. The next field was large, the space interspersed by a mixture of low growing trees. The sounds of the engines seemed to come from beyond the far boundary hedge.

Treading softly in the thick grass he crept through the broken gate, gripped the Sten gun with both hands and dodged to his right, holding tight to the hedge. Ten yards ahead, the first tree looked inviting, and bent double to reduce his profile, he hurried across. Working his way forward, weaving from tree to tree, he gained enough ground to get within twenty feet of his goal. The sound of the engines grew louder.

Wingham stopped and leaned against the nearest tree, a low-slung branch hiding him from the boundary hedge. He pulled out his map, found the corresponding grid reference and folded it to leave the location easily accessible. He tucked it back in his thigh pocket and stepped out from behind the trunk. At a small gap in the hedge he dropped to the ground and, very carefully, eased away a tangle of leaves that obscured his view. For a moment his heart raced. Underneath an assortment of large camouflage nets he counted twelve trailer-mounted mobile 88's preparing to make a move. And the sound of those engines belonged to a line of trucks reversing in from the lane.

He'd seen enough. He squirmed back in the lush grass, sprang to his feet, and ran. His only thought was to get to the radio. No dodging or weaving, just the fastest, shortest route back to Tierman. Lungs bursting with the effort he cleared the hanging gate, swept past the trough and powered his way through the hedge near Hernandez.

'Tierman! The radio, switch on!'

He folded to his knees, gasping for breath, sweat pouring from his face and neck.

Tierman screwed in the ten foot telescopic aerial and adjusted the dials on the control panel.

Wingham struggled to his feet, took the handset and waited for Tierman to give him the nod. Cupping one headphone to his ear he screwed his eyes closed to the sound of hissing static and pressed the switch to send.

'Hello, Baker-Delta. . , Hello, Baker-Delta, this is George, over.' He released the button on the handset and waited to receive. The whisper of static, an uninterrupted hiss. He tried again.

'Hello, Baker-Delta. . , Hello, Baker-Delta, this is George, over.'

This time the response came in clearly.

'Hello, George, this is Baker-Delta. Send, over.'

Wingham smoothed the map on the ground, pushed the button to speak. 'Hello, Baker-Delta. . , wait, over.'

He pushed his fingernail into the paper to highlight the location, traced the coordinates, scribbled them on his pad and matched the numbers to his letter codes. A final check of the figures and he lifted the handset.

'Hello Baker-Delta, this is George. Target is at, Foxtrot-Charlie-Mike, November-Alpha-Echo. I say again, Foxtrot-Charlie-Mike, November-Alpha-Echo. Over.'

He listened for the acknowledgement, word for word, and confirmed he wanted one round for observation. Lobbing the radio gear to Tierman he scampered back to the drinking trough from where he could see through the broken gate and watch the field beyond the trees.

15 Fury

Swaying into the offshore headwind *Brackendale* maintained her north-westerly heading with just enough forward momentum to counteract the coastal current. In the wireless room Leading Telegraphist Elliot answered Major Wingham's call, deciphered it against his decoding sheet, and transmitted the message through to the bridge. Seconds later, in accordance with his prior instructions, Elliot relayed the information to Lieutenant John McCloud in the Control Tower.

On the forebridge, Thorburn took the message and immediately altered course. 'Port fifteen. Steer two-oh-oh degrees. Make revolutions for twenty knots.'

From the wheelhouse voice-pipe, Falconer acknowledged the order. 'Port fifteen. Twenty knots. Steer two-oh-oh degrees. Aye aye, sir.'

Thorburn reached for the phone to the Control Tower.

McCloud answered. 'Sir?'

'I'm taking her inshore, Guns, 1,000 yards from the beach. Looks calmer in there. I'll come back to the northwest, slow ahead.'

'Aye aye, sir.'

Thorburn clipped the phone back on the bracket, eyeing up the ship's heading, judging the moment to bring her back parallel with the shore. He leaned towards the pipe. 'Starboard twenty, slow ahead. Steer three-one-five degrees.'

The Cox'n's acknowledgement echoed up the voice-pipe and Thorburn stepped across to the port wing. *Brackendale* settled, steadied in the relative calm of the inshore waters, a stable platform for the guns.

Abaft the bridge in the Control Tower, Lieutenant John McCloud jotted down the grid reference.

'Load all guns.' He looked up at the map board to his right, made a rapid calculation and manually inserted the range to target. A Transmitting machine automatically correlated the data: *Brackendale*'s relative speed, allowance for the north-westerly wind, a constant Force three on the scale. The forward pair of four-inch guns elevated to port and the quarterdeck mounting swung round in harmony. Three minutes after Elliot had taken the message all was ready. McCloud picked up the phone to the forward turret. 'For fall of shot, with one round only. Shoot!'

A thumping detonation from the turret and a shell streaked inland.

Wingham heard the shell whistle in overhead, saw the smoke rise from the explosion. For a first shot it was a remarkable piece of gunnery, as accurate as he could wish for.

Scurrying away from the stone trough he galloped back to Tierman and grabbed the handset. 'Hello, Baker-Delta. . , broadside, over.'

Brackendale's signalman came on, unhurried, precise. 'Baker-Delta. Wilco, out.'

Wingham straightened and called to the Rangers. 'In the ditch, this'll be close!'

They raced for the scant cover, wounded and healthy alike, tumbling into the bottom, sprawled out to await the bombardment. At less than five-hundred yards from the target, Wingham knew it was too close for comfort.

Three miles out to sea, Lieutenant John 'Guns' McCloud saw the smoke rise and trained the Range-finder to the spot. The turrets rotated slightly to compensate for

Brackendale's minimal movement. Elliot confirmed the precision of the sighting shot and with a swift check on his calibration, McCloud gave the order.

'Shoot!'

Brackendale's main armament roared, a blast of firepower. Thorburn braced against the shock of the broadside. Empty brass cases rattled to the deck. A second salvo crashed from the barrels and smoke billowed across the navigating platform. He leaned to the forebridge, watching the gunners in their acrid world of smoke and noise of the gun turret. Eight men, four per gun, oblivious to their surroundings; loading, firing, discarding the empties, reloading, No room for mistakes, trying to keep their feet, and Thorburn felt a humbling pride in their determined efforts. A third salvo ripped from the muzzles and the shells whistled away. He raised his binoculars at the smoke swirling above the fields. It wouldn't do to be on the receiving end of that lot.

2,500 yards from Utah beach, the field erupted in a flash of high explosive. Shattering blasts blew the guns into steel fragments, scything across the field. An ammunition wagon took a direct hit, instantly adding to the inferno, lethal missiles exploding in random chaos. White phosphorous sprayed and burned, melted flesh, dissolved bones. Caught in the mayhem, men died in agony, torn apart by the brutal fury of *Brackendale*'s guns. The gun crew of an 88 near the field's exit managed to hitch up to a truck and made a desperate attempt to escape the slaughter. The driver made a skidding right turn out of the gate and hit the accelerator. The next missile blew out the back of the truck and hurled the driver through the windscreen. He landed twenty feet ahead. His broken remains twitched in the pulp, an involuntary convulsion as he died. The towed gun sagged on the trailer's burning tyres and blocked the opening.

Against the hedge at the back of the field, the Headquarters half track had been demolished, the remnants burning freely, wreathed in smoke. The Commanding Officer's body lay nearby; face down in the grass, hit by shrapnel in the second salvo. Dark blood congealed into glistening pools.

Crawling along the perimeter of the hedge and nursing a savage wound to his right thigh, Brandt, who had only recently passed on Otto Reinhardt's orders, stared in horror. The destruction was mind numbing, and trembling with shock he mumbled in disbelief. He'd survived the attack on the observation bunker only to end up being pulverised in this field of death. The base of the hedge seemed to offer a little protection and he scrabbled in amongst the roots before pressing himself into the dirt. He wished it would all end.

Brackendale's final salvo ripped into the field in a hurricane of explosive force. The once deadly threat of an entire Regiment of mobile artillery was destroyed, annihilated. For Brandt it was one shell too many. It blew up near his head, and he was incinerated. As the smoke drifted clear through the maze of leaves in the hedgerows, only the decimated skeletons of men and guns remained, burning softly in the cratered earth.

Stunned, but unharmed by the ferocity of the bombardment, Major Paul Wingham and his few surviving Rangers climbed wearily from the ditch and brushed themselves down. Two stray shots had fallen short, one near the remains of the tank, the other on the road. Bill Tierman hoisted the radio out of the ditch and steadied the aerial, switched on and tuned back in. Wingham took the handset, toggled the switch and made the call.

194

'Hello Baker-Delta, this is George. Target destroyed. I say again, target destroyed, over.'

He listened intently for the response, eyes screwed up in concentration. The hiss of static cleared.

'Hello George, this is Baker-Delta. Target destroyed. Roger, out.'

Wingham sighed, mission accomplished. Time to move on. He straightened to his full height and stared at the wind driven clouds, occasionally rimmed in a sun kissed orange glow. In reality, the wind had moderated, the clouds thinning, and he drew back the sleeve of his battle dress. His watch showed ten to eight, and the 88's hadn't fired a shot. Utah beach would be open for the second and third waves of assault. General Douglas Carlswright could rest easy. Wingham had found the guns. His thoughts turned to more pressing matters, of secondary importance to Overlord, but for him, the more urgent mission of the day.

The Rangers moved around in silence, checking their weapons and collecting ammunition. The wounded tested their ability to move, to stand up and walk. Hernandez wore a fresh bandage and had returned to observe the adjoining field. It reminded Wingham that they'd all seen action before, weren't fazed by the trauma of battle. But now it was time to part company, his next mission wasn't for them. They were best suited to fighting as a team, for Wingham it was a return to the lonely game of hide and seek. Very deliberately he walked over to the middle of the group.

'If I can just have your attention for a minute.'

They stopped what they were doing, looking round in surprise, quizzical expressions on their hardened faces.

'This is a parting of the ways. You have to link up with the 82nd Airborne, and I have another job to do.'

Hernandez called over. 'Yeah? And where'd you think you're goin', Major?'

Wingham dropped his eyes and shuffled his feet. As always the Rangers gave you direct questions, no tactful subtleties, straight to the point. In the same vein, when he looked up to answer he spoke firmly.

'I have orders to link up with the French partisans, the Resistance. More than that I can't say.'

Vandenburg ran a cloth over the Browning's gun sight. 'Not sure about that, Major. We done looked after you all this way, reckon we can't just let you go wanderin' off all by yourself now, can we?' He glanced round at the others.

Wingham held up a hand. 'And I'll never be able to repay what I owe you, but this is a one man operation. If I'm seen with anyone else they'll be frightened off.'

Hernandez cradled his rifle, head questioningly to one side. 'I take it you done this sort of thing before.'

Wingham nodded.

'Guessed as much.' The sniper climbed to his feet, walked up and held out his hand. 'Luck go with you then, Major. We might meet again, if not, it's been good knowin' ya.'

Wingham shook the extended hand. 'Thanks,' he blurted out, embarrassed. Each man in turn made a point of wishing him luck and finally Doc Bell pointed at Wingham's blood soaked uniform, congealed into a dark patch on his battle dress. 'You gonna be okay?'

Wingham looked down and grimaced. 'Thank you, Doc. Looks ten times worse than it is.' Turning to the gate he jabbed a thumb at the body of Sergeant Chuck Rivers.

The Corporal held up the Sergeant's dog tags. 'Don't worry, Major, we'll see to it.'

With a reluctant nod, Wingham settled the Sten gun across his waist and moved out onto the road. He turned left, back the way they'd come, and as he strode off he cast a lingering eye over his shoulder towards the field. The Rangers stood in a line, grinning, hands raised in farewell.

Wingham half lifted a hand in salute, swallowed hard, and turned away behind the hedge.

Flight-Commander Chris Johnson taxied the Spitfire to the end of the runway, waited for the squadron to form on his tail and checked the grass strip was clear for take off. He called Flight Control.

'Hello Badger, ready for take off.'

'This is Badger. Take off now.'

'Wilco, Badger.' He switched channels. 'All sections, on our way.'

Goggles down, hood closed, brakes off; he pushed forward on the throttle heard the engine rise, the Spitfire trembling forward, and then felt the Rolls Royce Griffon howl into full power and leap up the runway. The tail came up and moments later he inched the stick back and the wheels rotated free of the deck. Airborne again. Undercarriage up, a check in the mirror and a quick glance around. The boys were closing up, two flights of six fighters, a tight formation.

Increasing the rate of climb he banked the squadron to the south and headed for the coast. Cloud base at eight thousand and he led them up to kiss the underside of the vapour. The green landscape slipped by below, the River Tamar beneath his starboard wing, winding to the sea. Streets of houses, ships in the estuary, and minutes later Plymouth drifting behind. He checked the bearing, one-oh-oh degrees, a direct flight to the Cotentin Peninsula.

Johnson looked round at the squadron, all weaving smoothly in his slipstream. He flicked on the R/T. 'Hello Gable squadron, this is Gable leader. Eyes peeled, don't assume they're friendlies. Blue Two, close in.' That was Johnson's wingman, too far out.

Blue Two yawed across, levelled, and the pilot nodded through the Perspex canopy, an apologetic wave of a gloved hand.

Ahead and below, the waters of the Channel teemed with a never ending flow of ships, convoys of every description, big and small, all converging on the embattled shores of Normandy. Ugly black smoke rose from the horizon where sea met the distant land, confirmation if needed that they were on the right course. Below left, gliding past the port wing, a full squadron of Typhoon fighter-bombers streamed south, closely shadowed by a flight of Hurricanes. Johnson smiled briefly. Every aircraft he'd seen bore the fresh black and white stripes of the Allied air force.

The radio clicked in his earphones. 'We have company at two o'clock, Leader. Angels six.'

Johnson dipped his nose, side slipped right, and regained station. 'Roger, Red Two, I see them.' They were P51 Mustangs diving away to their right, moving fast.

Again he craned his neck to check each Spitfire's position, watching their graceful rise and fall in the thermals. Helmeted heads and goggles peering through the canopies, swivelling from side to side, skimming under the sun flecked clouds. He pushed on towards the battle, ever watchful of the skies around. The course was east-southeast, and Cherbourg crept closer. He angled to the left skirting the northern tip of the Peninsula, steering clear of possible flak batteries. Arriving over the bay he banked right towards Utah beach and flicked on the R/T. 'Gable squadron, this is Gable Leader. Yellow and Red sections take the right flank. Blue and Green sections with me. Make sure of your targets. The US paratroopers are well inland. And don't forget, ground attack is our main aim, every man for himself.'

Answers came one by one. 'Yellow one, understood.' . . .'Red one, Roger.' . . 'Green one, okay Leader.'

Johnson made a final check of the sky. The Typhoons were boring in through the smoke, curling swirls whisping in their slipstream, the Hurricanes peeled out of formation and dived in for their targets. Barrage balloons swayed over the ships below and a cruiser spat flame from her guns, aimed at the shore. 'This is Gable Leader. Tally-ho!'

Flying down under the wind-torn clouds, Chris Johnson dipped the nose of his Spitfire and with his two sections over the beach, levelled out at 4,000 feet. He peeled left, weaved right, slipped lower, turned back towards the sea searching for a target. 3,000 feet below, the battle for the beaches unfolded on the narrow strips of sand. Vivid red explosions blanketed the German defences, dense grey smoke billowing in curls in the wind. Dozens of small assault boats trailed a line of white wakes, ploughing in towards the obstacle laden beaches.

The big guns of a battleship flamed orange in a massive broadside, the surface of the sea rippling under the concussion. He could see destroyers closing the land, a constant barrage of gunfire supporting the invasion.

Lifting the spinning prop he banked right, steadied the aircraft in line with Utah beach and flew on towards the town of Sainte-Mère-Église. He banked right again and swept north. He picked up the main road to Cherbourg and two miles south of a place called Montebourg he spotted a small column of German vehicles stopped near a line of poplars. Tracer and small explosions lit up the road and he saw the remains of a German scout car on fire. A half track had stopped behind it, the mounted machine-gun laying down a constant hail of shells. He banked into a circle, tightened in a wing down curve; and there were the Americans, fighting from either side of the road. They looked like paratroops, maybe the 82nd Airborne, and they were up against it. Johnson smiled inside the mask. This was a target of opportunity, the reason for the sortie, and he pushed the Spit down for an attack. Engine racing, he dived in.

Johnson levelled out at 300 feet, dipped to find the target, and hit the button. A shudder trembled his gloved fingers, the cockpit vibrated, and a stream of tracer lanced into the enemy ranks. Caught between the hedgerows there was no room to escape the hail of destruction. Mown down in a whirlwind of exploding vehicles the Germans vanished in the turmoil. The Spitfire screamed overhead and left a trail of carnage in its slipstream. With a grim smile of satisfaction, Chris Johnson pulled on the stick, rolled to his right and hauled the fighter skywards. Curving round in a wide arc he peered down at the smoking wreckage and nodded. There'd be no reinforcements advancing along that road for a while. An American soldier waved a hand in salute and Johnson waggled the wings. He pulled the stick back, climbed to a 1,000 feet and went in search of another target.

On *Brackendale*'s bridge Thorburn read the message from the wireless room and smiled. He looked up at the men around him, crowded with the full compliment bridge staff. 'Target destroyed, gentlemen.'

Armstrong grinned and thrust his hands deep into the pockets of his duffle coat. Labatt, just arrived up the ladder, spun round and slid back down to spread the news.

Thorburn picked up the handset to the Control Tower. Lieutenant John McCloud answered.

'Well done, Guns. Bloody marvellous.'

'Thank you, sir. We had a very steady platform.'

'Even so,' Thorburn said, dismissing the compliment, 'that was damned good shooting. Congratulate the gun crews for me.'

'Of course, sir, and thank you.'

Thorburn replaced the handset and turned to the wheelhouse voice-pipe. 'Starboard ten, half-ahead. Make revolutions for twelve knots.'

Falconer acknowledged. 'Starboard ten, speed twelve knots, aye aye, sir.'

Brackendale began her turn away from the beach, steering clear of the continued assault by the second wave of 4th Infantry Division.

Thorburn could easily see the tactical difference in the size of the landing craft pushing in towards the sand. Landing Craft Tank were off-loading from the surf, their yawning gull-winged doors churning out the Shermans, firing on the move, pushing through hastily dug fox-holes.

'Slow ahead. Steer oh-four-five degrees.' *Brackendale* idled towards the northeast, holding station 1,800 yards from the beach. Five large infantry boats crossed her path and Thorburn eyed them with appreciation, an impressive array of American manpower. He allowed them to close the land and turned the ship back into the prevailing winds. A line of Higgins boats chugged past, the helmets of the infantry crouched inside.

A shell exploded in the shallows and a boat swam through the ripples. The next line of boats followed them in, 1,000 yards out. One of them reared up to the force of an explosion, the bow ramp blown off. Men were hurled into the water. Weighed down by their equipment they struggled on the surface, swamped by the waves. Some never made it, pulled down by their packs. The other boats pushed on. They had strict orders, not to stop for anything.

'Number One! Get the motorboat over the side. Those boats are under orders not to pick up survivors, but I don't intend to stand by and watch.'

Inwardly, Armstrong smiled at the Captain's belligerent attitude. That's what made him stand apart, but it could also land him in hot water. 'Aye aye, sir.' Moments later he was on the boat deck calling for the crew.

Thorburn crossed to the starboard wing, not wanting to take his eyes off the struggling survivors. Not many remained afloat. Eight? Ten at the most, out of full boat of thirty.

'Stop engines.'

Brackendale drifted shoreward, rocking to the waves, helping to create a patch of calm water in the lee of the portside waist. Two of the swimmers saw what was happening and struck out for the side of the ship.

'Scrambling nets! Thorburn called.

On the quarterdeck, Labatt detailed the depth-charge crew to lend a hand.

The motorboat curled out from beyond the bows, gathering pace. A seaman stood on the foredeck, boat hook poised over the waves. Helping hands reached from the cockpit as the helmsman throttled back, easing in amongst the flailing arms. An injured soldier reached up for help, slipped, and fell back. He disappeared under the water then bobbed to the surface, coughing and spluttering. His life preserver flipped him on his side before a seaman stretched down and grabbed an arm. Two of the crew dragged him bodily into the boat. A swimmer at the back stopped moving, face down in the water. A man was dragged into the boat with an arm missing, barely alive. All the while *Brackendale* drifted closer. Two men made it to the scrambling nets and clambered onto the deck, gasping in sodden heaps. Eventually the motorboat's crew could do no more and the Bosun brought her back to the quarterdeck. A dozen hands helped them up, hanging onto the net with one hand and dragging them up to the guard rail. Doc Waverley inspected them one by one. The man with a missing arm was dead, a trail of blood washing down the side.

Thorburn stood in sorrow, waiting for the boat to be recovered. A pitiful few had survived, a platoon of vibrant young men, blown away in the blink of an eye.

Armstrong waved to signal the boat was secured.

Through his teeth he gave the order. 'Slow ahead, starboard thirty.' *Brackendale* came to life, turning out to the sea, seeking deep water.

Thorburn gripped the compass binnacle, anger welling. The toll of dead and injured was rising. There'd be many more before the day's end. He brought the ship out until she was on station with a fleet destroyer and turned northwest until the port beam ran parallel with the shore.

The Aldis lamp clattered. 'Signal, from commander, sir.'

'Yes?'

'Reads, "Thanks for your able assistance. Proceed to screen the right flank." Message ends, sir.'

Thorburn hung his head. So his job here was finished. He glanced over to the landings, at the grey curling smoke and burning vehicles: the occasional eruption of a shell hitting the beach and the scattered bodies. Now he would be on the periphery, the sideshow preventing any incursions by the Kriegsmarine. But at least *Brackendale* had played her part, right at the sharp end. He was glad he hadn't missed it.

'Very well, acknowledge.'

The lamp clattered and Thorburn called Lieutenant Martin. 'Pilot, set a course for our next station.'

'Aye aye, sir,' Martin said, and after a pause, called down the voice-pipe. 'Port ten, steer three-five-oh degrees.'

Thorburn settled for the chair and found his cigarettes. He wondered how the other landings were going? If it was anything like this, they must surely be a success. *Brackendale* cleared the sheltered waters of the bay and lifted her head to a long swell. She leaned and buried her bows, and Thorburn tilted his cap back. Free again.

Marianne Legrande cradled the hunting rifle and peered apprehensively up through the low canopy of leaves. At midnight she'd listened to the sound of aircraft flying in from the west, had seen the anti-aircraft guns firing into the night sky, the searchlights waving across the clouds. From before dawn she'd heard the bombers and the crash of explosions, seen the flames on the ground. And then shortly before daybreak came the roar of offshore guns, a never ending cacophony of rolling thunder. When the big guns stopped firing the sound of smaller weapons took their place, machine-guns and mortars and grenades.

Daylight had revealed dense clouds of dirty smoke darkening the northern sky and what she assumed must be Allied aircraft attacking ground positions, strange white stripes on their wings. Occasionally, the big guns fired again, two or three distant salvoes, followed by erupting balls of curling smoke. For the last hour the sounds of battle had waned, moving more to the southeast, over to her right.

Marianne took a small sip of water from her wine bottle and made doubly sure the cork was secured. She leant the bottle against the base of the tree and risked standing to take a look beyond her immediate confines. There was no sign of movement from the adjoining fields but with this amount of shooting she felt sure the Germans must soon mount a counter attack. They might well come this way. She'd made a large detour round an encampment of trucked infantry the night before, if they moved she was in their line of advance. Creeping forward to the edge of the trees she stared intently at the irregular line of hedgerows at the far edge of the field. In the left corner was a wicket gate and beyond that was a triangular shaped field, the most distinctive field out of many. She felt sure that anyone coming to meet her from England would use that as a reference point.

The sound of an aircraft interrupted her thoughts and she faded back inside the trees, squatting down behind a gnarled trunk. She must be patient, it was still early and London had not specified a time, only the day. She made herself a little more comfortable, snuggled the rifle in the crook of her arms, and settled down to wait.

Major Paul Wingham walked steadily towards the southwest of the Cherbourg Peninsula. It was familiar territory, a countryside where he'd spent two years working with the French underground. Then, as now, it had been full of Germans, but this time he felt they might be more preoccupied with the beaches than the old muddy farm track he'd used so many times before. The area was known as La Cavalaire and in that gentle rolling farmland the men and women of the Resistance had discovered a disused stone sheep shelter. Half hidden inside a low lying stand of trees they'd quickly made it a sort of temporary lodging in case of emergencies, a place of sanctuary to rest and hide.

Wingham slowed, wary now as he drew closer to the few isolated buildings. Having travelled across country he knew he was approaching the road that led from the east to Cherbourg, The Germans used it as their main arterial route, frequently driving supply columns both ways. He crept up to the hedgerow that ran alongside the road, found the line of least resistance, and pushed through the tangled thicket. A twig sprang back and whipped his face, a stinging cut to his cheekbone. A shallow ditch with a narrow grass verge bordered the roadway leaving anyone attempting to cross very exposed to the casual observer.

The thump of heavy gunfire echoed in from the sea, the distant chatter of machine-guns away to his left. Squinting against the lash of any more branches he forced his way his way through the last of the foliage and allowed himself to sink back and blend with the greenery. A long pause while he steeled himself for the effort and he jumped for the ditch. He could see the brown leafless branches of a dead bush on the far side which might give him access to the next field. He sprinted over and bulldozed his way in. Panting with the exertion he dropped to the ground and lay still. Ahead of him was the open expanse of a large triangular field, the point of the apex at the far end. Raising himself up he fumbled for the water bottle and took a swig, rolled it round his mouth. Give it a few more minutes, he thought, a little more recovery before the last leg.

16 Ambush

Otto Reinhardt abandoned the bunker and marched off at the head of his unit. Hitler's orders were to stand and fight but unable to make contact with any of his gun batteries, there seemed no point in staying to be slaughtered and he'd made the decision to quit the post.

'Neuman!' he snapped over his shoulder.

The machine-gunner trudged forward, the MG42 balanced over one arm.

'Herr Oberst?'

Reinhardt jabbed a finger at the long, winding lane. It stretched away for three hundred metres before turning right through the hedgerows. The sounds of battle reverberated in from the beaches, the staccato bark of heavy guns rolling across the land.

'I want you half way up that track. You set up that gun to give us covering fire. Clear?'

Neuman scowled and looked into the distance.

Reinhardt saw the reluctance and forced himself to be patient. 'Is there a problem, Neuman?'

The scowl softened and the machine-gunner met his eyes. 'Herr Oberst, we have served together for many years, no?'

Reinhardt nodded.

'And I have never disobeyed you?'

'That is true.'

Neuman pushed his jaw in the direction the road. 'Unless you give me at least one more man, I would be too far away, this would be suicide.'

Reinhardt studied the lane. Neuman was one of his original volunteers, had suffered the hardships of the

Russian winter and in all that time he'd never complained. He accepted the man's criticism and relented.

'You may have a point. Take Schulze, he has a good eye.'

Neuman pointed at Schulze and crooked a finger. 'With me, soldier.'

The man gave him a long look, then nodded and walked forward with his rifle.

Neuman settled the gun and the pair of them walked off up the lane.

Reinhardt waited, watching their slow advance. Eventually Neumann moved to the left and looked round for the best place to set up. He flicked open the legs of the gun and lay down facing the far corner.

Schulze moved to his right, covered another ten metres and disappeared into the bottom of the hedge.

Reinhardt turned to the only other men with combat experience. Four of them, out of a total of twelve in uniform. Of the remainder, there were two clerks and a cook, two wireless operators, a Telegraphist 1st Class and two Fixed Defence Gunnery Specialists, none of whom had seen front line service.

'You four!' he called, beckoning to the veterans. 'I want two of you, each side of the road. With a disdainful shake of the head he looked over the rest of them. 'Make sure your weapons are loaded with the safety catches on. I want no accidents.' If only he had his Bavarian Infantry Battalion; such strong warriors. No good dwelling on the past, he had to make do with what he had.

He took his first step along the road. 'Advance!'

Ahead of him the four veterans slipped into their old routine, 'move and cover', leapfrogging one another as they stalked forward.

Neuman saw them coming and brought the butt of the machine-gun to his shoulder.

Reinhardt strode brazenly up the middle, his motley crew of 'odds and sods' tentatively following his lead. As he closed in on the machine-gunner he made a cautious move to his right, hugging the safety of the hedgerow. The sun broke through the grey cloud, a dazzling swathe of light after the morning gloom. Just short of the turn the two pairs of veterans stopped moving, glancing back for orders. He raised a cautionary hand, removed his cap and edged forward to the corner of the hedge. Dropping to one knee he leaned slowly forward until he was able to study the road ahead.

It was empty. He relaxed slightly, holding his position. A thousand metres away the road turned left behind the ruin of a small chalet. A full minute passed as he stared into the distance, the warmth of the sun forming beads of sweat on his forehead. The road remained empty, no movement, quiet and still. He eased back and replaced his cap.

'Kruger . . . , there is a house at the far corner. You take the lead, same as before, stagger our advance and fifty metres at a time.' He hesitated. The machine-gun would have a clearer field of fire from the right side of the road.

'Neuman! Take yourself over to the right, twenty paces behind.' Once more he looked round at his odd assortment of followers. 'Stay behind the machine-gun. Clear?'

'Jawohl, Herr Oberst.'

'Then we go.' And to Kruger, 'lead on.'

Kruger took off, crouched forward in a fast run, and at fifty paces the pair flung themselves down and lay prone, weapons ready.

Reinhardt waved at the other two. 'Schnell!'

They bounded up the right side, and Neuman picked his moment, loping along in the rear. They ran past those on the left, by a further forty metres, and hit the ground, watching. Again Kruger came to his feet and led the way, fifty metres on from the others. Neuman scrambled to find a place and settled in a slight depression down the right.

Reinhardt estimated they'd moved to within five hundred metres of the house and gave the order to watch and wait. He took another long look at the dwelling. The upper floor overlooked their position, two small broken windows under a roof of scattered tiles. A rag of curtain flapped and Reinhardt felt a twinge of apprehension run up his spine. If the enemy had reached this far and his men were caught in the open . . . ? But he must get up this road.

He stepped out from the hedge, decision made. 'Kruger! We take the house.'

Beneath the left hand window on the upper floor, Hernandez squatted with his back to the wall, the Remington loaded and poised. He was about to take another look down the road. Crouched below the flapping curtain, Vandenburg had the muzzle of the BAR pointed high, resting on the window ledge. The rest of the Rangers were downstairs watching the front. Bradley had one leg propped up on a kitchen table guarding the window.

Hernandez eased up on one knee, swivelled round to the side of the aperture, and very slowly squinted past the wooden frame. He froze. A Kraut officer walked across the road and gave a command. Five soldiers lurched to their feet and appeared to be readying themselves for an assault.

He spoke from the side of his mouth. 'Krauts coming.'

Vandenburg grunted and slipped his forefinger inside the trigger guard, out of sight below the window.

Hernandez squirmed away into the darkness of the room, stood up and snuggled the rifle to his shoulder. The officer wearing the peaked cap loomed large in the telescopic sight. Aiming for the heart he closed one eye, steadied his breathing, and caressed the trigger. The

210

Remington thumped his shoulder. The bullet struck high, angled down above the breast pocket, punching him to the ground. In one practised movement, Hernandez opened the bolt action to extract the shell. It clattered to the floor as he reloaded the chamber and snicked the bolt back in place.

Vandenburg lifted the Browning over the window ledge and went for the nearest targets. He was very deliberate. Three or four short aimed bursts, a few rounds at a time. One of them staggered, stumbled and went sprawling. The second, hit twice in the right chest, spun backwards in a heap. Vandenburg changed targets, bullets chasing down the road.

Hernandez sighted on the Kraut with the Spandau. He was in a shallow ditch, half hidden. But the scope latched onto his helmet and the sniper found the man's eyes. He saw the Spandau shudder, spitting green tracer; and Hernandez touched the trigger. The bullet smacked into the left cheekbone. Blood spurted and he slumped over the butt of the gun, the side of his face torn open.

Panicked, one of the Germans shouted. 'Run!'

The remainder turned and fled. Vandenburg cracked another volley of shots at the running targets. A bullet caught one in the back and he fell, colliding with a man to his right. He too was hit, in the neck, died where he'd fallen.

The sniper rifle barked again and Hernandez managed to squeeze off two more shots before the fleeing rabble reached the corner and ran out of sight. Six bloodied bodies lay crumpled in the sunshine. The sniper held his position, watchful.

Vandenburg tipped his helmet back and fumbled for a Lucky Strike. 'You think they'll come again?'

Hernandez kept his eyes on the road, heard him flick the lighter. 'Not a chance.'

211

They heard a call from Bill Tierman downstairs. 'Hey fellas! I got a guy on the radio. The 82nd are holding Sainte-Mère-Église.'

The sniper glanced over to Hernandez and grinned. 'How far away, couple of miles?'

The machine-gunner blew a perfect circle of smoke. 'No, nearer five, maybe a bit more.'

On the bloodied road below all was still. The two Rangers held station, wary, and waited to see what happened.

Otto Reinhardt was not dead. The bullet had struck at an angle, deflected under his collar bone and severed his spinal chord. He lay where he'd fallen, blood on his chest, blood on the road, and paralysed. His eyes flickered open and he watched the clouds flying over, soft white balls against the blue of the sky. He felt the sun's warmth on his face and he remembered his youth, the lush valleys of the Bavarian Alps. His breathing became laboured, but without pain. A fly buzzed onto his right cheek, flitted to his nostril and landed on his partly open mouth. He made a vain attempt to blow it away and failed. Eyes wide open but unseeing, his life blood ebbed away. Otto Reinhardt became just another casualty of a long war.

Two miles away, Paul Wingham walked along the base of the triangular field and brushed himself down. About a hundred yards distant, almost hidden from view, stood a small wicket gate. If his memory served him right the stone shelter was at the southern end of the next meadow. The smoke of battle drifted up from the northern shore with more heavy smoke rising to his left, in the east. Cocking his Stengun he moved off towards the right-hand corner, took a chance and cut across, saving himself fifty yards. He pressed on, close to the hedge, sensed his heart pounding. He forced himself to take a breather; no good getting careless. Wiping a trickle of sweat from his face he set off again.

A thrashing flurry of movement made him start, and a bundle of feathers shot out of the hedge and flapped away. He cursed, breathed again and slowly released the Stengun's trigger. A bird's dark feather floated gently back to earth. With heightened senses and a tight mouth, Wingham controlled his breathing and walked on. The sound of aero engines caused him to look up and he stumbled on an uneven patch of ground. A Spitfire circled in a wide turn to the west.

Two minutes later he reached the gate, slipped quietly through and dropped to one knee. Almost there.

Before him the gently rising stretch of ground led up to the starkly silhouetted clump of trees he'd been looking for. He dropped to his belly and crawled into the sparse, tufted grass. Wriggling to his left allowed him to keep the hedge behind, hiding his profile against the darker background. Raising his chin gave him a clearer view and he took time to make certain that it was clear. A prolonged moment of careful observation and he was satisfied.

Wingham twisted on his side and checked the Stengun. He also had two frag and one smoke grenades left, along with his pistol and spare ammunition. It would have to be enough. And as for sneaking around the hedges, he'd had his fill of that; it would be straight up the middle to the trees.

He climbed to his feet, braced himself and lunged forward.

Charging up the centre of the field, Wingham felt his stamina begin to wane. At the midway point his shins ached, his lungs burned and the wound to his shoulder opened up and bled freely. But uppermost in his mind, overriding the hurt, was the desperate need to find the girl. And time was short.

He powered over the last few yards and crashed headlong into the shrubs. A sapling snagged his right ankle, tripped him up and sent him sprawling. Stunned and winded he spat twigs and gulped air.

A mud encased brown boot planted itself in front of his face and he looked up in concern. The muzzle of a rifle hovered above his head. As he focused beyond the barrel, the beautiful eyes of Marianne Legrande smiled down at him.

'Hello, Paul. Can't be too careful. Are you alright?' She squatted next to him and reached to touch his face.

He managed to roll on his back and bring his breathing under control.

Marianne stiffened, a sharp intake of breath. 'You're bleeding.'

'Not much.' He conjured up a smile. 'Just a graze.' He struggled up onto his elbows and reached out. 'Here, help me up.'

With both hands she pulled him to his feet and Wingham grinned at her worried face. He glanced down at the dark patch of blood spreading over his uniform. 'Really,' he said, 'it looks a lot worse than it is.' Dampness welled up round her eyes, tears of relief, and he reached out and pulled her close. For a moment she succumbed to his embrace, head under his chin. Then, with a hand on his chest she pushed gently away and wiped away the tears.

Wingham guessed she'd had a rough time, been through a lot, but he kept his thoughts to himself. She was proud, strong, and didn't take kindly to any sort of emotional outburst.

'That loaded?' Her hunting rifle had ended up propped against a tree.

'Of course,' she said, roughly palming the last tear from her face.

'Good, we might need it.' He looked around into the stone shelter to find a blanket and meagre provisions. 'I have to get you back to the landing beach. You ready?'

Marianne Legrande lifted her chin, placed her fists on her waist and glared at him.

'I'll have you know I've been ready for two days. Where were you? Running around playing at soldiers.' She pouted angrily. 'I am more than ready.'

Wingham couldn't help but laugh. When she calmed down he stopped grinning. 'Where's the map?'

She gave him a coy glance, and patted her left breast. 'In here.'

'Then get your rifle.'

With a petulant toss of her head, she picked up the gun, but then hesitated, pointing to the south. 'There are many Boche infantry, with trucks. They might come this way.'

'Well, we're going in the opposite direction. Come on.' He led them out of the trees, but this time chose the longer route, along the side of the hedge. He had someone else to think of now and Marianne was extremely precious, in more ways than one.

It took twice as long to get back to the gate and reach the road than when he'd come through the fields on his way to their rendezvous. But now he knelt in a small depression at the roadside and carefully checked both ways for signs of the Germans. Satisfied it was clear he turned and beckoned for Marianne to cross over. She lunged from the hedge, sprinted for the far side and threw herself into the opposite hedgerow. Wingham leapt after her.

Crouched in the waist high meadow grass she looked at him with a raised eyebrow. 'Now where?'

'Straight across,' he said. 'Stay low.'

She raised her head until her eyes cleared the top of the swaying seed heads. The chatter of machine-guns sounded close and she looked at him for reassurance.

He nodded. 'Straight down the middle, crawl if you have to.'

She pulled a face and frowned.

Wingham took the lead. He waddled awkwardly forward on his haunches and heard Marianne rustling through the stalks behind him. Every so often he stopped and carefully checked on their progress. The noise of battle faded, moving inland, occasionally interspersed by the thump of a warship's guns. Thighs aching, he dropped to all fours and pressed on over the uneven ground. It was hard going, and though he wouldn't say so, he felt for the girl. She couldn't have been prepared for this.

Finally they made the end of the meadow and tucked themselves into the spindly hedge for a breather.

'Is it much further?' she asked, brushing the dirt from her knees.

He reached for her arm and pulled her round to peer through the twigs. Ahead of them lay the shimmering expanse of flooded pastureland. Beyond that, an old stone wall. Wingham pointed at a causeway that led towards them from the beach. 'That's where we're going.'

He heard a sharp intake of breath. She was staring out to sea, mouth open in astonishment. He followed her eyes to the offshore waters and for a moment he too blinked in surprise. From beach to horizon and from east to west, a vast fleet of warships had gathered off the coast. Battleships and cruisers, troopships, destroyers and landing craft. Assault boats of every description, scurrying between the ships and the foreshore. And where once there'd been an empty beach, thousands of men poured up the sand, long trailing lines of infantry.

A squadron of Typhoon fighter bombers swept in low over the mastheads, racing inland. In close attendance came a flight of P57 Mustangs, engines howling.

Wingham found himself grinning at the overwhelming display of firepower. Try as they might, the Germans were never going to win this one. He even felt a moment of pity for those caught at the sharp end. Nazi Germany was facing defeat. A glance at his watch showed it was late morning and he still had to get Marianne down to the beach and into one of those boats.

17 Skirmish

To the north of Sainte-Mère-Église, Hernandez halted and raised a hand in warning. The Rangers scattered, melting into the side of the dirt track. The Sniper stared at a pillar of dense smoke coiling up over the hedgerows and wrinkled his nose at the smell of burning rubber, a physical, nauseating stink. Flicking the safety on his rifle he loped across to the hedge on his left and squeezed through a thinned out gap. Hampered by the wound to his arm he eased onto his belly and stuck his head out from the foliage.

Peering to his right he saw what remained of a small hedge and a line of poplar trees running at right angles to the squad's line of travel. A broken row of splintered telegraph poles indicated the presence of a road. Beyond the trees the smoke boiled black, harsh red tongues of flame flickering through the leaves.

He turned on his side and gestured for Vandenburg to join him. The machine-gunner flopped down and wriggled up beside him, looking along the hedge at the swirling smoke.

'Krauts?' Hernandez asked softly.

'Well the Airborne ain't got nothin' with rubber tyres.'

The Sniper nodded, thinking. 'We gonna have a look-see or go round?'

Vandenburg frowned. 'That's a helluva detour. Best I go take a look.'

Hernandez blew out his cheeks while he thought it over. 'Okay, just don't take all day.'

Vandenburg checked his Browning and slithered feet first down the small bank. Bending at the waist he took off at a run and disappeared from   view.

Hernandez glanced at his watch. Five minutes ought to be enough.

Vandenburg made it to the intersection of the two hedges and turned left on the grass following the line of poplars. Before he came level with the burning vehicles he paused at a hole in the low scrub and stuck his head out the other side.

A burning armoured scout car sat low on the steel rims, the rubber tyres a molten mess of dying flame. And there were bodies strewn all over, too many to count. Except for the dull red flicker of smoke shrouded flames, all was still. Cautiously he ventured onto the blistered tarmac, the Browning at the ready, and eased towards the carnage.

The nearest body lay face up with a gaping wound to the chest. A collar badge gleamed and he bent to take a closer look. It was the silver insignia of the SS. He straightened up in revulsion. Chuck Rivers had spoken the truth. The SS committed atrocities; both to civilians and prisoners-of-war. Hangings, firing squads and torture. It was the hallmark of Hitler's subjugation of the conquered. Fear was the key.

He looked away. There were no signs of anyone alive. The wounded had either died of blood loss or been recovered by the medics. Alert to the slightest movement he warily approached the back of a beaten up half-track. Peering inside only the dead met his eyes, the contorted remains of SS soldiers. A body hung out over the passenger door, an officer's cap with the Deaths Head badge lay discarded on the road beneath, a Luger clenched in his right hand.

Vandenberg's jaw tightened as he saw a red armband with the black Swastika, and an Iron Cross was fastened round the man's neck. He frowned, staring at the epaulettes. Some kind of lieutenant. He'd been dead awhile. Vandenburg coughed up phlegm and spat. Deserved everything he got. His feet crunched through a scattering of spent cartridge cases, the brass cylinders rattling as they rolled.

Skirting the burning scout car he trod watchfully toward the bend in the road. There wasn't much to see, only a row of three soldiers lying neatly to one side. Going down on one knee he took a keen look around, suspecting some kind of trap. When nothing happened he looked again at the three bodies and spotted the brightly coloured shoulder patches of the American Stars and Stripes; those guys were Airborne. Looking back at the number of dead Germans he pursed his lips in a soundless whistle. Must have been some fire fight.

Satisfied that the danger had passed he rose to his feet and made his way back to the gap in the trees. Hernandez was sat smoking, his Remington cradled across his knees.

Vandenburg waved him over, crossed his ankles and sat down to wait.

Belluci came first, stepped through the hedge and whistled.

Hernandez took a look, left him to it and walked back to Vandenburg. 'So, where now?'

'That road leads to Cherbourg. 82nd Airborne should be up that way, a place called Montebourg. The right flank, they were told to hold it.'

'Good a place as any. How far?'

Vandenburg scratched his forehead. 'Should get there by nightfall.'

Hernandez looked around at the depleted squad. Two walking wounded slowing them down. 'Anybody got any objections?'

Nobody put up any kind of argument so he called Belluci. 'We're headin' up the road. You wanna take point?'

Belluci was holding an Iron Cross. 'Pleasure's all mine,' he said, grinning. 'Got me a real nice piece of hardware.' He walked back through the hedge, a big grin on his face. The rest of the squad followed; there was a way to go to make it by dusk.

In the wrecked half-track behind the burnt out scout car, Oberleutnant Gerhardt Ziegler lay half in and half out of the door, nothing to indicate he'd ever been the proud recipient of high honours, the once glittering Iron Cross looted from his neck and now in the hands of a smiling Ranger. Death of an SS officer meant little in the way of anything special, just another statistic in the numbers of mounting dead.

Major Paul Wingham felt he'd waited long enough. It was imperative he get Marianne down to the beach and out to the ships. The bigger landing craft were emptying out on the sands, lines of soldiers trekking up to the low wall and the smouldering ruins of pill boxes. There were still the occasional explosions hitting the beach, heavy German mortars or long range guns, ineffective random shots. As he watched a soldier dropped his rifle and crumpled to the sand. Snipers? The men around him scattered, weaving up the beach.

'Do you feel ready for the next bit?' He asked the question without looking at her, knowing she was apprehensive. They'd done this before, a long time ago, not so far away. That had been at night, a desperate evacuation under the guns of the Wehrmacht.

'This looks easier than before.' She sounded confident.

He was quick to agree, bolster her confidence. 'Yes, probably, but we'll have to move fast, there's a sniper out there.'

She rolled on her side, and he felt her staring at his face. 'You think I am too girly for this?' The tone of her voice sounded petulant.

He turned his head, his eyes meeting hers. 'No, Marianne. I do not think it, and I didn't say it. What I am saying is that there are snipers. Once we make the move there can be no stopping. If you hesitate you will die.'

She looked away to the beach. 'Sorry, Paul. I know you are trying to protect me, but I'm okay. Really.'

Wingham nodded, came up on one knee and offered his hand. 'Up you get.' He stood for a minute while she readied herself for the move. A Sherman reached the causeway and lurched toward them. It wouldn't be long before there was a steady flow of vehicles moving this way, the least congestion the better.

From the corner of his eye he saw her lift the rifle. 'Ready?'

She nodded.

'See that gap in the wall?' The damaged German field gun was still there from earlier in the day. 'And that gun?'

She nodded again. 'That's where we're going.' He didn't wait for a response but stepped forward down over the bank onto the grass ahead. On his own he'd have started to run, but it was too far for her to keep up that kind of pace. Instead, he set off at a fast walk, weaving as he thought necessary. He was suddenly aware of being very exposed. A quick glance over his shoulder made him smile. She was half running to keep up. But her head was up and the rifle poised. He dodged right, angling across the field, deliberately changing direction. Another hundred yards and they'd be up to the old wall. From there, it was a stone's throw to the causeway.

The tank cleared the exit and squealed into a turn, the driver gunning the engine for power. A squad of infantry peeled out from behind the cloud of blue exhaust smoke, moving into line of march.

A bullet hissed past his left cheek and Wingham threw himself right, heard her follow, and checked his run. 'Straight for that wall!' He pointed, urging her on. 'Run!' He took off to the right again, putting distance between himself and Marianne. A sniper would be more likely to go after an officer than a woman. A second bullet plucked at his jacket and this time he heard the crack of the rifle.

The infantry saw what was happening and took up positions behind the wall, laying down a rapid screen of covering fire.

Breathing hard, he managed to spot Marianne getting dragged over the wall to safety. He sprinted to a section of brickwork with an overhanging tree, hoisted himself onto a branch and dropped behind the wall. The butt of the Sten gun smashed into his ribs and he winced in pain. He leant back and drew a deep breath. He was getting too old for this.

'Paul!'

He looked round to find Marianne running at him, bent from the waist, hugging the wall. He managed a feeble grin and waved a hand. She dropped to her knees and placed a hand on his shoulder, a worried look in her eyes.

'I'm alright, just winded. Stop your fussing.'

'What happened?'

'Sniper, but he missed.'

She relaxed away from him, sat back on her haunches. 'So you are not hurt?'

He shook his head. 'No, just got dug in the ribs by this.' He lifted the Sten gun and slapped the breech.

She laughed, a light-hearted giggle of relief.

Together, with her arm under his shoulder, they rose to their feet and stumbled off towards the tank and the waiting infantry.

The squad's medic stepped forward and grabbed Wingham's other arm. 'Easy, fella. You're losin' a fair bit of blood.'

'Just a flesh wound,' Wingham explained, and shook him off. 'Thanks for your help, but we have to get to the beach. We have an appointment in London.' He winked at Marianne and she smiled secretively in return.

The medic tilted his head to one side, speculative. 'If you're sure, buddy.' He swung his first aid pack behind his back and stepped out of the way.

Wingham nodded, straightened to his full height and turned for the causeway. There was no evidence of their fight with the Germans, no bodies, no wounded. He glanced down at her dark hair, met her trusting gaze and pushed off towards the beach.

Flight Commander Chris Johnson eased the Spitfire up to 2,000 feet and banked right for Cherbourg. He'd caught a brief glimpse of a house with no roof and troops moving towards the American right flank. Throttling back to 260 miles an hour, he levelled off and dipped the nose. There they were, Jerry infantry, at least company strength. No sign of any Americans. A quick look round the sky. Better safe than sorry. Three or four Spits circling inland of Sainte-Mère-Église and a flight of Hurricanes racing across Omaha beach. No enemy aircraft.

He rolled left away from the coast; the Jerries were more likely to be watching the skies over the sea. Two miles inland he slipped down to a 1,000 feet, banked right, and powered round to relocate the target. The ruined house was clearly visible, the infantry pressing forward inside the screen of a long hedge.

Johnson nudged the throttle back to take off speed, give himself time to home in. He jinked to starboard for better alignment, the ground a blur, rushing beneath the spinning prop. Nose down, gunsight on, thumb over the button. Less than 500 feet up, fast approaching the target. Upturned faces saw him coming and scattered in all directions.

Now! He jabbed the button and tracer lit up the ground, ripped into running soldiers, blasted a furrow through their tumbling ranks. A flame-thrower exploded, went up in an orange-red fireball. It was a four second burst and he released the button. Throttle forward, lift the nose and Johnson revelled in the power of the swiftly climbing Spitfire. He banked right towards the coast, turning into a wide flowing circle, holding the starboard wing tip down in line with the Germans. They were recovering fast, dispersing across the field in small groups. No visible interruption to their forward progress. There was an officer leading, waving his arms in remonstration, a soldier with a radio in close attendance.

Johnson tested the handling, waggled the Spitfire. Elevators, and ailerons, all the controls responded. Nothing to indicate he'd taken any hits. One more attack, more specific, aimed at the unit in command. A thorough check for enemy aircraft. Mustangs to the east, a squadron of Marauders heading for the Channel. No Messerschmitts, nothing.

Increasing the rate of turn, he slipped down to skim the hedges and wrenched her up to commence the strafing run. Over the final hedges, field dead ahead, locate the command group and open fire. Vibration from the guns, his tracer tracking over the grass and hammering into soft flesh. The bullets caught the officer and knocked him to the ground, three or more Jerries mown down under the hail of shells.

Then a line of tracer whipped up from the derelict house, a machine-gun catching him unawares. The crack of bullets tore into the port wing, and moved on down the fuselage. Instinct made him turn away, pulling on the joystick, pure reaction. Another burst caught him, pummelled the engine cowling and a plume of white smoke erupted from the nose. The engine coughed, caught again growled into power. He knew he had to gain height, a margin of safety. The white smoke was glycol; it would be just a matter of time. All thoughts of the Germans gone, now it was a matter of survival.

The coast lay ahead. If he could coax her round towards Utah beach he had a chance. Friendly territory. The engine coughed again, spluttering, roared, stopped, and the propeller feathered. No sound save for the whistling of the slipstream. He reached up and opened the perspex canopy, ready to use the parachute. But he was too low now, might make it to the sea. Not good with an air intake waiting to scoop up the water, usually ended with an arse over tit. The beach was coming up to meet him, fast. He tried to lift the nose, no real response. Stalling speed. The Spitfire was hanging above the western end of Utah beach, little traffic, even less soldiers. Where the surf foamed over the sand, Chris Johnson's Spitfire fell from the sky. There was an enormous jolt and the pilot lost consciousness.

As Wingham lead Marianne down to the sands he spotted a Spitfire flying low across the western end of the bay, White smoke poured from the engine and the propeller had stopped revolving. The fighter dropped, gliding poorly, weaving randomly. It was heading for a section of beach that had not been used for the landings, empty of troops. Instinctively, Wingham veered towards that end of the beach, knowing what was about to happen.

The Spitfire crashed in a welter of flying spray. Water caught the left wing, grabbed the skin and crumpled the flimsy framework. The tail broke away on impact, the fuselage torn.

'Marianne!' he called. 'Wait here.' He began to run. The airframe was half in the water, the propeller battered into splintered fragments. He could see a head in the cockpit, not moving. Jumping onto the right wing he found the canopy open, but what met his eyes made him hesitate. Blood dribbled down the side of the cockpit, smudged on the perspex dome. The flying helmet was ripped, the goggles smeared red. He reached for the straps, managed to release them, and then wondered how to go about getting the man's weight free of the cockpit.

The pilot groaned and raised his chin, held it for a moment, then lolled to the far side.

Wingham reached for the goggles and gently lifted them over the helmet. The pilot stirred, opened one eye and wiped the other with a gloved hand. Both eyes focused on the Major and the face broke into a faint smile.

'Am I still alive?'

'Looks that way,' Wingham said, unable to keep from grinning. 'You've taken a bang on the head, still bleeding. Can I help you out?'

'Bloody sore too,' he croaked. 'Name's Johnson, what's yours?'

'Paul Wingham. Now, can we get you out of here?'

'Indeed we can,' Johnson said, and levered himself up. 'Wait . . . , parachute's still on.' Freeing himself of the harness he accepted Wingham's helping hand and clambered out onto the wing. He felt the side of his chest and winced. 'Think I might have broken a rib.'

Wingham jumped down and helped him onto the sand. A wave lifted the fuselage and the Spitfire lurched sideways, the heavy surf foaming over their boots.

'Can you walk?' Wingham asked, wondering about the head wound.

Johnson nodded. 'Give me a moment.' He reached up and peeled off the helmet. Blood oozed from a laceration to his scalp. He took a deep breath. 'God, that feels better.' He took a last look over his shoulder at the wrecked Spitfire and with a shrug of resignation he turned away and they splashed forward through the surf.

Marianne ran to join them and moved in to take some of the load.

Johnson managed a crooked smile. 'What a darling girl. Maybe I did die and she's my guardian angel?'

'Stop chatting and save your strength.' Wingham could see they were approaching the main landing site and the 4th Infantry Division were piling in on the beach. Hundreds of soldiers filed past heading for the causeways. Tanks moved up and bulldozers criss-crossed the dunes. First aid stations tended to the wounded and two rows of poncho covered corpses lay respectfully to one side.

Wingham spotted an American Colonel directing the flow of traffic. It was a temporary Command Post for the beachmaster.

'Rest here,' he said, walked over and saluted, waiting for the officer to stop giving orders. The Colonel gave him a sideways glance. 'And what's your problem, Major?'

Raising his voice to be heard over the noise, Wingham kept it brief. When he finished explaining the Colonel waved a hand at the water's edge.

'Take your pick, just stay out of the way.'

Wingham saluted. 'Thank you, sir,' and made his way back to Marianne. Johnson was down on one knee.

'We can hitch a lift with anything that'll take us. Come on.' He and the girl hauled Johnson to his feet and arm in arm they waded out to the nearest empty Higgins boat.

The skipper had just finished transferring thirty men onto the beach and was bent down checking the fuel gauge.

Wingham led them up the ramp. 'Permission to come aboard?' he called, grinning.

The skipper straightened up and Wingham stopped to stare. 'Hello, Sub. Didn't expect to see you again.'

Sub-Lieutenant David Galbraith frowned. 'Do I know you, sir?'

'Not personally, Sub. You brought me in on the first wave this morning.'

Galbraith stared at him, mouth open, realised he was being rude. 'Sorry, sir. I didn't really expect anyone to survive that first attack. Glad you made it.'

The pilot stumbled and Wingham caught him and propped him against the side.

Galbraith turned to the Cox'n. 'Raise the ramp and give me slow astern.'

The boat reversed into the waves, made a neat turn to starboard and swung steadily out towards the waiting ships.

Wingham moved to the side and stared back at Utah Beach. Dozens of vessels jostled for space at the water's edge. Men and equipment littered the narrow strip of sand, a column of Jeeps and trucks driving away to join the battlefield. Smoke drifted on the wind.

He sighed, thinking of the Rangers, rembering Sergeant Chuck Rivers. They were good men. How many had survived? How many would live to see the end of the day?

The boat began to thump the waves and he turned away to sit beside Marianne. Not long now. Flight Commander Chris Johnson collapsed before they arrived alongside an American destroyer. The sailors took him to sick bay and the surgeon went to work. While Wingham talked to the captain, the surgeon came in to say the pilot had suffered delayed concussion but was out of danger. The captain arranged for Wingham and Marianne to be transferred into the care of the British navy.

Three hours later, in the cockpit of a fast moving Royal Navy gun boat, Major Paul Wingham, mission completed, and Marianne Legrande, field agent for General Scott Bainbridge, were fast approaching Portsmouth's outer reaches.

'Foxcub' had been rescued, and with her, the vital map of the Wehrmacht defensive installations of Cherbourg's deep water harbour. It wasn't long before the Allied commanders, examined Marianne's notes and began to make detailed plans to capture the port.

It was mid-afternoon when Hernandez stopped at a farm gate. He wasn't to know that two miles north the men of 82nd Airborne had taken the small town of Montebourg. The noise of battle had receded, coming from somewhere to the southwest, the sporadic rattle of small arms interrupted by the thump of tanks or field guns. From out to sea the deep rumblings of the battlewagons had faded to a few random shots.

Vandenburg caught him up. 'See anything?' he asked softly.

The sniper shook his head. 'Ain't seen nothing.'

'Might be a place to rest up. Wouldn't say no to a break.'

Hernandez didn't feel like arguing. His arm showed red through the bandage, oozing a fresh trickle of blood. He stepped forward into the entranceway. It was quiet. A high roofed barn took up most of the yard to his right, the rotten smell of manure assailing his nostrils. To his left was the farmhouse with two ground floor windows and a door set in the middle. Above the door was a small window on the second floor. There was something infinitely peaceful about the place, welcoming.

Turning to look over his shoulder he signalled for them to spread out. Bradley was standing with a makeshift crutch, Carson managing. Belluci had picked up a Thompson and Tierman his rifle. Doc Bell was helping

Bradley. There were nods and he whispered to Vandenburg. 'You gonna take the barn?'

'Yep, let's get it done.'

Hernandez made his move to the left, alert to the slightest movement. It was sticky underfoot, a thin layer of mud, some puddles from the overnight rain. His peripheral vision told him Vandenburg was on the move, angling away to his right. Behind him the Rangers advanced slowly, Doc Bell bringing up the rear.

Halfway across Hernandez looked ahead and spotted an unusual set of tyre marks. Three sets merging into two, then one crossing another, and back to two. In itself nothing too strange, it was a farm, there were all sorts of carts and wagons, horse drawn stuff. But he was looking at treaded tyre tracks, block pattern, not steel rims.

He hissed a warning. Something didn't add up. The tracks led across to the barn; must have happened after the rain stopped. Vandenburg was looking at him and he pointed with his rifle. They were clear enough and Vandenburg edged forward to follow the line of travel.

Hernandez suddenly felt uncomfortable. They were all out in the open, vulnerable. He glanced behind to shout a warning. Too late, he caught a movement at the top window and a machine-gun hammered into life. He swung the rifle and fired from the hip, the pane of glass splintering into fragments. He heard Vandenburg open up with the Browning and the brickwork shattered round the framework. A potato masher flew out, bounced once and exploded in mid-air. Carson dropped like he was pole axed. Shrapnel sliced through the sniper's right hand, a savage wrench, and he dropped the Remington. Diving to the muddy ground he reached for the pistol, trying to use his injured left arm. He cursed in frustration. He'd led them into a trap, let his guard down. A surge of pain made

231

him look at his hand. Blood flowed freely. He'd lost two fingers.

Anne-Marie was in the kitchen. She heard Gruber open fire, heard the grenade detonate and a machine-gun reply from outside. Crouching low, heart pounding, she crept over to the window and risked a peep into the yard. They were Americans! That brief glimpse was all she needed. The bottled up hatred of months of suffering boiled to the surface. Very deliberately she walked back to the big dresser and opened the drawer. She rummaged quietly inside and found the long, sharply honed blade of the bread knife.

From the bottom of the stairs she could see Gruber watching out of the window, saw him lift the submachine-gun and fire a short burst down at the Americans. A rifle cracked in reply and a bullet smacked into the ceiling.

Finally, summoning up all her reserves of courage, she took the first step up the stairs. Anne-Marie was a farm girl. She knew what it was to cut a side of beef, the bony resistance encountered. Now it would be a man, a loathsome fat man who had made her life a misery for too long.

Gruber leaned to the window, aimed and fired.

She lunged up the last pair of steps. His back faced her while he aimed again. With both hands she raised the knife, and at that moment, for some reason, he half turned. But there was no time left for Gruber. The knife slashed down with all her pent up fury. It penetrated to one side of his spine, glanced off a rib and pierced a lung. With calculated violence she twisted the blade and listened to his agonised scream. His pig eyes met hers in disbelief, the heavy jowls wobbling from the impact. He buckled at the waist, collapsed to his knees, gasping for air that wouldn't fill.

Anna-Marie held onto the blade and as his weight took him down she jerked backwards, both hands pulling. The sudden release made her step back to prevent a fall. His blood pumped from the gash, bright, arterial.

The gun fell from his grip and he slumped to the wall half sitting in the corner. A harsh rattling wheeze escaped from his throat and a trail of blood gurgled from the corner of his mouth. He shuddered.

She stood, the knife at her side, gazing at his death, a grotesque figure of revulsion. A reaction set in, a tremble through her limbs and she sobbed. It was huge, wracking sob, and she dropped the knife, put her hands to her head. There was silence in the house, silence in the yard, then she heard an American voice from outside.

'Think we got him?'

From what little English she'd learnt at school, she vaguely understood the question. From inside the window, not daring to show herself, she called to the men below. 'He is dead. No more.'

Hernandez heard the girl's call and squirmed round in the mud, looking for Vandenburg. He was down on one knee, an odd smile on his face, holding his side to staunch the flow of blood. Doc Bell got to him, forced him onto his back.

The sniper struggled to his feet, the stumps on his right hand dripping, the severed nerves feeding in waves of pain.

'Show yourself,' he shouted.

There was a movement at the window and a young, tear stained woman appeared, hair dishevelled.

Belluci pushed past moving for the door, wary.

Hernandez managed to unholster his pistol and closed in behind him. 'Easy,' he warned.

Belluci opened the door, let it creak inwards, machine-gun at chest height. The kitchen was empty and the only sound was a gentle sobbing.

Hernandez found the stairs, looked to the landing and saw the girl leaning against the wall, shoulders shaking. With the pistol in his left hand, just in case, he made his way up to the small space. There was an SS soldier slumped in the corner beneath the window, very obviously dead. Then he saw the bloodied knife and put two and two together. She'd probably saved their lives. Took a lot of guts. Physically she looked alright, probably shock.

'Okay?' he asked, as gently as he could.

She nodded.

'You wanna go down the stairs?' He motioned with the pistol.

She took a step away from the wall but hesitated. She turned to stare at the German, took a pace back and spat at the body. Then, head up, she made her way downstairs.

Hernandez nodded in approval. There was a bit more to that than met the eye, some underlying story. He let her go and checked the two bedrooms. Empty.

In the yard outside, Carson lay dead, Vandenburg was morphined out of it and Tierman sat fiddling with the radio, trying to stay busy. He shook his head, wondering. It didn't do to spend too much time thinking about the friends you were losing. He'd seen it before but that didn't make it no easier. And they'd lost a lot out of one squad today. They were only a few to start with, now they were even less

Downstairs in the kitchen the girl pointed to a small wooden door in the corner. She tried to speak, finding the right words. 'My mother and father,' she said haltingly.

Belluci went across and turned the big iron key, swung the door open.

The girl called out and there was a timid answer from the cellar. She called again and the old farmer and his wife emerged, blinking into the daylight. The mother saw Belluci in his Ranger uniform and started crying, kissed his hand. Embarrassed, Belluci stood there with a daft grin on his face and Hernandez smiled at the girl. The old man went for the cupboard in the dresser and produced a bottle of wine, a broad grin on his face, eyes wet with happiness.

Doc Bell pushed between them and grabbed the sniper's arm. 'Sit,' he said, and began to clean his hand. He bandaged the torn stumps of his fingers. 'How's the pain?'

'I'll live,' Hernandez grunted.

'Right, if it gets too much, holler. I want to bring Vandenburg inside. He took a bad one.'

Anne-Marie touched his arm. 'He can come,' she said, and pointed to the kitchen table.

Doc Bell smiled his appreciation. 'I thank you.'

With a jerk of his head to Belluci, he walked out to get Vandenburg.

Bradley limped supported by Tierman and Hernandez looked pointedly at the radio. 'You getting' anybody on that thing?'

Tierman shook his head. 'I can hear all sorts of stuff, but none of 'em seem to be hearin' me.'

'Keep trying.'

Doc Bell came back in with Vandenburg, Belluci carrying his feet, the Doc holding him under the armpits. They laid him on the table and Anne-Marie managed to get a pillow under his head.

Vandenburg groaned and opened his eyes.

The medic took a close look. 'Take it easy, just lie still.'

Hernandez hung his head, thinking it through. There was only Tierman, Belluci and Doc Bell uninjured. As for himself, he could still manage the pistol but his sniping days were done. If they came under any sort of sustained attack they wouldn't last long. He glanced up at the medic. 'Here a minute, Doc.'

He came over folding away a roll of bandage. 'What's up?'

Hernandez sighed. 'I guess we've just about had it. If we can't make contact then we best hole up until the cavalry get here.' He managed a faint grin, and then lowered his voice. 'Vandenburg ain't fit to travel, is he?'

'Nope, he needs a hospital. I can't do any more.'

'In that case, we're staying put. What next?'

The Doc turned to gaze at the room. 'Get some food and drink sorted.'

Anne-Marie stepped forward with a bright smile. 'You want food? We will make food. You must eat with us.' She rounded on her parents and spoke rapidly. Her mother clapped her hands in delight, and with an energy that belied the maturity of her years, quickly set about preparing a meal.

Hernandez nudged the medic and motioned upstairs. 'Better get rid of fat boy before he stinks the place out.'

Tierman looked up from the radio. 'Might as well do somethin' useful. Can't get a peep out of this heap of junk.' He dropped the earphones and followed Belluci and Doc up to the body. With some difficulty they brought the fat Sergeant down the narrow steps, struggled across the yard, and dumped him in the barn.

Tierman walked back out and stood looking at Carson's poncho covered outline. 'What about him, Doc?'

'Move him out of sight for now. Give it till the morning. If the infantry don't get here by then, we'll bury him out back.'

Belluci strode past and picked up Vandenberg's Browning. 'I'll go watch for anything coming. I'll be up at the top window. Good a place as any.'

The pleasant, pungent smell of brewed coffee drifted out from the kitchen and Belluci grinned, white teeth against his sweat stained face. 'Coffee's waiting.'

Doc bent down, lifted the poncho and snapped away Carson's dog tags. They moved him to the side of the house and returned to the kitchen.

Belluci took his coffee up to the landing, perched on the wide window ledge and settled down to wait. A short while later, Anne-Marie brought him a big plate of bread and cheese. She waited for him to take a bite and he nodded, mouth full. 'Good,' he managed between swallows, and she smiled sweetly before skipping back down to the kitchen. Still later, Tierman came to relieve him.

And so the Rangers waited, hoping for reinforcements, expecting an enemy assault.

It was late in the afternoon when Hernandez took his turn at the window, and shortly after he stiffened to the sound of approaching boots.

'We got company,' he called in a rasping whisper.

He heard movement from downstairs and Belluci bounced up beside him. 'What we got?'

Hernandez hushed him up and they swapped places. Belluci checked the ammunition and made sure the belt would feed in unhindered. It went quiet, no noise from the road.

Then a helmet made a brief appearance from around the far hedge, followed by the glimpse of a rifle barrel, quickly withdrawn. Hernandez held his breath. A soldier sprinted across the entrance and dived behind the nearside greenery.

The sniper leaned back and sighed, a big grin lighting up the lined face. 'They're ours.'

Belluci was peering over the gunsight. 'You sure?'

'Sure I'm sure. That there's 4th Infantry.

A second soldier nipped across the opening and Belluci nodded. 'Yep, they're GIs alright. We gonna call?'

'Go ahead, but keep that dumb skull of yours out of sight.'

Belluci moved to the side of the window, one eye peering round the frame. 'Hey!' he yelled. 'You guys with 4th Infantry?'

There was silence, a prolonged silence. Then voices could be heard, a restrained argument. 'Who're you?' came a shout.

'Rangers. Came in with the first wave.'

More conversation before someone yelled in response. 'Okay, Mac, we hear what you're saying. Now show yourself, real easy.'

Hernandez stepped forward and slowly stuck his head through the broken glass. There was a movement from below and an American officer appeared at the gate, and a dozen GIs came in at the run. They weren't taking chances, moving fast and covering each other as they moved.

Belluci let out a small whoop of delight and leaped down the stairs two at a time, got halfway down, turned around, and dashed back up for the Browning. Throwing it over one shoulder he made it down to the kitchen just as a Jeep came barrelling into the yard in a flurry of muddy spray.

Doc Bell walked out to find a Major in the passenger seat. He saluted.

'What's going on, Corporal?'

'Rangers, sir. I have wounded for evacuation.'

'Who's in charge?'

'Well, sir . . . , by rank, I am. We lost Sergeant Rivers and Corporal Donavon. And we did have a Limey Major for a while. Took off on another mission. So the sniper took over, name of Hernandez, sir. He's a fighting man.'

The Major studied the medic, saw the situation for what it was and kept his mouth shut. This was no time to start shouting the odds. He knew about war, had landed at Salerno in the Italian campaign, done more than his share of combat. From what he could see these Rangers were probably close to the end of their tether. He turned to his junior officer. 'Lieutenant, get the medics up here, the whole kit and caboodle. All of it.'

'Yes, sir!' the Lieutenant snapped, and started yelling at his men.

Hernandez walked unsteadily out into the yard and came to a standstill, swaying beside Doc Bell.

The Major took note of the bloodied bandage on his arm, and the fresh one, balled round his right hand. He looked at the man's face and recognised a kindred spirit. Tough, durable.

'Name?' he asked softly.

'Hernandez, sir.'

The Major nodded, confirmation of his own good judgement. 'I hear you're in charge.'

'Not really, sir. Just kind of happened that way.'

The Major grinned. 'Lieutenant! We'll take thirty. Do what you can for these men.' He stepped out of the Jeep and gestured at the vacant seat. 'Take the weight off your feet, son, and you can tell me all about it.'

Forty minutes later, the Americans prepared to move out. The five remaining Rangers were loaded into a truck; Hernandez, Belluci, and Tierman hauled themselves in over the tailgate. Vandenburg lay on a stretcher with Doc Bell administering plasma. The doctor with the medical team was convinced he would pull through.

239

Anna-Marie stood by the front door and watched the Americans take their leave. She thanked God for their arrival. She and her family would no longer suffer the indignities of living under the heel of the Nazi jackboot. As for herself, no longer the plaything of a slobbering, filthy, German pig.

They were free, liberated, something she'd always dreamt of but never wanted to pin her hopes on. Now, at last, mother and father would live in peace, might even live to see old age. As the wagons pulled out, she waved. She would never forget a handful of American Rangers who brought freedom to a small farm in northern France.

18 Those in Peril.

By 21.50 hours, *Brackendale*'s ship's company were out on their feet. It had been a long, sustained period without rest and with the coming of nightfall, the strain was beginning to tell. Men struggled to stay alert, but tensed at the slightest alarm, nerves jangling with the constant threat of attack. The men on the Pompom and Oerlikons displayed more signs of anxiety than most, desperate not to be caught out by the Luftwaffe. At this late stage, in the dwindling light of day, it was the return of the allied bombers which were causing the biggest headaches for the gun crews.

They had witnessed a sneak attack on one of the cruisers. As the American B17 bombers flew back to England, the Luftwaffe had attached themselves to the formations, indistinguishable in the poor conditions. At the most opportune moment they peeled away and dived at the nearest target.

They'd forced home an attack against fierce opposition from the guns of the cruiser, but nonetheless, one bomb struck the fo'c'sle and started a fire, and a second bomb exploded close to the stern and damaged the steering. The cruiser veered wildly out of station before being brought under control, and the fire had raged ever since, plumes of dense black smoke accompanying the ship's laboured manoeuvres.

For those who had witnessed the event, particularly the men aboard *Brackendale*, it was an unnerving spectacle, and further served to demonstrate the need to stay alert.

'Port ten,' Thorburn said to the wheelhouse.

'Port ten, aye aye, sir.'

241

He gave it a minute for the new bearing to come on. 'Midships.'

'Midships, aye aye, sir.'

'Steer three-four-oh degrees.'

'Three-four-oh degrees, aye aye, sir.'

Thorburn held a steaming mug of sweet, black coffee, glad of the warmth in his hands, reinvigorated by the caffeine. He was only too aware how easy it would be to succumb to the overwhelming desire to sleep, but he fought against it, remained in command. The adrenaline of the day's action had left him feeling sluggish; but his instinct prompted him to carry on. The ship dipped her nose into a wave and he balanced the mug, not wishing to spill a drop. A call from the radar room startled him.

'Radar. , bridge!'

Thorburn stepped towards the voice-pipe, bent down. 'Bridge.'

'New echo at Red one-hundred, sir.'

Thorburn frowned, checked the bearing. 'Portside?'

'Yes, sir.'

'Nothing to do with our ships?'

'Can't be, sir. If you look at the repeater they're all well to starboard.'

Thorburn glanced down at the radar-screen and peered intently at the array of echoes. The right side of the screen was a mass of luminous spots, so many they seemed to merge as one. Those were the convoys of the invasion forces. But as the radar swept round, there on the portside, a single small echo.

'Range?' To Thorburn it seemed a long way off.

'Six miles, sir.'

'That's not the 10th Flotilla is it?'

'The covering ships? I don't think so, sir. They've been up north beyond our radar.'

'What about a stray landing craft?' He asked the question even though he didn't believe it.

'I'd have picked it up before this, sir.' There was a subtle hint of exasperation in the answer.

Thorburn took a mouthful of the hot coffee and pondered. If this echo had only just appeared then it could well be a submarine, and if that was the case it must be a U-boat. Operationally, for obvious reasons, all Royal Navy boats had been ordered out of the area. And if the U-boat had just surfaced, it was hunting. *Brackendale*'s crew were already stood-to at Defence Stations, and reluctant as he was to disturb the off-watch crew, he had to bring the ship to total readiness.

He made up his mind. 'Action Stations!' And to the voice-pipe. 'Full ahead. Hard-a-port.'

He raised the binoculars from his chest, and then let them fall on the strap. The darkness of the night defeated him; nothing would show up at that distance.

Armstrong finished taking the reports and snapped the receiver back on the bracket. 'Ship closed up to Action Stations, sir.'

'Very well.' Thorburn peered at the muted glow of the radar repeater. He pointed at the display. 'I think we might have ourselves a U-boat.'

Armstrong studied the screen, taking his time. 'Might be, sir. . , might just be.'

Thorburn heard the reticence. 'Well it can't harm to investigate, we might get lucky.' He grinned in the faint light of the screen, made Armstrong smile.

'Midships, steer two-five-zero.' he ordered.

Brackendale took a wave on her starboard bow, slewed awkwardly, corrected, and ran on at high speed, knifing through the water.

'Guns. . , bridge.'

Thorburn answered. 'Bridge.'

'In contact. Range, nine-thousand yards. Bearing, two-three-five.'

'Thank you, Guns. Open fire if you get a visual. Don't wait for me.'

'Aye aye, sir.'

Thorburn squinted into the blackness and felt the tension in his muscles. He winced as an old wound stabbed him in the shoulder, a reminder of a previous conflict. The ship pressed on through the night, a fresh urgency of purpose.

Below the waterline in the hot, humid engine room, Lieutenant Bryn Dawkins kept a wary eye on the multitude of dials and gauges glinting out from the machinery. Sweat trickled down his skin and he wiped the corner of an eye. Under the call for 'Action Stations' the telegraph had rung up for Full Ahead, and so far there'd been no let up. The Welshman scratched his head with concern. He had discovered an almost indiscernible increase in vibration coming from the starboard propeller shaft. Whether it was due to a worn joint, or a bearing breaking up, he wasn't yet sure. He frowned at the spinning shaft, wiped his hands on his overalls and worried. All this was his responsibility and he was entitled to worry. Whatever the reason for the emergency the Captain was maintaining speed but he hoped the wheelhouse wouldn't be too long in ringing down for slower revolutions.

Until then the shaft would have to be monitored, continuously. He caught the attention of young Stoker Owens, a new lad who'd shown a lot of promise, and over the noise of the engines managed to explain what was wanted. The young man nodded vigorously and Dawkins felt confident enough to leave it with him. He stood for a moment longer, immersed in the technicalities of engineering. *Brackendale* badly needed a break for that boiler clean.

Kurt Schneider braced his chest against the bridge and focused his binoculars on the horizon ahead. Crowded into the small space with him were the two lookouts and the First Watch Officer, all with binoculars to their eyes. Nine kilometres on the port bow the ghost of a small warship had appeared and Schneider watched it thoughtfully. It appeared to have turned in their direction and he cursed under his breath. They could not have seen him in these conditions, not yet. But the radar might have picked them up . . . , possibly, he thought. Could they be sure of what they'd seen, doubtful. His face contorted in thought. Maybe he could attack this warship and be free to close the convoys. Never easy trying to kill a warship, they were agile and fast. So . . . , he must make a choice, make the attack or sneak away and hope to avoid detection. If he took on the warship it was all or nothing, but he shied away from wanting to use all the bow torpedoes on such a difficult target. He lowered the glasses for a moment, concentrating on his thought process.

Grand Admiral Karl Dönitz had taught them how to take a bowshot on a destroyer, but not on the surface. Schneider wondered if he might get close enough to be under the guns, hidden by their bows.

The bows of the boat twisted in the waves, spraying the bridge with stinging sheets of water. It dribbled off the peak of his cap and he wiped his face. The conning tower rolled through forty-five degrees and he grunted with the strain. He made up his mind.

'Battle stations!'

Thorburn clung to the bridge-rail and willed the ship onwards. He felt the power of the engines and

Brackendale trembled through his sea boots, quivering under his hands. She corkscrewed and steadied, thumped headlong into a wave, drifts of spray sweeping the bridge.

'Range?' he called.

'Eight thousand, sir.'

'Course?'

'Oh-eight-five, sir.'

Thorburn narrowed his eyes. Almost head on. That U-boat was attacking on the surface, otherwise he'd have gone under. Time to put him off. He unclipped the handset.

'Guns?'

McCloud answered. 'Speaking, sir.'

'That U-boat's taking us on. Open fire.'

'Aye aye, sir!'

The forward turret bellowed out a pair of shells, a blinding flash in the darkness. The smoke streamed aft and enveloped the bridge, stinging the eyes. Thorburn guessed the Gunnery Officer had tracked the U-boat from the first moment it had appeared on screen. The guns roared again and he preyed for accuracy. Another salvo, but the bows dipped in a wave, probably short.

He crossed to the radar repeater and peered at the glowing screen. The single dot had strengthened, small but definitely clearer. He heard a single gun fire from the quarterdeck and a starshell burst bright off the starboard bow, as if daylight had reappeared.

Then Jones shouted. 'U-boat! Dead ahead! Seven thousand yards.'

Thorburn threw up his binoculars just as the forward guns fired again, wreathed in smoke. He held the glasses in line with the bows. The smoke cleared, and he had his reward. There in the distance, the singularly ugly sight of a U-boat's conning tower. Columns of spray lifted from the

246

waves, well beyond the target. And still the menacing shape came on.

Schneider held his nerve.

'Open bow tubes one and two.' His voice was raised, calculating.

Two spits of flame belched from the shadow. The sounds of the shells ripped by overhead.

'Bow tubes one and two open,' came a call from below.

Schneider winced and shied away from shells plunging close ahead. 'Stand by,' he warned. A starshell, brilliant white, ballooned out to the port side.

'Lookouts below,' he snapped.

The bridge emptied and he found himself alone with the enemy. The warship was closing rapidly, the bow wave thrown high. He figured thirty knots. Torpedoes forty knots, closing speed, seventy knots, halving the overall range to the oncoming destroyer.

'Fire one!' He gave the warship five seconds.

'Fire two!'

A shell tore past the bows but Schneider hesitated. The torpedoes were on their way.

'Alarm!' he shouted. 'Alarm!'

He turned for the hatch, glanced back and saw the destroyer turning. The U-boat was sliding under, tilting down, and Schneider dropped into the tower, slammed the hatch above his head and secured it.

'One hundred metres,' he demanded from inside the tower. 'Right rudder, hard round.'

Thorburn had seen enough.

'Starboard twenty!' he called down the voice-pipe.

The Cox'n must have spun the wheel with extra venom. *Brackendale* heeled violently to port, white water surging over the bows, crashing along the fo'c'sle.

247

Another starshell, this time beyond the U-boat, leaving it silhouetted in the light.

Thorburn glanced from the enemy to the compass, gauging the moment to bring the ship back round to run parallel for a broadside.

'Port twenty!'

'Port twenty, aye aye, sir.'

Brackendale rolled upright, swayed through a dizzying arc and leaned hard over to starboard.

Still bent to the voice-pipe. 'Midships . . . , steady . . . , steer two-six-oh degrees.'

It was perfect timing. The conning tower was two-thousand yards off the port bow. 'Half ahead, both. Ring down for twenty knots.'

'Half ahead, speed twenty knots, aye aye, sir.'

Thorburn raised his glasses.

'He's diving, sir!' Jones yelled.

For an instance Thorburn ignored the call. He could see the nose going under, the foam washing over the deck plates, but it was the conning tower that held his attention. The light of the swaying starshell had revealed the unmistakeable image of a grey shark. That was *Glasgow Bay*'s executioner out there. 'Bastard,' he said aloud, and eyed the U-boat with loathing. The commander of that grey shark had indiscriminately machine-gunned the survivors of a lost ship, fellow sailors. There could never be an excuse for murder, and Thorburn's anger transformed itself into an icy calm.

Brackendale's main guns flamed out a broadside, hurling shells across the waves. The salvo straddled the target, plumes of water obscuring the view. The port wing Oerlikon hammered into life, a prolonged burst of tracer chasing the U-boat beneath the sea.

A shell exploded on the U-boat's casing, a lurid flash at the base of the tower. The forward lip of the tower found the surface, began to slide under, and the Oerlikon's tracer punched a row of holes in the steel.

Thorburn grimaced. Damaged, maybe seriously. Now for the coup de grâce.

In the engine room, Lieutenant Bryn Dawkins wore a worried frown. Vibration in the propeller shaft was threatening to unseat the bearing block and when the wheelhouse had called for a reduction in speed, the vibration had unexpectedly increased, indicating a serious misalignment somewhere in the transmission of power. The Welshman had begun to suspect a broken blade, either missing or torn, and that would need a frogman over the side. As Chief Engineer it was his duty to advise the Captain. In different circumstances the shaft could be disengaged with a consequent loss of power, but not when *Brackendale* was in the middle of a fight. He stepped closer to the spinning, gleaming shaft, struggling with how best to proceed. If it was a broken or dislodged propeller blade then the vibration would peak at a given revolution. That might be the current speed or something slower. At full revs there'd been less juddering.

Dawkins stared at the spinning shaft and worried.

Schneider made it half way down to the control room before an explosion threw him off the ladder. A rattle of shells thumped the tower as he fell. Landing awkwardly, he pulled himself to his feet and looked over to the attack table. In the dim red light, the First Watch Officer stood braced against the steep angle of the dive, counting off seconds on his stop watch.

A jet of water erupted down across the room, pouring in from overhead. Schneider stretched up, feeling for the opening. He found a fissure in the ballast main, the primary transfer line between tanks. No more than a crack.

But if he took the boat deep they would never get back to the surface. If he stayed shallow depth bombs would kill them.

'Call the Chief,' he spluttered through the water. He shook his head clear. 'We must seal this up.'

The shout went up and the Chief appeared, and with a cursory glance at the problem, issued a string of orders.

Schneider left it with him, climbed up into the control room. The depth gauge showed sixty metres and dropping lower. 'Make the depth for fifty metres,' he ordered. He checked their bearing. 'Centre the rudder. Make our course one-eight-five degrees.' South of their current position was the 'Deep' rift, running down towards the Channel Islands. If they could repair the pressure line and get to the rift, they might have a chance.

FlotillaKapitän Werner von Holtzmann squinted against the distant glare of a starshell. The swaying light hung eerily over the turbulent waters, and with his one good arm he lifted the binoculars in search of the reason. He spotted the ripple of gunfire and turned the knurled wheel to adjust the focus. The Schnellboat bounced under his feet, skidded sideways, forcing him to reach for a handhold. He heard the power feathered and the helmsman regained control.

Holtzmann returned the glasses to his eyes. A second starshell burst, closer this time, and the gunfire increased. He concentrated on those flashes and caught the gleam of a destroyer's upperworks, the White Ensign of a British ship. A line of tracer streaked out from a smaller weapon on the portside, aimed low at the sea. He followed it with the binoculars unable to find a target. Holtzmann dropped the glasses on the strap. His Schnellboats were hidden in the shadows outside the area of illumination. He guessed the range to the warship at nearly eleven-thousand metres.

He thought rapidly. Split his forces while the enemy was distracted. Three boats to attack from the south while he led the rest of the flotilla in from the north. Enough torpedoes to sink a battleship. And then they could get in amongst the troopships. He gave the order and the signal was passed. His flotilla divided and wheeled away to take up their positions.

Von Holtzmann smiled, a ruthless grin on his lean face. Glory might yet be his.

19 Frantic

Lieutenant-Commander Peter Willoughby caught the white shimmer of a magnesium flare as it curved across the southern sky.

'Starshell, sir.' His First Lieutenant reported at the same moment.

'I see it,' Willoughby said. He raised his binoculars over the port wing. The brilliant light drifted on its parachute, as much as twelve miles away, in line with Cherbourg.

'Check with Radar, Number One.'

'Aye aye, sir.'

Willoughby waited, and a second starshell floated skywards.

'Radar reports probable escort vessel moving west, sir.'

'Why probable? Aren't we certain?'

'They think it's a small destroyer detailed for right flank anti-submarine patrol. Radar reports regular search pattern.'

Willoughby let that sink in for a moment. 'Very well, keep an eye on it.' He looked round at the compass platform 'We'll break off the patrol, Pilot. Steer one-eight-oh.'

'South, sir?'

Willoughby took a deep breath. 'Yes, Pilot.' He restrained himself from raising his voice. 'I wish to satisfy myself as to the origins of that starshell. Can I assume that is alright with you?'

The Navigating Officer stuttered with embarrassment. 'Yes, sir. , I mean, I didn't mean to . .'

'In that case Mister Dixon, perhaps you'd be so good as to steer one-eight-oh degrees.' Willoughby turned away to hide his smile, peering over the bridge-screen. He heard Dixon pass the new course to the wheelhouse and felt the tilt of the deck beneath his sea boots. He brought his binoculars up towards the south and thought he caught a glimpse of a White Ensign. The momentary sighting of a small destroyer faded with the dying starshell but at least he felt he was doing something.

Thorburn watched the U-boat slide beneath the waves and cursed. Another minute and they might have inflicted enough damage to stop him going under. Now he was faced with the prospect of that old game of cat and mouse, and if he stopped to think about it, a game at which he'd not been very successful. He cursed again as the last starshell fizzled out and they were left blind in the inky darkness.

'Port twenty!' he snapped at the voice-pipe. 'Stand by depth charges.'

'Bridge . . Asdic. Contact, sir.'

Thorburn took note of the report, sub-consciously, but he only had eyes for that final swirl of water. He was fully intent on the immediate attack, a full pattern dropped across the U-boat's path.

'Midships,' he ordered. 'Steady . . . , steer one-one-oh.'

Chief Petty Officer Barry Falconer acknowledged. 'Steer one-one-oh, aye aye, sir.

The Asdic repeater pinged, shortening intervals between pulses. *Brackendale* rode on, closing with the unseen enemy. Thorburn ignored the Asdic, electing to go by instinct.

'Now!' he called.

The button was pressed and the depth charges splashed over the stern, fired out from the throwers, a shallow pattern searching for a sly wolf. As *Brackendale* ran on the first explosion erupted in their wake, dense towers of leaping water.

'Port twenty,' Thorburn said, turning the ship on a hunch, hoping to intercept the wriggling fish. Maybe northeast. 'Steer oh-four-five degrees.'

Passing down through forty metres the U-boat suffered a near miss off the stern quarter. Glass shattered tinkling on the deck plates. The boat shook, violently, a blur of deep explosions. Schneider lost his footing, grabbed for the periscope housing, managed to stay upright. His neck muscles twinged and his ribs felt hammered, hard to breathe. He had to shake this attack.

'Hard to port!' he snapped. Not near enough to be instantaneously lethal but with sufficient force to upset the trim and he felt there must be damage inside the pressure hull. The emergency lighting failed and torches flickered in the blackness, swathes of light playing over the gauges and control panels. A serious stream of water sprayed from an overhead flange and Schneider ducked away from the cold jet. He thought for a moment, how to avoid the next attack. 'Hard to starboard.' The sound of his voice cut across the noise, prominent, a helm order. 'Steer east.'

A call came in from the aft torpedo room. 'Inner door leaking on torpedo tube. Door buckled. Attempting manual seal.' The engine room followed. 'Fuel tank leaking, losing oil. Batteries giving off fumes. Starboard shaft warped.'

Schneider took a pace across the control room and looked at the depth gauge. Glass missing but the pointer still registered. Fifty-five metres and they were nose heavy. 'Equalise the trim.' The First Officer leaned to the wheels, but as Schneider guessed, he made no impression. The damage from the gunfire was too severe; the boat was slowly sinking.

'Forward planes to full rise.' The man on station obeyed, the instruments showing the angle achieved, and the boat hesitated, levelled slightly.

Thorburn frowned. The pattern of depth charges showed no signs of the anticipated result. Which way would that bloody U-boat turn? For all the sophisticated electronics, the modern equipment, the well trained operators on the Asdic, at this moment it came down to a matter of guesswork. His guess against the U-boat captain's decision. Nothing bettered the human brain. If he guessed wrong the U-boat gained vital time and distance. If he gambled correctly then he might finish it with a sinking.

Brackendale slid into a dark trough, twisted over the oncoming wave and corkscrewed through a rolling swell. Spray drenched the bridge-screen.

'No contact.' That was Asdic.

'Very well.' He rubbed his jaw, trying to put himself in the U-boat's shoes. If that commander was determined enough then he might still fancy his chances against the invasion fleet. A wide spread of torpedoes aimed at that amount of shipping and he had to get lucky. In which case he would hold course to the east.

Thorburn made his decision. 'Starboard ten.'

'Starboard ten, aye aye, sir.'

Brackendale leaned, shipped a foaming torrent over the port side, sluicing down the quarterdeck. At the depth charge rails crewmen fought to stay upright, the power of water tugging their boots.

'Midships,' Thorburn said, watching the compass. The ship swung upright, steadied. 'Steer oh-nine-five degrees.'

The Cox'n confirmed the order.

Thorburn had to give Asdic a clear sounding, decrease the noise of the propellers. 'Half ahead. Make revolutions for twelve knots.'

'Speed twelve knots. Aye aye, sir.'

Brackendale slowed, the vibration less pronounced. Thorburn shook droplets from his cap and wiped his face. They were steaming almost due east. If he'd guessed right ...?

'Contact! Moving ahead, sir!'

Holding his eyes beyond the bows he turned his mouth to the voice-pipe. 'Steady as she goes.'

'Wheel's amidships. Steering oh-nine-five degrees, sir.'

Asdic again. 'Course one-nine-oh. Range nine hundred, depth one-twenty, sir.'

Thorburn leaned on the compass housing and prayed. Shallow setting on the depth charges was one hundred and fifty feet. Was it holding depth or going deep?

'Range seven-hundred, depth one-twenty.'

There was his answer; he just needed a small correction left. 'Port five . . . , midships . . . , steer oh-nine-oh.'

'Oh-nine-oh, aye aye, sir.'

The seconds ticked by and *Brackendale* ran on, closing.

Asdic came back. 'Course oh-nine-oh, sir. Range five-hundred, depth one-twenty.'

Thorburn tensed. Another two hundred yards and *Brackendale* would be blind, the cone of electrical pulses too narrow, too shallow to pick out the target. And the U-boat would know, hear them coming. Make a last desperate move to limit the damage.

'Instantaneous contact!'

That was it, less than three-hundred yards. Now it was a judgement call, the final distance travelled to run over the submarine, an almost imperceptible wait before the fire button was pressed. He heard the faint sound of the bell, and the throwers coughed, tossing the canisters into the night. The explosions came. The sea erupted, drifted, a sheen in the broken grey of moonlight.

Time to bring her round. 'Starboard twenty.'

'Bridge . . Radar!'

Thorburn leaned to the pipe. 'Bridge.'

'Contact, sir. To the west.'

Thorburn leaned over to look at the small screen. A number of luminous echoes moving north and south. 'What do you make of it?'

'E-boats, sir. Moving fast.'

Unseen in the darkness of the bridge, Thorburn chewed at his bottom lip. He realised *Brackendale* was still turning, well to the west. 'Midships.' A glance at the compass. 'Steer three-oh-oh.'

'Three-oh-oh,' Falconer repeated. 'Aye aye, sir.'

Armstrong interrupted. 'Asdic report no contact, sir.'

'Very well.' Thorburn was distracted by the threat of the E-boats. It was a dangerous turn of events. 'Tell me when they change course.'

Time had slipped by, vital seconds, and the U-boat would have travelled hundreds of yards. He strode to the port wing and scoured the dark surface off the bow. No reports from the lookouts and nothing from Asdic. There was a muffled call from a voice-pipe. Armstrong took it. 'Depth charge report re-load complete, sir.'

Thorburn nodded. That was a quick turn round. 'Tell Mr Labatt, well done.'

'Bridge . . Asdic! Contact moving away on two-two-oh.'

'Can you give me a depth?'

'Hundred and fifty feet, sir. Holding steady.'

Thorburn squinted in thought. The U-boat had turned southwest, away from the invasion fleet. 'Port twenty,' he ordered. He took a moment to work out his options. He'd fulfilled his prime objective. The U-boat had been forced under and driven away from the fleet. How long before the E-boats got to him.

'Number One, where are the E-boats?'

'Still moving away, sir.'

'Very well.' That gave him enough time for another go at the U-boat and he leaned to the voice-pipe. 'Steer two-oh-oh, Cox'n.' That would shepherd the enemy further west.

'Two-oh-oh, aye aye, sir.'

Thorburn changed to the Asdic pipe. 'Range?'

'Twelve hundred. Depth, one-fifty. Course, two-two-oh. Speed, six knots.'

That was everything he needed. He raised his voice. 'Stand by.'

'Radar . . Bridge!'

Thorburn swore at the interruption, and then answered. 'Bridge.'

'E-boats turning to attack, sir, north and south.'

'Very well,' Thorburn said, calculating the priorities. He glanced at the radar repeater, picked out the northern flotilla and then identified the luminous pinpoints of light tracking up from the south. Calling up the Control Tower he waited for McDonald's calm reply.

'Sir?'

'Two E-boats flotillas, Guns. North and south. The U-boat turned southwest and I'm trying to keep him under. We'll shortly be head to head with the boats to the south. I suggest you concentrate on them first. Starshell and main armament. I'll turn north when I can.'

'Aye aye, sir.'

Thorburn moved forward to the bridge-screen. 'Where's that U-boat?'

Armstrong called over. 'Bearing two-three-five degrees, sir. Range, one thousand.'

Thorburn squinted into the darkness, working out the odds. If he could just hang on to the sub for a while longer, keep driving it away from the fleet? But he couldn't ignore the threat from the E-boats 'Make revolutions for fifteen knots. Steer two-four-oh degrees.'

Armstrong passed the order to the wheelhouse.

Thorburn tightened his jaw. 'Depth?'

'One-ninety feet, sir.'

The crash of a gun in the forward turret made Thorburn wince. A starshell flared into the night sky and swung on the parachute, drifting.

'E-boats! Fine on the port bow!' Jones shouted.

Thorburn reacted. 'Starboard twenty.' He needed to give Guns every chance with all the four-inch mountings. He raised his binoculars, searching for the enemy. A glint of white bow-wave and he had the nearest boat, two more in line abreast.

A blast of flame from the forward guns across the port side, and smoke swept aft in the wind. With *Brackendale* turning, the quarterdeck four-inch joined in to hammer a pair of shells at the bouncing targets. Plumes of spray erupted in their midst.

'Midships! Steer two-eight-oh!' The ship was heading a few points north of west. The guns crashed out an explosive torrent of shells, blazing away at the elusive targets.

An orange flash lit the water and an E-boat vanished in a ball of fire, trails of incendiary curling through the darkness. Enemy tracer lifted from the bows of both remaining E-boats, peppering the bridge, ricochets whining off the steel structure. Another starshell burst into light.

Thorburn instinctively ducked, hanging onto the rail, and heard Armstrong acknowledge a voice-pipe. 'Radar reports display inoperative, sir.'

'What?'

Armstrong tried again. 'Radar reports display inoperative, sir.'

'I heard the first time, Number One. Find out what the problem is.' Thorburn frowned, annoyed. They were blind and there were more E-boats to the north, unseen. A swirl of acrid gun smoke swept the bridge and he coughed. A hail of machine-gun bullets whipped over his head and rattled the Range Finder.

Armstrong came back to report, fell up the ladder and stumbled onto the bridge. 'Radar's in pieces, sir. We won't get that working again.'

Thorburn swore over the noise of the guns, controlled his emotions. 'Very well. Thank you, Number One.'

He snatched up a handset and called McDonald. 'Guns?'

'Sir?'

'I need starshell to the north.'

He saw the forward mounting traverse to starboard and a gun lift skywards. The shell burst, radiant.

A lookout shouted an alarm. 'E-boats! Green nine-oh.'

Thorburn called McDonald. 'Change target. Main armament to the north and I'll take control of the secondary.'

'Aye aye, sir!'

Thorburn half smiled. He sounded busy. He turned to Armstrong. 'Number One. Get the Pompom on the E-boat to the left, the Oerlikons and Lewis guns to the right.'

Below the port bridge-wing the Oerlikon gunner hit the trigger and a stream of twenty millimetre tracer lanced across the sea. In seconds the quadruple Pompom joined the fight, a satisfying thump-thump-thump, hurling two pound shells into the melee.

Jones gave a shout. 'Torpedoes!'

Thorburn grimaced through the oncoming machine-gun fire, caught the splash of two cylinders from the left-hand boat. Then the second boat let loose. He leaped for the voice-pipe. 'Full ahead! Hard-a-port!' Now for the waiting game; and were they acoustic or the old contact? He saw a torpedo break the surface, porpoise out of control and squirm away to the east, well abaft the stern. Three to go. *Brackendale* leaned hard over to starboard, straining to turn and Thorburn squeezed the bridge-rail willing her on. The forward turret fell silent, unable to target the northern flotilla as the ship twisted south. The quarterdeck was still in contact banging a fusillade of shells towards England. Two of the three remaining torpedoes passed astern but the third looked as if it would hit beneath the depth charge rails. Thorburn bit his bottom lip and prayed.

Brackendale took a jarring hit to the stern side plates, the force of it felt on the bridge. But the torpedo bounced and turned, the propellers driving it toward the stern, the detonator still intact, inert.

Thorburn closed his eyes, released his grip on the bridge-rail. A dud. The chance in a million failure, and *Brackendale*'s nine lives had saved them yet again. He checked on the compass. The ship was swinging through 360 degrees. 'Midships. Half ahead. Revs for twenty knots.'

The Cox'n acknowledged, his voice far away.

'Ship! Bearing, Green-one-oh,' a lookout called, and Thorburn hurried to the starboard wing. Fresh starshell arced into the sky and the stranger's forward guns flashed into action. Tracer criss-crossed the waves, east to west beyond *Brackendale*'s bows and he watched as the flotilla of E-boats scattered.

On the bridge of H.M.S. *Rosefinch*, Willoughby picked out the flash of guns, squinted under the glare of a starshell and ordered an increase in speed. His binoculars found the distant silhouette of a Hunt class destroyer turning west away from the convoys, her main armament spitting flame. In the light of the flare he spotted the E-boats attacking up from the south. Lines of tracer swept into the destroyer's upperworks and she answered with Pompoms and Oerlikons.

'Bridge . . Radar!'

'Bridge,' Willoughby confirmed.

'Fast moving echoes at Green twenty. Range two-thousand, course one-nine-oh.'

Willoughby glanced into the darkness beyond the starboard bow, guessing it was another pack of E-boats. He grabbed a handset. 'Guns? What can you see at Green twenty?'

There was a pause as the Range Finder Director traversed to the right, fine over the starboard bow.

'E-boats, sir. Four . . . , no, five. Thirty plus knots, heading for that destroyer.

Willoughby reacted. 'Let's have a look, Guns. Starshell if you please.'

Moments later one of the four-inch in 'A' turret banged out a shell to the heavens and the brilliance of the incandescent flare turned black night to day and the charging E-boats lay exposed to their guns, caught unawares. 'Open fire!'

The four barrels in 'A' and 'B' turrets ripped out a salvo, and two of the twin barrelled Oerlikons joined the fray.

20 Open Fire

Willoughby had his glasses trained on the small destroyer, trying to fathom out who he was assisting. His forward guns crashed out again. An E-boat disintegrated, a fiery flash on the water. Now the sea was aglow with the light of starshell, nothing left to hide. 'Signaller!' he called. 'Challenge that destroyer.'

A hand held Aldis lamp flicked a beam over the waves. There was an instant pulse of light in return, too quick for Willoughby to read. The signaller shuttered the acknowledgement. 'H.M.S. *Brackendale*, sir.'

Willoughby let his binoculars drop on the strap. For a split second he smiled, shook his head in disbelief. *Brackendale*. A ghost from the past, a name to be savoured. A survivor.

'E-boat turning to starboard!' a lookout shouted.

Willoughby responded. 'Port twenty.' He wasn't about to let *Rosefinch* get sandwiched by the enemy. She heeled under helm, heading for the convoys before he brought her back under control. 'Midships . . . , steady, steer, one-seven-oh. When he looked again all the E-boats were concentrated to his right. More starshells flamed bright and the six-barrelled Pompom thumped into action. A torrent of shells erupted from his guns, round after round raking the fast moving boats. A twin Oerlikon bracketed the lead boat, orange tracer biting at the cockpit. The power boat skidded sideways, bounced into the air and somersaulted backwards. The upturned hull glistened in the swaying lights. Twenty millimetre shells punched holes in the keel before the Oerlikon went after another target.

Bullets lashed the quarterdeck and hammered at the turret of 'Y' gun. Men were caught by flying splinters, cut by ricochets, died. Blood flowed under their feet.

An E-boat launched both torpedoes and slewed away, racing for safety, attack complete. The sea around it erupted, a flurry of shells chasing the fleeing shape.

Willoughby sensed the danger. 'Hard-a-starboard!' The warship leaned wickedly, changed course rapidly, pounding into the waves. He caught a momentary glimpse of the phosphorescent wake careering towards the stern. 'Midships! Steady!' *Rosefinch* straightened and the torpedoes slid past the stern. Willoughby pushed his cap back and gave a low whistle. Touch and go.

Hidden at the outer circle of the starshell's light, one of the Schnellboats had wriggled south, undetected. Werner von Holtzmann clung to the cockpit's control panel and narrowed his eyes in grim determination. The boat was bouncing on the limit, veering from side to side, stability on a knife edge. But the starshell had served a dual purpose, heaven sent for the defenders but also perfect for the attacker. And Holtzmann wasn't going to give this one up. He was fast approaching the best solution, a thousand metres on the destroyers port bow.

He spat out the last of the chewed cigar. 'Ready, Lieutnant?

'Jawohl, Herr Kapitän.'

Leading Seaman Allun Jones was stood at the port bridge-wing quartering his sector of watch through the binoculars. A lustrous white bow wave whipped past the lens and he inched back to check what he'd seen. An E-boat powering in to the attack.

He screamed a warning. 'E-boat on the port bow! Range, one-thousand!'

The shout was so loud McDonald heard it in the Range Finder and swung the forward guns onto the target. The four-inch barrels steadied, there was a moment's pause and with an explosive roar they hurled a pair of shells across the waves. One missed short in a plume of spray. The other struck the sharp stem and detonated, tearing the vessel into oblivion. For those aboard death was instantaneous. FlotillaKapitän Werner von Holtzman perished in a seething inferno, obliterated.

Thorburn looked over at Armstrong and grinned, a broad reckless show of teeth. 'Bloody marvellous,' he said. 'Bloody marvellous.'

The U-boat had lost the battle to maintain buoyancy. While the battle raged overhead, Kurt Schneider cursed in anger. They were steadily sinking, and the deeper they went the more the pressure opened up the tear in the hull. The Chief had done his best but the power of the incoming water had beaten them and Schneider knew it was only a matter of time. With the sea water in the batteries the fumes would kill them anyway and he was determined not to die in vain. If he went to full power and blew the ballast tanks they could still make it to the surface. It might give him one last chance to take the Englander with him. The forward tubes had two 'eels' remaining. Mind made up Schneider unclipped the microphone and spoke to the entire crew.

'Men of the Grey Shark,' he began. 'We have failed to stem the leak, there is too much damage. If we do not surface then we perish in the depths. Our family and friends will soon be lost to the enemy but I will not give up without a fight. If we must die then let us die in battle. We can still take some of them with us.' He raised his voice. 'Are you with me?'

A loud chorus of shouts and cheers greeted his announcement, full of bravado, together in death.

'So be it. Man your stations!' He turned to his First Officer and gave the order.

'Surface the boat. Blow tanks. Full ahead! Steer north.'

Around the control room the men's faces turned in his direction. He knew what it was. He'd just signed their death warrant. Resigned to their fate the men returned to the wheels and the gauges. Some hoped they might survive, make it out onto the deck, get clear before the charges detonated. If they were lucky. U-boat crews were seldom lucky; too many lives had been lost to think anything but.

The hiss of air accompanied the needle swinging up in the depthgauge, the compass turning slowly as the bows came round to the north. Schneider prepared to go topside. 'Gunners! Stand by.' He clamped his teeth, steeled himself for the onslaught. All he asked was time enough for one attempt.

The boat hit the surface in a seething mass of foam. The bows reared up clear of the water, then returned with a crash, and Schneider lost his grip on the ladder. He clamped a hand on a rung and hauled himself up to the hatch. Braced inside the conning tower he heaved up against the surge of water and flung himself out.

'Engage the diesels!'

Over the forward bulwark two warships turned across his path, heading west. The forward hatch sprang open and his gunners poured on deck, the glint of ammunition as they cleared the gun and opened the breech. On the anti-aircraft platform behind him the pair of twin machine-guns prepared for action. He called down to the control room. 'Make your course two-nine-oh.' Knifing through the waves the grey shark swung to the left and the diesels drove them on. Schneider concentrated on the nearest ship, the small destroyer. That was the one which had water bombed him. He wanted revenge.

'Deck gun ready, Herr Kapitän,' a crewman shouted and Schneider nodded his approval.

'Tubes three and four stand by for firing on the surface!' he ordered, controlling his voice. He must ensure the men didn't panic, understood his commands.

The torpedo room replied. 'Tubes three and four flooded. Ready for firing.'

Schneider clarified his orders. 'I will take command of the firing, from the bridge. No offset. I want them to run true.'

An Oerlikon on the destroyer began to pump shells at them.

'Open fire!' he yelled, and the deck gun recoiled with a bang.

'U-boat on the surface. Red one-hundred!'

Thorburn lunged across to the port wing. He saw it immediately. A small, swaying tube of conning tower, a forward deck all but covered by the foaming waves. He could see it turning to port, cutting the angle to *Brackendale*'s course, positioning for a torpedo strike. But it was on the surface and Thorburn wasn't about to pass up the invitation.

'Number One. Tell Guns to open fire.' He moved to the voice-pipe. 'Hard-a-port.' He needed maximum turning power. 'Full ahead starboard engine. Stop port.'

The Cox'n's reply was lost in the noise of the Oerlikon hammering into action. *Brackendale* leaned out, commencing her turn in towards the U-boat. An orange flash from the U-boat and Thorburn hunched his shoulders. The armour piercing shell struck high on the forward turret, ripped through the thin steel and flew harmlessly out the other side.

267

Below the waterline in the engine room, Bryn Dawkins saw the telegraphs ring up the two variables on the drive shafts, and broke the port beam and maximised the output of the starboard propeller. He peered at the spinning shaft, could feel the extraordinary vibration, and prayed it would hold together. Should he ignore the call for maximum revolutions and decelerate, even by a few rpm? But the Captain was relying on the ship's machinery, fighting for survival. Dawkins was in no position to overrule the command. He wiped the sweat from his worried face and stared in anguish.

And then, in the space of a millisecond, a shrieking squeal of tortured steel pierced the noise of the engine room, and the shaft shuddered to a grinding halt. Smoke swirled up from the main drive coupling and Dawkins slapped the emergency cut-out. He reached for the other lever, brought the clutch into play and engaged the port shaft. Better to have at least one working. He grabbed the handset on the bulkhead and called the bridge.

The First Lieutenant answered, well aware something was wrong. 'What happened, Chief?'

'We've lost the starboard shaft, permanently. I've engaged the port for now but you'll only have half revs.' Dawkins heard him pass the message, and then it was Thorburn's speaking. 'Do what you can, Chief. It's a bit busy up here.'

Dawkins grimaced, knowing it was futile. There'd be nothing he could do to help, but he didn't need to admit it. 'Aye aye, sir,' he said, sounding full of confidence. 'I'll do my best.' The connection ended and he turned his attention to the needs of the moment. The smoke had cleared a little and he crossed to the offending article. In all his years at sea he'd never lost a propeller; just his luck it had to happen now.

On the bridge, Thorburn recognised the slackening of the turn, the port engine opposing the helm. *Brackendale* had only come round ten degrees and although still turning, it was wide, slow. The main armament exploded into action, the four-inch barrels blasting out a salvo, straddling the U-boat's low profile. The Pompom pumped a steady stream of two pound shells across the void, high velocity projectiles forming a curtain of steel.

The deck gun on the submarine fired again, another 88 millimetre round whipping over the waves. It blew up in the fo'c'sle and started a fire. Bullets sprayed around the bridge and Thorburn ducked. He straightened enough to peer over the bridge-screen, trying to gauge the turn, watching the U-boat take up an ideal position. Eight hundred yards, he judged, unavoidable at this speed. *Brackendale*'s guns fired from every mounting and yet nothing seemed to stop that boat.

Schneider spat salt water and blinked through the sheets of foam enveloping the tower. Fountains of spray danced from the sea, every enemy salvo leaving its mark. Small calibre stuff ricocheted and whined from the steelwork, tearing holes as bullets punched in from the destroyer. He saw the ship begin to turn, reducing her profile, making for a difficult strike. And then for some reason the turn loosened, taking a much wider arc. He held his breath checking through the darkness. A starshell blossomed, fired from the second warship hidden by the destroyer, and night changed to day, glaringly bright. The deck gun spat flame, began a reload. A British shell detonated on the deck casing, blew the gun to fragments. The men were slaughtered; cart wheeled into the sea, cauterised and drowned, gone in an instant.

A shell from the Oerlikon smacked the periscope, deflected off and ripped into Schneider's stomach, driving down to his pelvis. He screamed with agony, fell against the bulwark and saw his blood run red. Pain wracked his body, unbelievable torture, and he'd been so close to winning. He forced a hand to the rim of the tower, dragged himself upright, no feeling in one leg. The destroyer was still across his bow and he made a last desperate effort. He shouted. 'Tube three. . Fire! Tube four. . Fire!' He hung on, blood haemorrhaging from his mouth. In the dazzling glare of the starshell he caught a glimpse of bubbling wake. His 'eels' were free, out to kill.

He clung on through the pain, grimly determined to see the end. A shell hit the waves, shrapnel flaying the saddle-tanks. A machine-gunner screamed, sliced by a fragment, left arm torn away. The conning tower rattled to a hail of bullets, chewed at the attack periscope and left it dangling by a splintered shard.

Schneider hung by an arm, light headed, eyes glazing from lack of blood. With an enormous effort he forced himself to watch. Any moment now.

Unknown to all those on board the small destroyer, the U-boat's final torpedo slid harmlessly beneath the keel, a failed guidance system pushing it ever deeper. Thorburn raised his binoculars, found the U-boat and focused on the conning tower. A man's head appeared, a peaked cap slanted over his forehead. A bloodied hand clung to the steel lip, his face contorted in pain. Thorburn tracked the flash of bullets as they struck the panels. Lines of tracer hunted along the U-boat's deck, punching at the plates.

The enemy returned fire, machine-guns hammering at *Brackendale*'s bridge. A stream of tracer whipped in and raked the upperworks. Sparks flew, bullets ricocheting off stanchions, punching ragged holes in the fragile steel. A section of glass starred, shattered, and Thorburn flinched below the lethal shards.

He straightened for the voice-pipes. A bullet smashed across his forehead and gashed his temple. He staggered from the hit, buckled at the knees, shocked by the impact. A searing shaft of agony burned his scalp. He scrabbled for a hand hold and dragged himself upright. Blood flowed freely down his cheek, warm and wet, soaking his collar. His cap was gone and he searched aimlessly on the deck to find it. A voice came from far away, disjointed, a strange echo.

'Sir!'

He looked up, disorientated. A hand grabbed his elbow and a grim faced Yeoman met his eyes. 'Alright, sir?'

Thorburn squinted in an attempt to clear his blurred vision. He bared his teeth against the blinding pain and shook his head. It helped. 'Thank you, I'll manage.' *Brackendale* lurched and he swayed, steadied himself on the compass binnacle.

The Yeoman nudged him, holding out the Captain's cap. Thorburn nodded briefly and gently balanced it on the back of his head. Feeling for the wound he touched the sticky mess and wiped blood on his jacket.

Thorburn cursed his luck, not at his own misfortune but at *Brackendale*'s lack of agility, her inability to sharpen the turn. The forward guns bellowed, thumping shells at the elusive target. The hanging flare swayed lower, dimmed. This might be his last throw of the dice.

21 Vengeance

Thorburn blinked, blood trickling into his eyes; the pain was intense, throbbing at the side of his head.

'U-boat turning towards the stern!'

Thorburn looked quickly. It was Jones, glasses still trained on the enemy. A starshell burst bright, hung on the wind, and Thorburn again caught sight of the ugly shape, the hated grey shark reflecting off the conning tower. It was swinging round, running parallel down *Brackendale*'s port beam. The quadruple Pompom had it over open sights, a constant stream of shells whipping across the waves. At the same time he realised the quarterdeck four-inch couldn't engage, unable to depress low enough. The situation called for something more and he wracked his wounded brain to come up with a solution. *Brackendale* corkscrewed awkwardly, beam on to the westerly wind. The movement caught him unawares, made him lean out over the port wing looking down the length of the ship. And he spotted a possible answer to his prayers.

He lifted the telephone to the depth charge station.

'Yes, sir?' came a shout over the noise of the guns.

'Mr Labatt. One depth charge, port thrower. Set for shallow. Quick as you can.'

'Aye aye, sir!'

Thorburn wrinkled his brow, desperate to think straight, eyes glued to the U-boat's continued progress, steadily turning into an ideal position for the thrower, forty or so yards. He leaned out again staring aft beyond the four-inch barrels, and two men appeared at the launcher. He saw a hand reach for the firing pistol, a thud of explosive, and the canister curved into the air. A high elegant arc, then a splash off the U-boat's portside, descending below the waves.

Thorburn waited, watched, held his breath. The depth charge exploded, muffled, and erupted in a seething column of foaming spray. The shock wave lifted the U-boat's stern, the conning tower reeling sideways, the saddle tanks exposed, the ugly belly of the shark. Abaft the conning tower the machine-gunners plunged into the sea, a tumbling cartwheel of arms and legs. Gallons of water poured into the open hatches adding weight to the dive, driving the boat into the depths. Thorburn watched the image on the conning tower, the light grey of the shark, as it succumbed to the waves. Two spinning propellers glinted and were gone, the sea closing in behind. A pair of gunners were sucked to their deaths, drowned in the powerful turbulence. A bubble of oil belched to the surface, swirled in the vortex, smoothed and settled. The starshell faded, darkness prevailed, and an unseen figure lifted on the swell.

Kapitänleutnant Kurt Schneider was dead before he surfaced. His lifeless body rolled and twisted, and finally, face down in the grimy oil, he vanished in the waves.

For a precious moment, Thorburn allowed himself a grim smile of victory. The *Glasgow Bay* had been avenged and he hoped Edward Fitzpatrick would be satisfied. On the quarterdeck, the crew yelled and cheered and Thorburn wasn't about to intervene. They deserved it. As for himself, it had taken him three attempts before he'd managed to sink a bloody U-boat.

Time to check for survivors, easier to turn away and come round with the port propeller's assistance. 'Starboard thirty. Full ahead port.'

'Starboard thirty. Full ahead port. Aye aye, sir.'

And Thorburn felt *Brackendale* heel over, only a little, but she definitely leaned. She described a fairly tight curve and it was good to know the old girl could still respond. Ploughing round to the south a lookout called a warning. 'Debris off the starboard bow.'

'Midships,' Thorburn ordered, and *Brackendale* swung up onto an even keel. The ship was running parallel to the sinking and he gauged they were a hundred or so yards to the east.

An enormous collision rocked the ship and *Brackendale* staggered under the force. They'd struck something very solid. The watertight compartment beneath the forepeak took the brunt of the impact. The fo'c'sle heaved upwards grinding and splintering. The small destroyer groaned under the strain, ripping joints, tearing rivets. She lurched drunkenly, almost stopped, her stern lifting. Thorburn was thrown off his feet into the port corner of the forebridge. His right kneecap hit a steel panel, a stab of pain jolting through his thigh. Pulling himself to his feet he limped heavily to the engine room voice-pipe and waited for Dawkins to answer.

'Chief?'

'Yes, sir?'

'Stop engine. I'll get back to you.'

'Aye aye, sir.'

'U-boat along the starboard side!'

Thorburn jumped for bridge-wing. Half submerged, the submarine scraped and banged along the side plates. The moonlight glinted off the torn saddle tanks, a long open scar cut deep into the pressure hull. As the weight of water surged through the gaping wound the U-boat dissolved beneath the waves, and finally, the Grey Shark sank to the depths.

But no time for self congratulation, *Brackendale* needed his attention. She was nose down, stable for the moment, holding their own. The question was, for how long?

'Number One, the forward bulkheads!'

Armstrong had already begun to move. 'Damage Control to the boat deck!' he yelled, and slid down the ladder. Uppermost in his mind were casualties. How many had been caught below? What would they find at the bulkhead? Were the watertight doors capable of withstanding that kind of damage? Within a couple of minutes the men had gathered by the ship's motorboat. They stood quietly, waiting for orders, ready to apply well rehearsed procedures.

'Right lads, here we go.' He led off through the bridge superstructure and down below to the forward bulkhead passage. He walked along what should have been a level platform but the weight of water made for an obvious tilt down to the bows. He frowned, at least the electrical circuits still functioned, enough light to see where they were treading. Even so, he switched on his torch, the powerful beam slicing through the background glow. Down here, in the quietness below decks the sounds emanating from ahead were not encouraging. Strange creaks of tortured steel and the heavy slap of water.

The searching beam of his torch found the main bulkhead, the main division between the fo'c'sle and the waist of the ship. The men bunched behind him, aware of the danger and how quickly the steel might give way. He moved the torch to the watertight door and the locking lever in the middle. He followed the rim looking for the slightest leak. He thought there was a dampness, took a pace forward and rubbed a finger on the joint. Relief to find it was just discoloured paint. He listened, eyes closed, straining to hear any signs of life beyond the steel panels. And then the lever moved, swung to the open position and Petty Officer 'Ginger' Peterson stood on the far side of the coaming. 'Glad you're here, sir. Got some strange noises coming from beyond the forward bulkhead.'

Armstrong nodded with relief. The men in the forward magazine had survived, no flooding in there. 'We'll see to it,' he said, and led them on through the bosun's storage to the bulkhead of the bow compartments. He carefully checked where the bulkhead met the ship's side and up at the deckhead. The central panel above the door showed signs of warping, a convex dome, as if struck by a giant sledgehammer. From beyond the door came the sound of gurgling water and the screech of tearing steel. There were no leaks, not even a trickle. She'd always been a tough old girl, but after such a powerful collision, he was amazed by how strong she was.

'I want a man to watch this. Any volunteers?' He was asking a lot. It could have been an order but he chose to ask. If the bulkhead or the door gave way . . . , well, there might be a warning, there might not.

'I don't have anything planned, sir.'

Armstrong looked over their heads to see Leading Seaman Carrick with a half raised hand. He was a Liverpudlian, six years in the Navy, three with *Brackendale*, and as reliable as a man could wish for.

'Well done, Carrick. Torch working?'

'Yes, sir.'

'Good. Let the bridge know the minute you see a leak.'

'Aye aye, sir.'

Armstrong nodded, meeting his eyes. 'Right, the rest of you with me.' He checked on the men in the magazine, shaken but visibly relieved to be still in one piece. He told Peterson the bulkhead was holding and left them to it. The passage had become steeper, forcing them to lean in as they made for the main deck. Petty Officer Rawlings met them at the bottom of the ladder and Armstrong handed him the torch. 'Check on casualties first then do a visual of the fo'c'sle. And no heroics, we don't want to lose anyone.'

'Aye aye, sir,' Rawlings said, and led the men up the ladder.

Armstrong made it back to the bridge and reported. 'Forward bulkhead holding, sir. Damage Control are checking the fo'c'sle.'

'Casualties?'

'Nothing reported as yet, sir.'

'Right,' Thorburn said, and Armstrong watched him struggling with his thoughts.

'Who's looking after the bulkhead?' he asked suddenly.

Armstrong reacted. 'Carrick, sir. Leading Seaman, good man.'

'Very well. Let him know I intend getting under way. Have the Bosun join him. We'll try very slow ahead, see what happens.'

Armstrong nodded. 'I'll pass the word, sir.'

Thorburn peered at him in the darkness, then turned to the bank of voice-pipes. Armstrong heard him speak, subdued, a small break in his voice. 'We're going to try and get her home, Number One. Just once more.

Lieutenant-Commander Peter Willoughby stood in the darkness of *Rosefinch*'s bridge and with both hands cupped to the voice-pipe he called down to the wheelhouse. 'Slow ahead, both.'

Over the port side he could just determine the stricken outline of *Brackendale*'s silhouette. The bows were low in the water the fo'c'sle angled forward. It left the stern sitting higher than normal but the propellers underneath the surface. He wondered what had happened, whether she was actually sinking or somehow managing to keep herself afloat.

'Port five,' he ordered. That would bring *Rosefinch* in alongside *Brackendale*'s starboard beam. They might need to transfer some of the crew. 'Number One, get the searchlight on her fo'c'sle. Let's see what's going on.'

'Aye aye, sir.'

Moments later the powerful beam of light flashed over the forward plates of the small destroyer. The water was halfway up the bow plates.

'Starboard five. Stop engines.' He was taking a chance, but they'd destroyed the E-boats and the Asdic was clear, only the convoys to the east showing up on Radar.

Rosefinch swung in slowly, a ship's width between them. He called across the gap. 'Hello, *Brackendale*! Who's in charge?'

After a short pause he got his answer. 'Commander Thorburn!'

Willoughby wasn't sure he'd heard right. 'Say again,' he yelled.

'Lieutenant-Commander Richard Thorburn.'

Willoughby shook his head and cleared his throat, grinning. 'This is His Majesty's Ship, *Rosefinch*. Lieutenant-Commander Peter Willoughby at your service, sir.'

There was a prolonged silence as the two warships wallowed unevenly in the choppy seas. From the peripheral glow of the searchlight he saw a figure come to the destroyer's bridge-wing.

'Small world, Peter. We keep meeting like this and they'll start talking about it. What brings you this way?'

That was the confirmation Willoughby needed, the sound of a voice he knew so well. 'Just happened to be passing. Need a hand?' He chuckled to himself. What were the chances of the two of them meeting again under these circumstances? Entirely opposite to their last encounter. Then, it had been his old ship *Veracity*, torpedoed and sunk by an E-boat, and Richard had performed the rescue. Looked like he was about to be able to repay the compliment.

'Not sure yet. Bloody U-boat resurfaced somehow and we collided. Damaged the bows, but the bulkhead's holding and we've just started the pumps. I was about to try and get under way.'

Willoughby gave that the dignity it deserved. Nonetheless he wasn't going to leave *Brackendale* to her own devices. 'Right, I'll get out the way. Give you a bit of room.' He turned away. 'Number One, kill that searchlight.' Darkness returned and he leaned to the voice-pipes. 'Slow ahead. Starboard ten.'

Rosefinch eased out from *Brackendale*'s side and Willoughby squinted at the inky night. He spoke to everyone within earshot. 'I want everyone on their toes. We don't want to be caught unawares. And that goes for you lookouts especially. Number One, check the Asdic, make certain it works. We'll be a pair of sitting ducks and I want good warning.'

'Aye aye, sir,' the First Officer said, and they settled down to watch and wait.

Richard Thorburn was having difficulty coming to terms with the situation. *Brackendale* was still afloat and he was determined to get home, if he could. His people deserved that much. And Willoughby wouldn't leave them, that he could be sure of. He glanced up at the White Ensign rippling in the breeze. In all the time *Brackendale* had sailed under that flag, she'd never totally succumbed to the enemy's fire. But now she needed all his help and he wasn't about to let her down.

He picked up the handset for the engine room.

The Welshman was quick to answer. 'Dawkins.'

'Hello, Chief. Captain here.'

'Yes, sir?'

'We rammed the U-boat and we have serious damage to the bows, we're not even sure how much. The forward bulkhead seems to be holding so I'm going to try and get her home. Can you give me a few revs on the port shaft?'

Dawkins seemed to be thinking as he spoke. 'Well, we've still got steam . . . , and the port propeller might give us enough thrust. Depends on the damage, sir. Whether we can steer against the drag. Push comes to shove, we might do better going in reverse.'

Thorburn winced. It wasn't quite the image he had in mind. 'I think I'd prefer going ahead if possible, Chief. Let's give it a try, maybe five or six knots, and obey the telegraph. I know you'll have your hands full, so could you leave somebody on the telephone, just in case?'

'Aye aye, sir. Of course.' There was a few seconds silence. 'I'm sure we'll manage.'

Thorburn nodded in the darkness. 'Yes, Chief. I think we will.'

A weakness in his limbs made him grope for the chair. He took a moment to recover, regain his composure. The wound was worse than he thought and he couldn't shake the feeling of nausea. He knew it was shock, the damaged nerves ends translating into waves of pain. And he was still losing blood, continuously weeping down the side of his cheek. He took hold of himself and gulped in a lungful of sea air. It steadied his pulse rate, took away the sickness.

Rising slowly to his feet, he tested his weight on the damaged kneecap. There was a niggling twinge but he found it was stable.

Brackendale rose and fell sluggishly, her starboard plates caught in the westerly seas. The waves had pushed her round to the south and Thorburn limped to the bank of voice-pipes. He bent to a tube.

'Who's on the wheel?'

'Cox'n, sir.'

Thorburn furrowed his brow, squinting into the darkness. 'Every thing all right down there?'

'I think so, sir. I can still feel a response to the wheel.'

'Good,' Thorburn said. 'Now listen, Cox'n. I'm going to try and get the old girl moving. The starboard shaft is out of action. The bulkhead is holding fast at the moment so I've had a word with Mr Dawkins and we'll try for five or six knots to start with. We'll use the telegraph but I might overrule that by phone. Afraid you could be pretty busy on the helm.'

'Aye aye, sir. Understood.'

'Very well.' Thorburn paused, looked around the dark bridge, the fitful gleam of the moon highlighting the outline of the watch keepers. 'Slow ahead port'

'Slow ahead port. Aye aye, sir.'

Thorburn heard the ring of the telegraph and waited. He felt the almost imperceptible turn of the single screw, high in the water, biting for purchase. A subtle change in the ship's attitude as she slowly pushed ahead. *Brackendale* began to make tangible headway and Thorburn wondered about the bulkhead. He cursed in annoyance. He should have had a messenger to bring news, and it was a bad mistake. But he could rectify his error.

He squinted through the gloom to the back of the bridge and found a signalman waiting for orders. 'Get yourself down to the forward bulkhead and let me know what's happening.'

The man disappeared from sight and again he waited. At least the ship was moving, the next problem was the steering.

A minute later the signalman reappeared out of breath. 'Bulkhead holding, sir,' he panted. 'No sign of a leak.'

'Well done. Now get yourself back down the bottom of that ladder and let them know you're there. They can shout if need be.'

'Aye aye, sir,' and he was gone.

Thorburn put a hand to his head, feeling unsteady. He forced himself to concentrate, glanced at the compass. The ship was facing almost due south. Now for a change of course. Take her starboard, round to the west, away from the invasion fleet, and if all went well he would complete the turn by heading north. He put his mouth down to the voice-pipe. 'Cox'n!'

'Sir?'

'We'll try a change of course. I want to come round to two-seven-oh. Give me starboard five on the wheel and let's see how she takes it.'

'Starboard five, aye aye, sir.'

Brackendale floundered. What remained of her bows took the weight of breaking foam, surging unevenly down the distorted sides. Without the cutting edge of her stem, the bluntness of the distorted plates pushed randomly through the waves. The compass began to revolve, little by little, half a degree, swinging awkwardly . . . , two degrees.

Thorburn was transfixed, eyes glued to the dial. The pain in his head receded and he even managed a weak smile. *Brackendale* was answering the call, through ten degrees. He looked up over the broken screen. To the north across the starboard beam he could see the vague outline of *Rosefinch* standing clear and he guessed Willoughby was watching anxiously, waiting to lend a hand. *Brackendale*'s quarterdeck lifted to a swell and the ship rode lengthwise over the long wave, corkscrewed slightly and settled down on even keel. When Thorburn looked again the compass showed the bearing as two-seven-five degrees, a fraction north of west.

He bent to the voice-pipe. 'Well done, Cox'n. Hold her on five. Might not be so easy now, we'll have the weather on the port beam.'

'Aye aye, sir. Starboard five of the wheel on.'

Slowly, very slowly, *Brackendale* fought her way round to the north. She lurched sideways with every wave that hit her port beam. One moment she was turning, the next she was thrown off course; to begin the turn all over again. But with the single propeller driving her on, and the Cox'n battling to bring her round, Thorburn eventually, gratefully, bent to the pipe. 'Midships . . . , steady.'

'Wheel's amidships . . . Course, three-five-eight degrees, sir.'

'Nice work, Cox'n. Maintain heading: anywhere within a few degrees of north.'

'Aye aye, sir. Bit wobbly, but manageable.'

Thorburn grimaced, almost smiled. Sometimes the Cox'n had a rather pertinent turn of phrase. He straightened and reached out for the chair. He leaned on the back not trusting himself with the comfort of the seat. He might not get back up.

'Yeoman,' he called to the flag deck. 'Make to *Rosefinch*, "I have one shaft turning and steering under control. Will try to increase speed," and get me someone from the wireless room.'

The hand held night lamp flicked into action and he waited while *Rosefinch* made her reply.

'Message from *Rosefinch*, sir. Reads, "Will act as escort until Saint Catherine's Point. Am standing by. Good luck." End of message, sir.'

Thorburn climbed weakly into the chair. 'Reply, "Will try not to take too long. Thank you." And then you can take a signal for the W/T office.'

'Sorry, sir, but the wireless room is out of action.' As the Yeoman gave him that unwelcome piece of news he flashed Thorburn's reply over to *Rosefinch*. There was a brief flicker of acknowledgement.

'What's the problem?' Thorburn allowed his chin to rest on his chest.

'Shrapnel, sir. Took out the equipment.'

Thorburn mumbled. 'Very well.' He was almost at the point of not caring. No radar, no wireless, bows buckled, all he wanted was to rest. He sat for some time before Armstrong climbed up to the bridge and saw him slumped forward, fresh blood glistening on his face.

'Sir?' he queried quietly, and when there was no response he called to the nearest person. 'Get the Doctor, now!' And made the situation clear. 'I have the bridge.'

In Portsmouth's busy dockyard, in the brightly lit offices behind the heavy drapes of blackout, First Officer Jennifer Farbrace turned into the corridor outside her office and then heard the insistent ring of the telephone. With an exaggerated long drawn out sigh she hesitated. It had been a long day. From the moment the first of the dawn landings had begun a constant flow of signals and messages had poured into Pendleton's office. It was late now and she was tired. Balancing the sheaf of files in the crook of her arm she craned her neck to glance at her wristwatch. An hour till midnight.

The strident ring of the phone dragged her back to the office and with her free hand she picked up the receiver.

'Pendleton's office.'

'Signal for the Commodore,' came the reply.

Jennifer dropped the bundle of paperwork and reached for her notepad. 'Go ahead.'

The signalman cleared his throat. 'Message reads, "From HMS *Rosefinch*. *Brackendale* severely damaged. Limited power and steering. Will stand by as escort." Message ends.'

Jennifer stared at her scribbled notes, not wanting to believe what she'd written.

'Did you get that, Ma'am?'

She struggled to answer. 'Yes . . . , yes, I've got it. Any news on casualties?'

'No Ma'am.'

'Did you get a position?'

There was the faint sound of paper being shuffled. 'Thirty-five miles north of Cherbourg.'

'Thank you,' she muttered, and slowly replaced the receiver. With one hand on the desk for support she swivelled into her chair, still clutching the notepad. Her mind raced. Thirty-five miles north of Cherbourg, in other words, seventy odd miles to safety. Could *Brackendale* really manage that sort of distance? No word on casualties. What about Richard?'

She suddenly felt sick, her heart pounding, hands clammy. If only she'd gone home earlier or someone else had taken the message. By morning the worst would have been over. *Brackendale* either safe in harbour, or not. But she knew that for her there'd be no going home now, far better to keep busy, stay in touch. Pendleton wouldn't be in the office before six o'clock and there was no point in disturbing him. There was nothing anyone could do except wait.

She loosened her tie and unbuttoned the collar of her blouse. The nausea eased and her heart stopped thumping. She rose from the chair and walked into the small kitchen, poured herself a glass of water and took a few sips. Regaining some of her composure, she adjusted her collar and tie, and took another swallow. The telephone rang. She almost ran back to the desk and snatched up the receiver.

'Yes?'

'Signal, Ma'am. Third troopship convoy for Utah taking station twelve miles south of St Catherine's Point.'

For a moment Jennifer just stared vacantly at the office door before realising it was an update on Operation Neptune.

'Thank you.' Dropping the handset on the cradle she gathered up the forgotten files and made for the corridor. As she headed for the typing pool she wondered how many more times that damned phone would ring before she heard whether Richard had survived. She straightened her back, tossed her head to settle the strands of wayward hair, and strode into the room full of typists.

'Hi, Jenny. Busy night?' Linda girl was smiling brightly, bobbed hair, sparkling eyes. She hit the typewriter carriage and the bell tinkled as it returned to the start.

Jennifer forced a smile and nodded. 'Hectic,' she answered lightly, and stacked the manila files onto the 'In' table. No one glimpsed the anguish, her hidden fear inside. She managed a relaxed smile and turned away for Pendleton's office. As they always said, worse things happened at sea. Just for once she desperately hoped they were wrong.

Lieutenant-Commander Richard Thorburn regained consciousness just as Doc Waverley ordered two sick berth attendants to bring a stretcher. His head throbbed and he screwed up his face against the pain. 'No, forget it, Doc. I'm not leaving the bridge.'

Waverley controlled his obvious annoyance. 'Sir, I cannot be held responsible if you won't allow me to tend to you in the sick bay.

Thorburn shot him a weak smile. 'Sorry, Doc, have to countermand that order. Patch me up the best you can, I won't tell anybody.' He smiled again.

Waverley snorted in disgust and turned to Armstrong for support. 'Number One, can't you talk some sense into him?'

Armstrong made an exaggerated pretence of thinking it over and slowly shook his head. 'No, Doc. Not my place to interfere.'

Waverley stood for a moment and then accepted the inevitable. 'Get me a light here,' he snapped, and delved inside his medical case.

In the dim light of a shaded torch, muttering and moaning about a Captain's all pervading dictatorship, he cleaned and dressed the wound, insisted Thorburn take two pills, and stormed off the bridge still muttering under his breathe.

Thorburn turned to Armstrong and grimaced. 'Thank you, Number One. You have my undying gratitude.' He stood up from the chair and waited for his head to stop aching and stepped forward to the bridge-screen. 'How's the bulkhead?'

'Holding, sir. Mr Dawkins has been to inspect it. Keeping a close eye on the seams.'

'And do you have a report on the casualties?'

Armstrong hesitated before speaking. 'Six wounded, all in the sick berth.'

Thorburn stared down at the bows. Beyond that there were only the waves and the strange pattern of curling foam breaking against the misshapen plates. Six wounded, a lot to have out of action. Men who were just performing their duty, but vitally important duties, feeding the guns, fighting the ship. They were husbands and sons, brothers and dads, and their families would be waiting for news, hoping and praying they were all well.

He straightened from the screen, clearing his mind. There were things to be taken care of; they weren't yet out of danger. He took a pace closer to Armstrong and lowered his voice. 'I suggest we clear the ship's boats, have them ready in the falls. And the Carley floats, too. Make sure they're all available. And where's *Rosefinch*?'

'Standing off the starboard quarter, sir. Commander Willoughby's on the bridge.'

Thorburn cast a glance that way and caught the faint shimmer of the bow wave. 'Very well, carry on.'

Thorburn levered himself out of the bridge-chair and stepped up to the shattered screen. With the coming of daylight, St Catherine's Point appeared dead ahead, shrouded in a mist of breaking surf. He gripped the rail and straightened to his full height. He'd managed to snatch a short break and make himself look reasonably presentable. Washed off the worst of the blood and changed into his shore-going jacket. His cap sat somewhat precariously on one side, Doc's dressing giving him a rather piratical appearance. The worst of the pain had gone leaving a permanent ache. The knee was a different matter, tender and swollen.

Armstrong handed him a mug of coffee. 'Isle of Wight looks peaceful, sir.'

Thorburn took a sip of the steaming liquid, let the bitter taste roll over his tongue. He glanced at his First Lieutenant. The two of them had been together for a long time. 'Yes, Number One, a sight for sore eyes after last night.'

'And you bagged your first U-boat.'

Thorburn was quick to correct him. 'No, we bagged our first U-boat. You, me, the mess stewards, the galley cooks, everyone. The entire ship's company.'

Brackendale twisted in the rolling swell, the damaged bows tossing a fine sheet of spray over the fo'c'sle chains.

Thorburn swallowed more coffee, contemplating the future. Nothing of course, was ever quite what it seemed.

He recalled an advisory order. It strongly recommended captains not to ram submarines owing to the amount of damage that could be sustained by the warship involved. Expensive and time consuming repairs. From his earliest days in command, Thorburn had always been at loggerheads with authority, intentional or otherwise. Their Lordships conceded he was an excellent seaman, a 'leader of men' even, but he was far too quick to break the rules. So here he was again, this time reporting the accidental ramming of a U-boat and knowing his actions might well be construed as reckless behaviour. He would probably end up facing a Board of Inquiry.

The coffee was going cold. He took a last mouthful and curled his lip in a lopsided smile. To hell with the Admiralty, he thought. At least *Brackendale* had got her U-boat and the sinking of *Glasgow Bay* had been avenged. What was the saying? He struggled to recall, then bobbed his head with satisfaction. Vengeance is mine.

'Signal from *Rosefinch*, sir,' the Yeoman reported, and flicked an acknowledgement.

Thorburn looked over at the warship watching the twinkling light.

'Signal reads, "Will leave you now. Casualties to offload. Good luck." Message ends, sir.' *Rosefinch* began a turn to starboard, increasing speed, the superstructure of her bridge coming into view. Thorburn reached for his binoculars and found Willoughby in the starboard wing.

'Reply, "Thanks for being the good shepherd. God speed and good hunting," and Yeoman, get yourself a relief. You've been up here too long.'

The lamp clattered and he saw Willoughby raise a hand in farewell. He waved in return, and they parted company.

Jennifer Farbrace had worried through the night and it wasn't until 04.50 hours that *Rosefinch* sent a second signal. The message was passed through immediately and she found herself crying with relief. He was alive. Richard was safe and *Brackendale* would be entering harbour. She grabbed her cap and coat and rushed through to the typing pool. Linda was still on duty and looked up in surprise at her flustered arrival. Jennifer bent down closer. 'Linda, I have to go. Can you take over my desk, answer any messages? Won't be long. Thanks!' She left her open mouthed and hurried out and down the stairs. Walking the short distance to Victoria Road, her unbuttoned coat flapping round her legs, she turned and made for the quayside. The harbour was quieter now, the troopships and sweepers mid-channel. Most of the destroyers were out screening the convoys and the hurly-burly of embarking soldiers seemed more organised, less frantic. She threaded her way through to the dock she found a less crowded berth between two tugs and waited for *Brackendale* to appear. The repair basins were round to her right, the harbour entrance to the left; the ship would have to pass this point.

In the fresh breeze of early morning, she stood with her face to the sea, hugging her coat and wishing Richard Thorburn would hurry up. During those final hours of the night she realised she was truly in love and, whatever it took to achieve, she was determined to marry him at the earliest opportunity.

With the wind tussling her hair, occupied only by her thoughts of a ship's Captain, she waited.

Brackendale's White Ensign fluttered at the mast head and for the first time since the previous morning, Lieutenant-Commander Richard Thorburn allowed himself to relax. Once again she was almost home, slower now, hurting from her wounds.

He thought about all that had happened on the 6th of June, 1944. It had been a fateful twenty-four hours, and he knew they would live long in his memory. From the thunder of D-Day's dawn and the roar of the Allied guns, to the landing of the boats and the fight for the beach. He gazed out across the ship's bows and remembered. Many of those men had died, many more had survived, and some day, when he was grey and old, the tale would be worth the telling.

He leaned to the wheelhouse voice-pipe. 'Starboard twenty.'

The Cox'n's firm acknowledgement echoed in reply. 'Starboard twenty. Aye aye, sir.'

Armstrong joined him and together they watched the majestic sweep of a fleet destroyer surging past for the enemy coast.

'Midships.'

Brackendale steadied in the lee of the land and tired though he was, Thorburn slapped Armstrong on the shoulder. 'That's it for us, Number One. Dry dock and a spot of leave I shouldn't wonder.'

'Yes, sir,' Armstrong said with a peculiar smile. Then he turned to look aft. 'Haul away, Yeoman!'

The semblance of a white flag flapped to the top of the mast, and painted roughly in the middle, the black outline of a U-boat rippled in the breeze.

Armstrong grinned happily. 'Congratulations, sir. Thought we'd mark the occasion.'

Thorburn nodded slowly, and swallowed hard, squinting up at the masthead. He found it difficult to speak. 'Well done, Number One. Very appropriate.'

He turned to face the bows, let the spray hide his emotions, and shoulder to shoulder with his First Lieutenant, the Captain of a valiant little destroyer, duty done, brought her home from the sea.

Made in the USA
Columbia, SC
17 December 2022

74265512R00161